THE LAZY DRAGON
AND THE
BUMBLESPELLS WIZARD

KATH BOYD MARSH

The Lazy Dragon and the Bumblespells Wizard

Text Copyright © 2016 by Kath Boyd Marsh

For more information, write:
CBAY Books
PO Box 670296
Dallas, TX 75367

Children's Brains are Yummy Books
Dallas, Texas
www.cbaybooks.com

Paperback ISBN: 978-1-944821-00-5
ebook ISBN: 978-1-944821-01-2
Kindle ISBN: 978-1-944821-02-9
PDF ISBN: 978-1-944821-03-6

Printed in the United States of America.

For my parents Clarence and Mary Ann, who gave me honor, perseverance, and the magic of books. Without their absolute belief in Cl'rnce and Moire Ain, this book would never have been.

CHAPTER 1

Cl'rnce Merlin Clan Principus River Dr'gons—or as his twin sister called him, "waste of dr'gon scales"—crumpled the poster in his paw and stared into his school's main hall. The Dr'gon and Wizard Technological School and Knights Academy students filed past him. None of them looked at him and most gave him a wide berth.

Cl'rnce didn't care. He had plans. "This is war. My sister is going to pay," Cl'rnce whispered, too low for any of the other students to hear.

Hazel was one snarky sister, and it was over-the-top mean of her to make and hang that poster. He un-crumpled it and read it again:

Fair Warning. Cl'rnce Merlin Clan Principus River Dr'gons has stolen the baby Barforamous from the zoology department. Be on the lookout. Cl'rnce most assuredly plans a messy and smelly practical joke for the annual Students' Assembly.

Cl'rnce sighed. Hazel was a spoiler. Most of what she wrote was true, except for the part about him having the Barforamous. Bubbles had escaped yesterday during Cl'rnce's mid-afternoon nap. The smelly little fart-machine creature was probably eating all the stinkweed on the river's edge and would work his way back to Wiz-Tech all on his own by tomorrow. But that was too late for Cl'rnce's long-planned prank.

"Being brilliant, and the best practical joker at Wiz-Tech, of course I have a backup plan." Cl'rnce sniggered. Three hours before, he'd snuck in and set a robe-shrinking spell. It would go off in less than an hour.

He was pretty good at magick, although he kept that a secret. *Magick 101* was one of the few classes he didn't sleep through, but he preferred to preserve his title as school slacker and practical joker. No point in ruining his reputation by letting anyone know how good he was at magick. Besides, as much as he liked magick, it was a lot of work.

Bouncing from foot to foot, Cl'rnce kept glancing at the giant hourglass floating above the hall's stage. Cl'rnce wished he'd thought to plant a Speed-Up spell. The program was taking too long. The Senior Knights, always first up during the Students' Assembly, clanked up on stage so slowly Cl'rnce thought they were trying out to be statues. Finally up on stage, they took forever to stand still and stop making creaky armor noises. At last they recited the school oath.

Almost as slowly, they clanked off the stage and plunked themselves down in their rows of benches neatly lined up on the left side of the hall. Next up. This was what Cl'rnce was waiting for—the Senior Dr'gons and their Wizard Partners, including his sister Hazel and her wizard Gaelyn.

He had two surprises for Hazel and Gaelyn. The first was to create chaos, always a special ingredient in Cl'rnce's jokes. But the second was the part that he looked forward to most. He usually set his jokes to go off on their own so he could observe and enjoy. But since part two was only for Gaelyn, Cl'rnce had to be present, casting the spell so it didn't leak over on anyone else.

When part one went off automatically, the entire student body would be in an uproar. During the confusion, running about and shouting, Cl'rnce would cast the Borrow spell he'd selected from his extensive repertoire of borrowing spells. Cl'rnce maintained such a large category, because he "borrowed" a lot of items, returning them after the fun wore off or the former owner complained to Professor Gralph.

This time Cl'rnce intended to borrow Hazel's Wizard Partner. "Borrow" was all he wanted. No one ever kept what they borrowed. They gave it back. Didn't have to worry about it anymore. Perfect.

Hazel could definitely have her Wizard Partner back.

Cl'rnce was not interested in any long-term commitment, like what was supposed to happen when taking on a Wizard Partner. He'd let Wizard Gaelyn believe she was his partner just long enough to convince her to cast a small spell on Hazel, the one that would make all of Hazel's eyelashes disappear. His sister was inordinately prideful about those eyelashes. And not simply because only royal dr'gons ever had eyelashes, but because she was . . . Hazel. Cl'rnce shouldn't have needed Gaelyn, but eyelash magick was really hard work. And he hadn't bothered to learn those kinds of spells yet.

It was when the Senior Student Dr'gons and Wizards were supposed to follow the Student Knights that it went wrong. The dr'gons and wizards stood up from their benches scattered in zigzags and careless circles, but then immediately sat back down. Professor Gralph rose from his deep chair in front of the platform and walked up on stage. What was wrong with Gralph? Professors didn't interfere in the annual Students' Assembly. Cl'rnce leaned back against the wall and decided to enjoy it. As Professor Gralph, who was almost as cranky and mean to Cl'rnce as Hazel, crossed the stage to the podium, his robe shortened. It was above his knees by the time he'd trod halfway. The professor's face glowed red with anger. Dr'gon Professor Smith ran onstage with a new robe to throw on him. But as she sprinted, her robe and the one in her paws, shrank faster than Professor Gralph's. The two teachers dove behind the podium.

Cl'rnce cackled while the rest of the students gasped and murmured. When Professor Gralph stood, keeping the podium between him and the students, his face was so scarlet it could have been made of tomatoes. Which made Cl'rnce laugh even harder.

"Cl'rnce Merlin Clan Principus River Dr'gons, present yourself to me at once!" Wizard Professor Gralph roared. His arms were bare to where his robe sleeves rubbed his armpits. Gralph extended his skinny arms and whipped the air with a complicated design.

Cl'rnce gulped back his laugh when the enchantment forces flew at him. The air churned and froze as cold silver chains formed, racing to capture him. He didn't have the magick to counteract a Chained spell. Worse, fear made his tongue stick against his teeth, and he couldn't get the Borrow spell's words out fast enough to enchant Gaelyn to get help. All he had was a paw full of rope enchanted with a Tangle-Their-Feet-Until-I-Get-Away spell, which he always kept with him just in case.

He threw the spell out into the hall and turned and ran through the door and on out of the school's main building. He darted behind the warhorse barns of the Knights Academy. Passing the refuse pile topped with the Student Knights' old armor and broken stuff,

Cl'rnce tossed the last bits of rope he had used to create the Tangle-Their-Feet-Until-I-Get-Away spell. The paw full of cut rope was no longer usable, but the moment it hit the hill of rusted and broken armor, a peasant darted out, snatched it, and ran back into the stables.

"Odd fellow." Cl'rnce shrugged and kept running. In seconds he was near the secret tunnel where he napped in winter. He dove inside at the same time he heard the roar of the whole student body chanting a spell to bring him back. His sister's voice was loudest.

Tucked just inside the spell-proof tunnel opening, Cl'rnce turned for a second, stepped back out, and, with a flick of his claws, threw up a simple reflecting spell to cast back all magick onto his pursuers. They'd be extra mad when they all bounced into each other. He was sorry to miss it, but he wasn't sticking around.

By the time he reached the end of the tunnel, he couldn't hear the mob. But his sister would never give up, so he squeezed out of the tunnel and ran harder, wishing for once that he could fly. If he could soar like his sister, Hazel.... But he made a point of not doing anything like his snarky twin. So he raced on.

At last he spotted ahead of him something moving but not screaming. He squinted. Yep, the rushes at the river edge were blowing in the wind. "Almost there. I am so good." He raced headfirst into the cattails and waded downstream until he came to his favorite tree.

"Home at last."

Cl'rnce climbed and balanced on a thick branch high enough that he could see all the way to the school campus. The leaves were thick, so he was hidden while he watched tiny knights and wizards run about searching for him.

"Busy, busy." Cl'rnce stretched and yawned. "Time for a nap." He rested his head on his arm and dozed off. He felt himself fall into the same dream he'd had for the past week. He was sure this dream, and all the ones like it, was about the Wizard Partner he'd have one day. The dream unrolled as before, and again he wanted to peek under the vision-wizard's hood but couldn't get close enough. It annoyed him that he couldn't learn who his partner would be. But he laughed it off. After all, he liked being on his own. He didn't need anyone else. Not now.

And then his dream changed and turned into a nightmare. His sister's voice stabbed into his head like a hot lance. Cl'rnce kept his eyes closed trying to believe he was still asleep. But he knew better. Had she smelled out the Barforamous poop at the base of his tree? Probably. He should have cleaned up after Bubbles.

"I know you're rolling your eyes under those lids. Stop it, or I'll give you something to roll your eyes about," Hazel snarled.

He heard her wings snap shut near his head. She thumped down on his branch, hard. The tree limb

dipped so low Cl'rnce floated above it for a minute before the limb snapped back up, nearly slinging him into
the air. He wound his claws into the small side branches
and wished for her to go away.

"Doesn't my little brother look like the perfect in-
nocent. Like he'd never do a thing to embarrass the
professors or *me*! Don't you dare try to go back to sleep!
Open your eyes. Wake all the way up. *Wake up!* Now's
not the time for your fantasies. The River Dr'gon has
superannuated!" his sister screeched in his ear.

Squeezing his nap-heavy eyes tighter, Cl'rnce drew
one scaly arm over his muzzle. "Leave me alone. I don't
have time for you. And besides, I'm pretty sure Mother
had Dr. Pendr'gon give you and me shots for superannua-
whatsis last year. We're safe."

He hated how Hazel could locate him when nobody
else at Wiz-Tech had a clue where he was. If he'd cleaned
up after Bubbles, this time she would never have sniffed
him out. She couldn't have seen him in the thick foliage.
He'd improved his camouflage high in the mulberry tree
by weaving extra leaves around his nap branch.

Cl'rnce could tell from the snarlier-than-usual frac-
tured-glass sharpness in her voice that Hazel was in one
of her bigger M-A-D moods. She had a lot of them, and
usually she shared them with her little brother, because
she always assumed he was at fault for whatever had
gone wrong. Admittedly, after that last prank, she once

8

again was right. Cl'rnce wondered what it would be like to have a sister who was sometimes wrong and maybe smiled instead of screamed at him.

He smelled the rising fire in her. For a moment, he thought he might have gone a little far with this practical joke. She had never been the one to personally hunt him down when he was in trouble. He certainly had expected her to wait for someone else to do it this time. This was Bad.

Only something that would get Cl'rnce in big trouble would drive Hazel to venture past what she so elegantly referred to as Wiz-Tech's "smelly old stables, which are stuck behind the knights' section of the academy for a good reason." That she hadn't used her usual flunky to fetch him meant this was going to be a dr'gon's flight past bad. Had something happened after his practical joke?

Hazel kicked his branch until, eyes still closed, he turned his head in her direction.

"You need to stop loafing and pay attention. We have one grand mess," she snapped.

An instant too late, he heard the scratch of her razor-sharp talon along the trunk end of his branch. The limb cracked, and Cl'rnce plummeted. He snapped open his almost-never-used wings to slow himself.

But he didn't open them all the way, and he wasn't quick enough; butt first, he landed in the muddy riverbank. Cl'rnce stared up to where his sister hovered. He started to plan. That was his motto: Always have a plan.

With a snort and a quick extension of her perfect jade wings, Hazel flapped down in front of him. Tidily on dry ground, she stood a pace beyond his muddy landing spot. "Cl'rnce, you big lummox! You are not worthy, but it's time for you to step up as the heir, as the next River D'rgon." A burst of angry flame slipped between Hazel's fangs.

Cl'rnce's paws were stuck under the mud. With a muddy squish that sounded a lot like hot air escaping his bottom, Cl'rnce rocked backward to get up. But the mud sucked him forward. He lost his balance and landed muzzle first in the muck. He slit an eye open to peer up at Hazel. "Huh?"

Cl'rnce worked hard not to flinch as he stared into the angry purple edges of the world's meanest sister's snout. Hazel was older by a measly seven minutes and seven seconds, but she acted like she knew everything and treated him like a too-dumb-to-be-out-alone troll. He struggled to get up, but his legs were stuck in the slippery mud, wrapped together in the tangled strings of crushed rushes.

Hazel flicked open her razor claws; with one swipe the weeds snicked apart.

"Hey, be careful. You might slice me instead." Cl'rnce stood and slogged through the sludge.

He kicked the shredded plants. The severed cattails

flew at his sister, missing her by an inch. She squinted at him. Cl'rnce pretended not to notice she was even angrier now. He said, "Do you know how long it took me to steal the maps to find this place?"

"Aren't we proud? Now we can add thieving to your many talents." Hazel leaned close. "Are you paying attention to me?"

Rubbing his eyes, Cl'rnce turned away from her breath. Hazel'd been eating gardenias again. Not only were they his least favorite flower, but they made such a smelly combination with her normal rotted-eggs-and-sulphur breath.

Cl'rnce said, "Depends. Why are you stalking me? I thought after assembly you were scheduled to make the First Year Dr'gons' lives miserable. You'll be late if you don't hurry back to their caverns."

"As if I don't know what you did. No matter. Right now I'm making your life miserable," Hazel said, leaning even closer, pouring out scalding gardenia-sulphur breath.

Cl'rnce had an uncomfortably close view of her front fangs, which were sharp and even. Not like Cl'rnce's, with his right fang longer than the left. Hazel could bite really hard with her perfect fangs. She'd made a point of biting him almost every day when they were young dr'gonelles.

"I know. I know everything," she said, raising her

eye ridges.

Cl'rnce shivered but managed not to run.

Hazel continued, "You're the worst. For months Wizard Professor Gralph and Mother have been asking me to talk to you, about how you make trouble and . . .." She took a deep breath, rolling her eyes up. "No. You're not getting me off topic. What's happened is too important." She pointed a claw at him. "You can't go on like this." Hazel stared at him, slowly nodding her horned head. "Are you listening?"

"I can't go on like what?" Cl'rnce stretched to his full, twelve-foot height. Around Hazel there were three rules to survival. Rule Number One: always be taller than Hazel. Rule Number Two: always be ready to dodge and run. Number Three was the same as Number Two. "I was just napping. It's not like I was busy setting any knights on fire."

"No, not today. Today it was shrinking robes, and that's not the point. Did you know Mother got The Letter? The school's Board decreed you have until the end of this term to make up the last fifty credits you failed toward your Dr'gon Arts degree; if you don't, you're out. This is a disgrace. No Merlin Clan River Dr'gon has ever been expelled from Dr'gon and Wizard Technological School and Knights Academy. You're an embarrassment to our family, the Merlin Clan, and all River Dr'gons."

Hazel's snout was now an impressive red and purple. Not too far from explosion point, Cl'rnce thought. It wouldn't take much to get a world-class tantrum out of her, maybe distract her from the whole assembly fiasco. He smiled at his sister. "Hazel, you're the only one who ever rolls out the school's whole, long name. Why do you do that? Personally I go with Wiz-Tech. But I guess being so *you* is how you got to be valedictorian of your class, huh? Is that the way all your friends say the school name? Oops. My bad. You don't have any friends."

"Stop it! I know what you're doing. And *my* class is supposed to be *our* class, except you've flunked Wizard Training three times." Hazel snorted three tight streams of flame at Cl'rnce.

He ducked the first two, but the last burst hit Cl'rnce's left hind paw. "Ow! What'd you do that for?" He hopped away.

"Pay attention!" Hazel's paws were clenched so tightly they were almost white through her purple scales.

"Okay. Go ahead, Viper Breath." Cl'rnce bent over his burned paw. "Will you look at this? I'm singed all around my claw." He glared at his sister. "And it stings a lot!"

"I'm going to ignore your whining," Hazel snarled, "but only this once. Listen up. This is the important part. As mad at you as I am for your failures here at Dr'gon and Wizard Technological School and Knights Academy, there is something far more significant. Are

13

you listening this time? *The River Dr'gon is superannuated."* She stared at him.

Cl'rnce couldn't believe it. She either didn't suspect about his Borrow spell or for once wasn't interested in punishing him and letting everyone know what a dope he was. Nope. She wouldn't miss that opportunity. She didn't know. He was safe, at least until he made sense of why she was really after him.

She'd said something about a superannuated dr'gon. He didn't know what that meant, but the way she was glaring, he had a feeling it meant something awful—like dead. Cl'rnce patted his chest and felt his heart. It was okay—he wasn't the one dead.

He couldn't resist poking her again, so he shrugged. "Which dr'gon?" He patted his chest. "You and I are both River Dr'gons. And we're both here. I'm not dead or super-whatsit . . . well, it's true I am super." Cl'rnce opened his eyes wide, giving her his most doubtful look. "Are you super?"

Hazel breathed in so deeply her chest expanded to twice its usual size, and her muzzle glowed an even angrier red. "Listen, waste-of-dr'gon-scales—" She poked Cl'rnce's chest with a knife-like talon. "—not *a* River Dr'gon. *The* River Dr'gon. The Primus! The First Dr'gon among all River Dr'gons and Dr'gon Nations, the Dr'gon Council leader, *the* River Dr'gon."

"So what?" Cl'rnce felt a tickle of alarm but decided

to ignore it.

"You know so what. By our royal birth you are it, the next Primus, *the* River Dr'gon. Why you and not me is just plain stupid. Why should a lazy, selfish trickster like you be First among Dr'gons? Just because you are the last male Merlin Clan River Dr'gon? Every other dr'gon clan allows royal females to be considered, but not ours. And our clan rules." Hazel spit a flame ball into the puddle beside Cl'rnce. "Phooey!"

When hot mud splashed him, Cl'rnce flinched. "Don't hold back, sis. How do you really feel?"

Hazel glared, clacking her glistening teeth. "Letter or no letter from the school, you're out, leaving at once. The point is even though you will never graduate like all the Dr'gon Nations rulers before you, you must find a Wizard Partner and undertake the Journey immediately. You and your partner must return the Whisper Stone to the Dr'gon Council Chamber as every potential Primus before you has."

She closed her eyes and droned out the next words. "You must overcome the perils of the Journey and prove yourself worthy of being Primus." Hazel took a deep breath and held it long enough for her red muzzle to pale to its normal light-purple edges. "I've always feared this day would come. The decision is made. You have no choice."

Cl'rnce pulled up an Essence of Life flower. The

flowers protected against disease, which he thought he'd need if he was stepping in where this super-whatsit diseased River Dr'gon had been. But the flowers also gave visions. As he snorted its fragrance, a vision of the dream-wizard unfolded. This time he watched her throw back her hood. She was a freckle-faced short person engulfed in a too-long blue robe. She didn't look like any wizard he knew, but she was saying how he was special. He let the dream image melt. If he couldn't stay at Wiz-Tech, it was sort of possible getting a Wizard Partner who adored him as Primus could be good. Also being Hazel's boss could be good. And fun was his middle name. Cl'rnce shrugged. "Okay. Anything else?"

Hazel took a deep breath and blew out slightly less scalding air. "Yes. Repeat after me: I have to get a Wizard Partner. I have five days to complete the Primus Journey and deliver the Whisper Stone to the Uamha."

"Where?" interrupted Cl'rnce.

"The Dr'gon Council Chamber." Hazel snorted three hot puffs of angry steam in his face. Cl'rnce felt the run-now-or-get-flamed heat rising in his sister. Her muzzle started to glow scarlet again. "I said to repeat after me." Flame-edged steam slipped through her fangs. "I have to get a Wizard Partner."

Just one more poke at his angry sister and Cl'rnce would get going. "Hazel has to . . ."

Hazel let loose, and Cl'rnce leaped up and over her

long flaming shot. "Good one, Hazel. You almost got me in the—"

She fired again, but he was too slow, and she nipped his muddy rear.

HAPTER 2

Cl'rnce swatted out the flames, checking to make sure his perfect scales were not damaged. Only a foot away from him, standing as still as a statue, with that look that said Cl'rnce had gone too far, Hazel hissed, "Focus, little brother. Five days." His sister's voice softened to her scariest tone. "Wizard Professor Gralph says there are five wizardry students who haven't yet paired up with a dr'gon. Any of them would be honored to have the next Primus as their Dr'gon Partner." Hazel choked on the last words.

She clicked her claws together once; a small parchment appeared in her outstretched palm. Hazel read from the paper. "'Bosberous.' He's from the very old and distinguished Pendr'gon wizard clan." She glared at Cl'rnce as if she could force him to say yes to stupid old Bosberous.

He shook his head. "Don't think so. I made Bosberous's wand fire backward."

"So? That's nothing next to some of the tricks you've

pulled on other wizardry students." Hazel shrugged.

Cl'rnce flicked a fluff of dandelion off his chest. "Yeah. That's how I saw it. Too bad you weren't there to defend me at the Disciplinary Court. It's been over a year, and Bosberous still won't speak to me." Cl'rnce smiled. "Not that his speech is all that clear, what with that chin-length lip hair." Cl'rnce circled his talons outside his ears. "I'm not sure if he hears all that well through the stylish orange and blue ear tufts. Funny what a backward-firing wand can do." He laughed.

Hazel drew a claw through the first name. "Well, there's Norman. As a Slipstream he has a real gift for transportation spells. You'll need those to get to the Council Chamber with the Whisper Stone in time."

Cl'rnce shook his head.

Hazel sighed. "Fire again?"

He gulped. She knew about the stables. He nodded and shrugged. Hazel scratched at her paper. "There seems to be a theme here. You need to stay away from fire spells. You're not that good at them, you beady-eyed cretin."

"Are not beady. My eyes are large and lustrous. Mother said so." Cl'rnce rolled his eyes away from Hazel. He kept it his own secret, but he was pretty good at non-fire magic and could have gotten highest marks in *Magick 101,* if he'd shown up for the final practical test. But it interfered with nap time, so . . . .

He walked to the river edge and bent to admire himself in a pool as still as glass behind a fallen log. Cl'rnce waved at his reflection, enjoying the graceful motions of his digits.

Hazel read the next name. "Jeremiah. No, never mind. I remember him. He has a brutish temper." She eliminated number three.

Cl'rnce choked. "Yeah, let's stay away from the cranky ones." He eyed his crabby sister.

Hazel didn't look up as she read, "Halbert."

"Fire." Cl'rnce scraped a bit of mulberry leaf out of his fangs and smiled at his reflection. "Don't you think I'm uncommonly handsome?"

Hazel snorted and zipped her claw through *Halbert*. "That leaves Wilhelmina Wanderlust. An excellent choice. She was one of the most promising First Years . . . ."

Cl'rnce jerked away from his watery image. "She's like you!"

Hazel growled, "So what?"

Bossed and tortured by Hazel for four hundred and twenty years, Cl'rnce shivered at the thought of a partner picked out by, and resembling more than a little, his own sister. He grabbed for an excuse. "Uh, Willy is afraid of caves. Don't I have to take the Whisper Stone to the Council Chamber inside Ghost Mountain? The Council Chamber is nothing but a big cave. What good is a wizard who won't go in a cave?"

Hazel scratched the last name and tossed the paper into the air. She shot flame at it, turning it into a fiery ball. Cl'rnce ducked as the blazing paper whizzed a scale's width from his head.

"Fine, Cl'rnce. I'm done. Find your own Wizard Partner. And wipe that crafty look off your face. I know what you're thinking. You will not talk my partner into helping you. Gaelyn has more sense than to hitch her entire life and career to the likes of you. Find your own sucker—I mean wizard."

When she pointed her paw and snapped her claws, Cl'rnce winced from the sharp magickal thump behind his right horn. His sister had learned too much magick and used it to torture him. "And don't go back to napping. You have only five days from today to complete your mission and claim your inheritance."

"What if I don't want to be the next leader?" Cl'rnce asked, hoping to move Hazel to the edge of fury again. She was so entertaining when she was almost trying to contain her temper.

Hazel stomped on Cl'rnce's burned paw. "Think, you lazy, self-absorbed slacker. It doesn't matter that I'm twice the royal River Dr'gon you are and would work harder than you've ever dreamed of working. You, Mom, and I are all that is left of the royal Merlin Clan River Dr'gon line. But the Law dictates that royal male

21

River Dr'gons be considered to inherit first. Until all the royal male River Dr'gons are gone, you are it!" She mumbled something about current Primus Thomas, but Cl'rnce couldn't quite hear it.

A cloud scurried over the sun, sending down a shadow and a chill through Cl'rnce. He was pretty sure it was the cloud, not the picture flashing in his head of him dead and Hazel smiling.

She took a deep breath and continued, "Is this very clear? Even if you said no, I could not take your place without a contentious vote in the Dr'gon Council. Think about the chaos that would ensue if the Primus was up for grabs among the royals of the other clans. Who would kill to claim the Primus? Philomena Flannach from the Geilt Dr'gon clan, that's who. How many of her kin have turned killer? How many Merlin Clan River Dr'gons have they slain? I suspect her uncle killed our father."

Hazel stepped closer to Cl'rnce.

He shrank back from her.

"In what cobwebbed corner of your ill-used mind," she continued, "do you truly believe Philomena wants you alive, if you become Primus? Even if you'd be a lazy slug who would let anyone who asked do your work for you. If she wasn't a Geilt, she'd just wrap you around her claw and manipulate you, but she's a killer and she wants—"

"See what I mean about females?" Cl'rnce stepped

away two more paces.

"What?" Hazel screamed. "Do you really mean to say my friends and I are like Geilts?"

"No." Cl'rnce backed up again. Hazel's explosion wasn't nearly as much fun as he'd thought it would be.

Hazel snatched the ridge of his wing. "For the sake of all the Dr'gon Nations, you will get a Wizard Partner and return the Whisper Stone to the Uamha by midnight five days hence. You will not allow the Geilt clan to become Rulers of all the Dr'gon Nations! You must follow law and custom, so you have the backing of all the other clans."

Hazel reached into her neck pouch and pulled out a small black rock. "I was going to give you the Whisper Stone when you had your partner and were ready to head to Ghost Mountain, but I've had enough. Take it. And don't lose it." She tossed the rock to him.

He recognized the soft vibrations in the stone. There went his last hope. There was no pretending this was just Hazel bullying him. The Council really had sent her. She'd been entrusted with the Whisper Stone. Whatever this superannuated meant for the old Primus, Cl'rnce had no way out. His whole clan, and the peace-loving other dr'gon clans, were depending on him. Cl'rnce tucked the disk-shaped stone in his neck pouch. Keeping his eyes on Hazel, he lifted his painful back paw.

Hazel returned his stare for a few seconds. "For crying out loud, stop licking your toes. I can't talk to you when you look stupider than usual." She snorted a medium stream of flame.

Cl'rnce jumped away and up to a low branch.

"I'm going to find Gaelyn. We have work to do with the First Years," Hazel said.

As his sister started to stride away, Cl'rnce dropped down in front of her, shoving his un-singed paw under her feet. "Have a nice trip." He laughed.

Without missing a step, Hazel skimmed over Cl'rnce's foot, then ripped open her broad wings and launched skyward. "Trip. Amusing, Cl'rnce. Just what the Dr'gon Nations need. A clown." She clacked her claws three times and disappeared.

Cl'rnce shrugged off her insults. Throughout their childhood, she'd said worse to him. He was glad to be rid of her, even if she'd left him with a lot of work and a puzzle about super-whatsit. He was bothered that Hazel hadn't told him what that was. But maybe it wasn't important. Maybe.

Whatever it was, he needed a new plan, preferably one where he found someone else to do this quest for him, or at least most of the work.

At least for now Hazel was gone. He did a little dance, kicking up dandelions so that their fluff showered him like snow. Soon the dandelions were worn down to stems, and Cl'rnce was tired out with so much exercise.

"Nap time again. The one good thing about the Primus Journey is that I won't be here to get blamed for the assembly prank."

He stretched his scaly arms and yawned. "I'll nap up a plan to get the Whisper Stone quest done, maybe even without a Wizard Partner. Although it's too bad my vision-wizard isn't around. She's kind of okay. She knew I was special, so she's smart. She probably knows all about super-whatsit."

Cl'rnce wadded some weeds into a pillow and curled up in the deepest shade beneath the mulberry tree. "If only I could unload this Primus thing on Hazel. She's mean enough to keep the whole Geilt clan in line. I'm just too nice."

He sighed and plumped his pillow. "Hazel's right about one thing; if I had a Wizard Partner, I wouldn't have to do the hard magick. Too bad all the wizardry students hold grudges. A couple of crispy body parts, and no one speaks to me."

His words felt fuzzy as his muscles relaxed. "No wizards here desperate enough to volunteer to partner with me. School needs a new student like my vision-wizard who thinks I'm great," he muttered and dozed off. She walked into his first dream. He could see her freckled nose, but the rest of her face was hidden by her hood.

CHAPTER 3

Hugging her secret under her tunic, Moire Ain ran toward the village. Over her skinny shoulders, the sun poured midday heat, a scalding reminder of the awful fury Hedge-Witch would be in. Hours ago Moire Ain should have returned to their hut with the herbs, including the pale and odorous tuber she was sure was poisonous.

For once Moire Ain didn't care how bad a beating she would get. She finally possessed the one treasure she had never expected to own. Moire Ain had found her own magick book. Finding a place to hide it was more important than Hedge-Witch's wrath.

Running past the first village hut, Moire Ain thought a thanks to Goodwife Greenfield for the reading and writing instructions. Not that the goodwife knew she had been teaching the witch's foster child. For the last few years, Moire Ain had hidden in a tree and soaked up the lessons the goodwife taught to her brood of children. No one knew Moire Ain could read and write.

As she sped past more village huts, the peasants

turned their backs. For as long as she could remember, the villagers had hurried inside their homes whenever she passed. But this time, she couldn't slow to wish one of them wanted to know her, become her friend.

Where the book touched her, her skin prickled again. Strangely it was the same feeling she'd gotten when she'd spotted the piece of leather-wrapping sticking up out of the earth. She'd quit digging for Hedge-Witch's poisonous plant when she caught sight of the leather. At first she feared that the plant and the buried book were one and the same—evil. But curiosity got the better of her, and when she'd unwrapped the book and held it in her hands, she felt the good. The happiness.

Moire Ain had magick in her. Not much. Not as much as she wanted. But she knew the feel of good over evil. She knew which herbs would counteract the poisonous ones Hedge-Witch fed to the villagers' animals in order to force the peasants to pay for cures. When Moire Ain could, she secretly cured the animals before Hedge-Witch could do any real damage.

This book prickled and tickled with good magick, even if it was mostly written in a language she didn't know. Enough of it was in her own language for her to be certain of the good. She could become a great wizard with this book. But first she had to find a safe place for it.

She stopped thinking of hiding places when she spotted a horse tied to one of the haphazard branches that made up the walls of their hut. Not only was a horse unusual, but Moire Ain had seen this horse once before. Last time, Hedge-Witch had taken off and been gone for three days. She'd returned in an abnormally good mood, with gold to hide under the dirt in the corner of the hut. For a week afterward, the old witch sang of murder and mayhem and giggled like a wrinkled little girl.

Moire Ain veered behind the villagers' huts. She would come up behind her home, away from the front opening. There was nowhere to hide around her shack. Unlike the other homes, there were no trees or bushes shading Moire Ain's home. It was hot in the summer and cold in the winter. All the saplings Moire Ain had tried to plant close to the hut died at once. Moire Ain was sure the noxious gases scattering from the carcasses that dried on racks in the yard had killed the plant life. Or maybe it was the gathered plants, also set out to dehydrate, since many were poisonous instead of curative.

Moire Ain wanted to hear what the crone was up to with this visitor. So Moire Ain snuck up to their hut, sliding along the side. She was pretty safe since their hut had no windows. Even better, the walls were thin, and Moire Ain's hearing was acute.

"I tell you she is ready," Hedge-Witch said. "She will do the deed within the five days."

A voice, which creaked low but could have been either a man or a woman, answered, "You are certain?

Your life depends on it."

"I am certain." Hedge Witch's voice took on a whee-
dling tone Moire Ain had never heard before. "The king
will die. You will rule. Do not fear. You have entrusted
the right witch to do the job."

"You mean the girl will kill him?" the voice said, a
bit louder and more annoyed than even Hedge-Witch
usually sounded.

"Yes. Yes. Of course. I control her. She will do my
bidding. Now about the payment."

"When the job is done."

The voices grew fainter as they argued, as if they
had walked farther into the hut.

Moire Ain slapped a hand over her mouth before she
could gasp. The old witch was talking about turning her
into a killer. No! This was not going to happen. Moire Ain
had to escape.

But she heard the voices get louder, as if the stranger
was approaching the hut's opening, leaving. She didn't
dare run yet. Hedge-Witch would hear her pounding
feet. It was eerily quiet now. The only noise was that of
birds scolding a crow or a hawk. And then silence again.

There was no more conversation. At last the beat
of the horse's hooves could be heard trotting down the
road, out of the village, heading toward the woods to
the south. Moire Ain listened for Hedge-Witch. She
heard pounding. It sounded like Hedge-Witch was

29

beating something. Moire Ain leaned farther around the hut to see.

Hedge-Witch stood in the road, muttering and smashing her rod into the dirt. Even though everything else was still, her straggly hair whipped about like a tornado had hold of it. Moire Ain had seen the crone this angry only once before. Anger made her meaner and more determined. Not only was she furious, but there was payment to be had. For gold, Hedge-Witch would do anything, no matter who got hurt. This time she was going to use Moire Ain to kill a king.

Moire Ain didn't care if Hedge-Witch was angry about the way the stranger had spoken to her or if she was mad that Moire Ain was late. She was not going to stay to find out. Slinking back around the hut, Moire Ain pulled out her book. She flipped through, looking for anything she could use. Maybe something to silently call her pet raven, Raspberries, warning him to escape. But all the spells went on for pages, and none now seemed to be in her language. There wasn't time to master one, even if she could have deciphered the language they were in.

There was no choice. She had to run and hope Raspberries followed, but first she would take care of something. Since Moire Ain would not be around to cure the poison Hedge-Witch would make from the white tuber that reeked of evil, she would destroy it. Moire Ain threw it into the coals of the cooking fire burning behind the hut.

As it hit the flames, the plant screamed.

Too stunned to move, Moire Ain was still staring when Hedge-Witch hurtled around the hut shouting, "What have you done? Get in the hut. I'll deal with you later. You are too incompetent to even gather a . . . ." She stopped. She stuck her staff in the fire and dragged out the blackened plant. Throwing dirt on it to smother the burning parts, she picked it up and stroked it like a pet cat. A crafty look crossed the old crone's face, and she shook her finger at Moire Ain. "You will find out what that was when I—"

"Feed it to me? You plan to poison me to make me kill a king?" Moire Ain tried to scream, but her throat had closed, and everything came out as a whisper.

The old witch smiled and started to chant.

By the third word, Moire Ain recognized the spell. Spider webs would fly out of Hedge-Witch's fingers in a moment. Moire Ain would be imprisoned in sticking silken ropes.

So she ran.

She heard Hedge-Witch screaming behind her. "Grab her. Grab the rotten thief!" Her howling brought out every villager who wasn't already outdoors. But they slunk back into their doorways as Moire Ain fled by. They were too scared of Hedge-Witch to help Moire Ain.

Jumping over a washing tub, Moire Ain knew where

to go. The river. Water was the thing the old witch hated most. Moire Ain sprinted faster, hugging the book so close its worn beige cover could have melted into her skin. She didn't waste breath yelling the truth that she had stolen nothing.

At the river end of the village, Moire Ain threw herself into the lush bushes surrounding the Greenfields' home. She only meant to stop for a moment and then run again, but her shrunken stomach betrayed her.

The smell of baking bread drew her onto her feet. She stood up, breathing in a warm meal, the kind she rarely had. She closed her eyes and tasted food shared with a smiling family. As she pictured steamy slices of bread passed down a long wooden table, she watched her own hand try to take a hunk, but the bread vanished, and she was jerked back to reality by shouting voices.

Moire Ain turned to run again, but she slammed into the soft bosom of Goodwife Greenfield. The woman grabbed Moire Ain by both arms and pulled her into the family's hut.

Moire Ain's heart nearly broke. She'd been captured without even getting out of the village. The goodwife she had pretended was her mother was about to turn her over to the witch.

"Quiet," Goodwife Greenfield said. She shoved Moire Ain deeper into the hut, keeping a hand on her arm. Not letting go, the peasant turned and blocked the doorway.

Moire Ain knew there was only one escape. Unlike Hedge-Witch's molding straw shack, this thatched home had a small window opening. Moire Ain eyed it, sure she was skinny enough to fit through. No one was keeping her prisoner until Hedge-Witch arrived.

Moire Ain tried to shake them away, but tears of betrayal stung her eyes. That the goodwife would give Moire Ain back to the witch hurt more than she could bear. How wrong Moire Ain had been about Goodwife Greenfield. It didn't mean a thing after all that unlike the rest of the village, she had never shooed Moire Ain away or hooked her fingers at Moire Ain in the sign to fend off evil.

Moire Ain wriggled as hard as her dirt-encrusted body would allow and finally pulled out of Goodwife Greenfield's grasp. If she was going back to Hedge-Witch, first she'd save her book. She'd hide it. Somehow, but where?

"Quiet!" Goodwife Greenfield said again. "Hide." With a hooking motion, she shoved Moire Ain behind her tall, well-padded self.

Moire Ain's heart whispered with hope.

"Did you see the little thief?" Hedge-Witch's shrill voice pierced the hut.

"Why, good morning to you, Goodwitch," Goodwife

Greenfield said, ignoring the question. "What brings you to my home? I need no cures. We do not have illness here, but I think the Brownbarks' cow is not giving milk. They'd welcome you, surely. Where is your assistant?"

"She's run away, the little thief!" Hedge-Witch hissed.

"A thief? What did she steal?" Goodwife Greenfield moved back a step, and Moire Ain danced backward with her.

For a second, there was silence, but finally Hedge-Witch spit out, "My book!"

Moire Ain stifled a gasp. How did Hedge-Witch know about her book?

"Book? But I thought you did not read. You said you gained all your knowledge of healing from the gods." Goodwife Greenfield's arms flailed toward the ceiling.

"Oh, indeed," Hedge-Witch stammered. "I said my boot. Didn't you hear me?" she said, acid lacing her words.

Goodwife Greenfield snorted, and Moire Ain knew the goodwife wasn't fooled. "Boot?" Goodwife Greenfield said. "You wear boots? How you've prospered. No one else in the village can spare animal hide for boots. I see though that you are not wearing even one boot now. Did you own just a single boot?"

"Never mind," Hedge-Witch snarled. As angry as she was, the old crone would not dare to strike someone as beloved by the village as the goodwife. With the crowd gathering out in the road, she would not be able to do anything to Goodwife Greenfield. Her next words were extra angry with the frustration. "If you see the little thief, send her back to me."

"Because she stole your boot?" Goodwife Greenfield said with more than a little sarcasm.

"I don't like the tone of your voice, Goodwife Green-field," Hedge-Witch hissed. "It would be a shame if your pigs died."

Goodwife Greenfield stepped forward, away from Moire Ain. "*Are* you threatening me, Hedge-Witch? I would not like to report to the warden that you threatened a free citizen of Albion. Such things are frowned on. Even from old women with only one phantom boot."

In all her years of living with Hedge-Witch, Moire Ain had never heard anyone challenge the old hag. Hedge-Witch had made a point of telling Moire Ain that everyone believed it was always Moire Ain's fault when a cure went wrong.

"Hrumph." Moire Ain heard the slap of Hedge-Witch's bare feet as she trotted back over the stone threshold and down the dirt road.

Goodwife Greenfield turned to Moire Ain. "Little one, I think you must get far away. I know you stole nothing, but she's a vengeful old crone. Whatever she's furious about, it is better if you flee. It's past time you made your own way, struck out on your own."

"Yes. Yes." Moire Ain nodded. "Thank you for not telling her I was here. You were brave."

Goodwife Greenfield shook her head. "I'm glad it appeared such, but I was most certainly fearful. Hedge-Witch is more perilous an enemy than many believe."

Goodwife Greenfield reached a calloused hand out and stroked Moire Ain's tangled hair before she could dart away. "If any of us were truly brave, we would have freed you years ago. Don't think for a moment that any in the village credit Hedge-Witch when she blames you for the evil she attempts. She's a vile old troll. I wish we were all free of her."

Moire Ain wanted to tell Goodwife Greenfield about the murder conspiracy and the old book she'd found buried by the river, the book she still hugged close to her skinny chest beneath her ragged robe.

But Goodwife Greenfield walked over to a thick wooden shelf upon which a stone pot sat. Lifting the cloth covering, she took out a hunk of bread and a chunk of cheese. She wrapped them in the scrap of cloth that had been the pot's lid. "Do you have a pouch to carry food in?"

Moire Ain shook her head. Goodwife Greenfield untied the leather strap around her tunic and slipped off an old leather pouch. She laid the contents, a few herbs, on the small table under the shelf. Waving her hand over the plants, she said, "I do not call Hedge-Witch to cure my family or animals. I know a little about potions, but I'd prefer no one was aware of my skills." She looked into Moire Ain's eyes.

Moire Ain nodded. Keeping secrets from Hedge-Witch was always a good idea.

Tucking the bread and cheese into the pouch, Goodwife Greenfield said, "If you have anything else to hide in your pouch, I think you can have privacy in the corner. I suggest you hurry. I hear my children outside shaking river water on each other. Do you like to swim?" The goodwife bit her lips.

Moire Ain knew Goodwife Greenfield was afraid she'd insulted Moire Ain. Witches did not swim or go near water. Which was one way Moire Ain was definitely not like Hedge-Witch. "I love to swim," Moire Ain said.

Moire Ain took the pouch from Goodwife Greenfield's outstretched hand. "I give you thanks." She gulped, her throat swollen on the words. For the second time, tears she'd sworn many beatings ago never to shed tried to slide out. All this kindness overwhelmed her. Moire Ain ducked her head to hide her eyes at the same time she tucked the book into the pouch, behind the cheese.

Goodwife Greenfield squatted down until she was even with Moire Ain's swampy eyes. "I trust the lessons were sufficient, and that you can read the book you are willing to steal and run away with."

"I didn't steal the book." Moire Ain looked up, tying her rope belt and securing the pouch to her ragged robe. "You knew?"

Goodwife Greenfield smiled. "Of course. It wasn't just to entertain my children that I taught them out under the trees. And I would not normally speak so loudly as to enable a child hiding in a tree to hear me. Or flail my arms in the air to demonstrate how a letter or word is made before scratching it in the dirt."

Moire Ain wiped her running nose on her tattered robe's arm. "I give you my thanks," was all she could squeak.

"I wish I could have done more. The whole village wishes we could have done more. But we are a cowardly bunch."

Moire Ain patted Goodwife Greenfield's arm. She didn't blame the village for their fear. They didn't even know how truly wicked or powerful the hedge-witch living in their tiny village was. Moire Ain had no idea why the old crone lived here, but she was certain that secret was connected to the trips Hedge-Witch took every few months. She'd usually return grumpy and muttering about "waiting, and better be worth it." To cheer herself, Hedge-Witch would give Moire Ain some horrendous cure to deliver, up a cow's butt or down a pig's gullet.

Goodwife Greenfield gathered Moire Ain in a hug. "Start your journey, Moire Ain. And the gods be with you."

Moire Ain hugged back, awkwardly, since she'd never had a hug before, or given one. It felt better than warm bread.

After a couple of seconds, Moire Ain ran out of the house. Stopping behind a bush, she listened. The Greenfield children chattered around the side of the hut. Down the road nearer her own hut, Hedge-Witch screamed at the villagers to stop lying and tell her where Moire Ain hid. Crouching low, Moire Ain dashed behind the Greenfields' hut and into the woods. She was headed for the one thing Hedge-Witch hated and feared—running water—the only protection she could think of for herself and the book.

CHAPTER 4

Before Moire Ain could get far, she heard the Greenfield children coming. She climbed into her favorite tree to hide while they filed into their home. Farther off she saw Hedge-Witch storm up and down the village demanding the peasants allow her to search their huts. But each villager had an excuse for not allowing her entry. As her screaming grew louder, first a haystack, then a chicken coop caught fire.

Moire Ain wanted to jump down and help the villagers, but Goodwife Greenfield popped around the back of her hut and shook her head at Moire Ain's tree. "Go!" the goodwife said.

The goodwife was right, but Moire Ain gripped her branch harder, forcing herself to wait for the chance to run. Below her, as each peasant refused to help, Hedge-Witch screamed that she would burn the entire village.

Goodie Ash shook her head at Hedge-Witch and said, "I do not believe the girl be evil. The child was nowhere around when my mam died. But you were."

40

Goodie Bram yelled from her hut, "It wasn't the girl who gave me that black potion that killed my ailing pigs. Leave the girl alone."

Never before had the villagers protected Moire Ain. Butterflies brushed soft wings across her heart as she realized Goodwife Greenfield wasn't the only one who didn't believe Hedge-Witch's awful lies.

As the villagers marched out of their huts and banded together to put out the fires, Hedge-Witch's face flushed redder and redder. Moire Ain felt guilty. If the old crone did something even more horrible to the villagers, it would be Moire Ain's fault. She had run from Hedge-Witch to avoid murdering a king, but if she didn't step forward, she'd be the reason a whole village burned to the ground or got the sinking sickness and died.

Hedge-Witch was only yards from the Greenfields' hut when the crone's fingers began the tracings in the air to bring the illness miasma from the rotted place.

Moire Ain had to surrender. She'd stay and find another way to stop Hedge-Witch from using her to murder that king. Maybe her new book had an easy spell she could cast to send Hedge-Witch into a deep sleep. That would give Moire Ain time to find a way to stop Hedge-Witch for good.

Her hands making the final bigger circles to call the sickness, Hedge-Witch stomped up to the Greenfields' hut. The old crone stood screaming that she would see to it that all the Greenfield children died horrible deaths if her slave was not returned. Before Moire Ain could drop down out of the tree to surrender, Goodwife Greenfield sailed out her front door. Carrying a huge cauldron of water, she stumbled on the threshold and lost control of the pot.

The crystalline water Moire Ain had seen the two oldest Greenfield children tote home splashed over Hedge-Witch. The old hag howled in pain.

Goodwife Greenfield yelled, "Hedge-Witch is possessed! Look how a demon has taken her. Hear how the clear spring water burns her skin."

The villagers ringed around the old witch as she whirled, screaming for someone to bring her rags to soak up the water. While the murmuring circle surrounded Hedge-Witch, the smallest of the Greenfield children slipped behind their home and scampered beneath Moire Ain's tree.

"Momma says run. Run through the river. Go fast. Go now. Old witch won't hurt us. Old witch too afraid of water." The little boy tugged at the hank of hair covering his eye and scooted back to the circle. He grabbed hold of his mother's hand. She leaned down, and he whispered into her ear. Neither looked Moire Ain's way, but she was certain he was reporting back to his mother.

Moire Ain dropped out of the tree and ran faster

than she ever had. The villagers were distracting the witch so she could escape, and she would. When the river came into view, she hesitated. If she jumped in and swam, she'd damage her precious book. She looked around. Nearly submerged in racing water, spanning the river from one side to the other stretched a slippery road of boulders. In the late summer, the boulders weren't wet, rising above the river in that dry season. But today the high water made the rocks too dangerous to use as a bridge. Moire Ain looked for another way to cross the river while protecting her book. She spotted a bright rag and hemp rope hanging from a tree branch that nearly stretched all the way across the river. She'd watched the village children play here, swinging out on the rope and dropping into the deep middle of the river.

If the branch had only grown out over the river a few more feet, she could have used it to cross. Moire Ain would have to use the rope to swing far enough out that she could let go and sail over the river bank onto the other side.

Trees had always been special to Moire Ain, so she was sure this was the answer she was meant to find. She climbed out onto the overhanging branch, her hands in front and her toes gripping the thick branch as best she could. She inched along like a woolly caterpillar.

Halfway across, still three feet from where the rope hung down, the limb cracked. Moire Ain froze. She willed the branch to not break. There was silence. She took a relieved breath and inched again, but the limb cracked again. She had to get to the rope and swing as hard as she could. At worst when she got close enough, she could throw her book to the opposite bank and drop into the river to swim.

Before she stretched to the rope, a soft chirrup made her look up. Above her a big branch stretched from a different tree on the opposite side of the river. The higher branch was thicker than the one she was on. If she could reach it and climb up, she could shinny over the river and not risk throwing her book.

She stretched her arm up, and the branch under her snapped louder. Sitting back, she pulled the book out of her bag and clutched it close, sighing. The plan wouldn't work; her arm was too short.

Her branch cracked and creaked again dropping another inch. She couldn't imagine how her slender weight could be too much for the branch she was sure the Greenfield children had just played on. It didn't make sense until a tingling in her nearly asleep arm made her look at the book. No bigger than her two hands, the book no longer felt light as a leaf. Trapped over the river, her precious book was becoming too heavy to hold. Too heavy for the branch.

She didn't dare move for fear she'd break the branch. She couldn't think what to do. And then a very strange thing happened. A whisper snaked into her ear. "Awake."

She stared at the book, but she wasn't surprised. Why shouldn't a magick book speak? She asked, "Are you ready to do magick?" She waited, but the only sounds around her were the distant yelling from the village and the chirp of the tree frogs above her.

She was disappointed that the book didn't answer, but she believed in it. There had to be an important reason that she'd found it just when Hedge-Witch was about to force Moire Ain into being a murderer. It was like its title: *Magicks Mysteries*.

Maybe it was not a chatty sort of book, but she was certain it was reaching out to her, to teach her magick. If the book didn't like to talk, maybe it could read her thoughts. She concentrated hard on what she needed most.

She had to get to the rope tied to her branch, swing out so she could drop on the other river bank, and . . . escape. And she needed to accomplish all of this before Hedge-Witch caught up to her.

Hoping the book was listening and would help, she edged forward an inch, her right hand sliding toward the swinging rope's knot around the branch. The limb cracked louder and sank closer to the river. She closed her eyes and thought as hard as she could, praying her book would help. "Rope. Rope. Rope."

Moire Ain pictured her hand grabbing the hanging rope, standing, and jumping off, swinging far into the air. She pictured the rope in her hand. In her head, she'd looped it around her wrist. But then the vision reformed. At the last second, instead of swinging on the rope, she saw herself throw the rope a dozen feet through the air at the tree limb above her.

There was a tug at her wrist. She opened her eyes and stared down at the rope still tied on her branch. Was she being told to throw a lasso? How? She couldn't reach the rope. But the next moment Moire Ain yelped when a tug at her waist nearly spilled her off her branch.

The rope belt around her waist stretched. One end spun out, sailing up and looping around the branch above her head. Moire Ain didn't move for fear she'd break the branch she clung to, but she watched the other limb dip down close until it was even with her cracking branch. She slowly slipped one leg and then the other over the new branch. She was safely on it when the lower branch gave a final crack and broke off, slamming into the river and bashing the water into a giant wave.

Riding the new branch, Moire Ain laughed even when river water swamped up at her. But as the broken branch rode the wave up past her and then fell into the river, it caught her ragged robe, nearly dragging her down. For the first time, she was grateful for the thin fabric of her robe when the cloth tore away. Her clothing bore a new hole, but she was still safely on her new branch. Moire Ain took a shaky breath and watched the broken wood float down-river, the shred of dull cloth waving like a small flag.

Moire Ain crowed to her book, "Wow! That was great. Even the part where my robe ripped. Hedge-Witch will see the branch and think I've gone in the river and drowned. I hope."

The book remained silent. She inched quickly across the new branch and was standing on firm ground in a minute. "I did that with my mind and you, book. That's more magick than I've ever done. I'm already a great wizard! And I haven't even really started any mastery lessons. That's mighty great. I'm mighty great. I'm great and mighty."

She placed the book on a dry rock and inspected it for damage. Despite the splashing she'd gotten, it looked the same. Moire Ain was amazed. She'd gotten across water Hedge-Witch wouldn't cross. She hadn't damaged her book. The only thing she was sorry about was that when she'd run, she hadn't had a chance to get back in her hut and bring her pet raven, Raspberries. He'd been her only friend forever. Now she was alone with an uncommunicative book.

Picking *Magicks Mysteries* up again, she was about to tuck it back into her pouch when a blur of ebony feathers squawked through the tall trees and plopped on her shoulder. Moire Ain's heart soared, and she couldn't help grinning.

She rubbed her raven between his eyes, just above his beak. "Now that you're here, everything is perfect. You are the smartest raven in the world to have figured out how to get out of your cage. I wish I'd been able to get that lock off long ago." Moire Ain noticed a bit of woven wood caught on the tip of the raven's beak. "You chewed your way out? My, brave, strong, smart Raspberries. I didn't mean to leave you behind. It all happened so fast. I had to run."

The raven ducked his head and made contented growly noises.

"You weren't here to see what I just did. You are going to be so proud of me. I'm on my way to being a great and mighty wizard," Moire Ain said.

The raven cocked his head at her and made his threatening noise.

"No. Don't worry, Raspberries. Not like Hedge-Witch. Truly. I promise I will never kill anyone. Or make people sick or their animals die. I will only be a nice wizard and a great one."

Raspberries growled out, "Great and Mighty Wizard."

Moire Ain laughed. "You can talk! Hedge-Witch tried at least three spells to teach you to speak, but you never did."

"Great and Mighty Wizard," Raspberries said again, and butted his head against her chin.

"You believe in me? You think I'm great and mighty?"

She felt like a beginner, but maybe she was on her way to being great and mighty. If she could rescue herself with a magick rope, it was time to believe in herself. It was time to change her name to Great and Mighty Wizard and become what she wanted to be. She'd begin her future.

"Great and Mighty Wizard it is." She rested her head against her raven's side. "We're going to do great and mighty things, you and me, and my book."

For a few moments, she stood imagining all the magickal good things they would do. Raspberries tugged on her hair, bringing her back to the present and the riverbank.

She took a deep breath. "But first we need a good hiding place for the night. We may have a river between us and Hedge-Witch, but she'll find a way to get to us. We need a safe place so I can get started learning some of *Magicks Mysteries'* lessons." She tucked the book into her pouch.

"Rsssppp!" Raspberries said, and flew off her shoulder.

Moire Ain watched him fly high around the trees, circle, go low, then fly back to her shoulder. "Rsssppp!" He ducked his head, turning and pointing at the deep woods behind them.

"Lead on." Moire Ain started to walk while Raspberries grumbled. They hiked through the woods for only ten minutes before they came to a cliff. Moire Ain looked along the cliff face and then up it. She spotted a cave with a lot of shrubbery growing on either side of the opening.

Raspberries growled.

"In that cave?" she asked. "It was awfully easy for us to find this cave. Surely it will be at least as easy for Hedge-Witch to find it."

Raspberries snorted and hopped off her shoulder. He flapped up to one of the shrubs and tugged it over the cave opening.

"Hide the entrance! Good idea!" Moire Ain said.

She climbed the short distance up the cliffside. Once she was inside the cave opening, she broke off branches from the bushes and wove a covering to hide the entrance.

"That'll hide us. Plus from up here we should hear Hedge-Witch and be able to get inside before she can see us."

With Raspberries perched on her, she sat down in front of the cave covering and dug out the bread and cheese Goodwife Greenfield had given her. The food had been meant to last a few days, but she decided to eat it at once. She was so hungry, and she knew Raspberries would be too, since Hedge-Witch fed him so little. She hoped the book would help her find more food.

After their meal, the raven napped, and Moire Ain opened her book. She skimmed through *Magicks Mysteries*, figuring out that it was divided into lessons, thirty, about how to become a true wizard. When she learned to read from Goodwife Greenfield, she'd hoped learning the common language of Albion was all she'd ever need. But most of the book was filled with funny scratching that seemed sometimes to move.

"How do I get started if you're written in some kind of magick words?" She thumped her book closed. Staring over the woods below the cave, she tried hard not to let the tears come back. She'd escaped Hedge-Witch, and it was for nothing. If Moire Ain couldn't learn to be a wizard, and because of that Hedge-Witch caught up with her and got the book, the cruel crone would be too powerful. Moire Ain would be forced to do what the old crone ordered, to be part of the murder.

"Rssspppbbb," Raspberries slit open an eye, grumbled, and moved a step farther from her.

"Don't fret, Raspberries. I can puzzle this out. You know I can. No one but you and I know Hedge-Witch never even tried to cure anyone. She made a commotion of ordering me to learn to be useful, and I did it. She didn't really mean me to, but I was the one who figured out what plants would cure a fever or make blisters go away."

Moire Ain ran her fingers over the edges of the book's closed pages. "I have to learn magick, but how, if I don't know the magick language?" She held her breath for a moment, hoping the book would say or do something that would make its words appear in the Albion common language. But nothing happened. She fanned through the pages just in case the book communicated silently, and she would suddenly understand. But the indecipherable words still cluttered each page. "Magick should be just. This is not justice! It's not!"

Closing *Magicks Mysteries* again, Moire Ain drummed her fingers over the emblem on the front of the book. Almost worn away, it was a long rectangle with the title embossed on it. "It's shaped like one of those banners the Woosley kingdom's king puts out to announce how great he is. I remember last year he put out hundreds of banners to announce his birthday, and that everybody had to come up with a present. I wonder what it's like to get a present on your birthday? Or to know when your birthday is."

Moire Ain snuffled up her running nose. All her bravery was leaking out her nose and leaving her with too many sad thoughts. Stupid sad thoughts.

Her raven shuffled over closer to her and gently tugged on a strand of her curly hair.

"Thanks, Raspberries." She patted his head.

But he gave a sharper tug, pulled out a hair and dropped it on the book. Quicker than she could swat at him, he hopped onto the book cover and carefully arranged the hair so that it looked like a rope threaded through one corner of the embossed rectangle. He gave the hair a peck, and the cover seemed to ripple like a sail filling with wind. For a moment it looked exactly like one of the king's banners snapping in the wind.

"Make banners?" Moire Ain asked. "Make banners about . . . what?"

Raspberries stared at her.

"I don't get it. What good does a banner do? I mean, how does that teach me to read my book?"

Raspberries squinted at her.

"Teach? A banner about teaching? Wait. A banner about getting a teacher so I can learn from my book! You're so smart!"

Moire Ain put the book down and started pacing in and out of the cave opening. "The Woosley king uses his banners, and he gets lots of presents. Could I do the same and get a teacher?"

Raspberries tucked his head into his shoulder and made snoring noises.

Moire Ain wasn't a bit sleepy. "Where will I get banners? I don't have any money. Cloth and paint and such cost money." She sat, leaning her elbows on the cover of her book.

Raspberries' head popped out of his feathers. He snorted and leapt into the sky.

"What! Where are you going?" Moire Ain called after him. But the raven was a black blob, and she didn't dare run after him or yell any louder. Hedge-Witch might hear and find her.

With nothing to do but wait for Raspberries to return, Moire Ain flipped through her book again. From time to time, she looked up at the sunlight drifting down into the treetops. Where was Raspberries? Where was Hedge-Witch? As long as she heard the birds singing, and the squirrels chittering around her, she knew Hedge-Witch had not caught up.

Moire Ain let her eyes droop closed. When she jerked awake, everything was dead silent. Too quiet. She sat up, holding her breath and scanning below her for the old witch.

At first Moire Ain saw nothing. Then loud clanking and cursing burst through the woods. Into the clearing below her stomped a knight in rusted armor. He led a horse that snapped at the knight's rear every three steps. The knight was so busy smacking the horse's head away and studying the ground that he didn't notice behind them the length of fabric unraveling from under the horse's saddle.

Finally the knight stopped and bent over something on the ground. He straightened up and said, "That's his print. The dr'gon went that way!" He pointed straight at the cliff.

"Dr'gons," Moire Ain whispered. She'd never seen one, but she'd studied the pictures in her book. Even if she couldn't read all the words, she'd found a few bits and pieces in her language that said dr'gons and wizards stood together as partners. If dr'gons and wizards worked together, and she meant to be a wizard, then dr'gons were good. At least dr'gons were one thing she didn't need to fear. Hedge-Witch was enough.

Moire Ain wondered if that was why this knight was hunting for a dr'gon. She'd never seen a wizard. What if this knight was a wizard looking for a dr'gon? Maybe she should follow him and find her own dr'gon.

The knight spun on a rusty heel and pointed away from Moire Ain's cliff, deeper into the woods. When he held his hand out, his arm's armor fell off. When he bent to grab it, the horse took its opportunity and bit him in the rear.

The knight jumped and yelled at the horse, "If I didn't need you, you miserable excuse for a knight's warhorse, I'd strike you down." Holding his loose armor over his butt with one hand, the knight reached for the sword stuck through his rusty metal belt.

The horse snorted. His eyes glared a hot-coal red.

Moire Ain scooted back into the cave and behind the branches covering the opening, then peeked out. The horse's eyes still flamed, but the knight showed no fear. He swatted the horse on the side and lifted a leg to get up in the saddle. But he was still holding his broken armor and only had one hand to hoist himself up on the horse. The horse turned as the knight flailed about trying to pull himself up. When the knight fell back on the ground, the horse nickered. Moire Ain was sure the sound was horse laughter.

Now the knight rolled on the ground, jerking this way and the other trying to get up off his back. Finally he rammed an armored foot into the dirt and managed to lever himself onto his feet. When he was upright, he pulled a leather strap out of the chest piece of his armor. He used the leather to tie his arm armor back on, then marched to the horse and snatched the reins. This time he stilled the horse for a second, but not long enough for the knight to struggle back on top.

As he tried a fourth time to mount, the knight finally spied the long fabric hanging off the back of the turning horse. One leg in a stirrup the knight roared, "I say *stop!*"

The horse froze. The sudden lack of movement hurled the knight over the horse's neck. The rusty knight landed on his narrow dented bottom. The horse nickered again.

"Not much of a rider, sir knight?" Hedge-Witch strolled into the clearing.

Moire Ain scooted farther back from the ledge, clinging to the shadows inside the cave. She held her breath, hoping neither of them had seen her move.

But Moire Ain's thundering heart told her the truth. Hedge-Witch had found her. Moire Ain was trapped.

"I will have no sass from you, peasant," the knight screamed. "And get away from my horse."

The old witch backed away but grabbed the length of trailing cloth.

"Let go of that, you old crone," the knight yelled. "That's not yours."

The Hedge-Witch glared at the knight. "Have you seen a girl? A scrawny thing a bit taller than I, with mud-brown hair tinged with hellion red? No more than ten, maybe twelve, sun cycles old."

"No! Let go of it!" he yelled again.

This time the horse, his eyes flaring brighter red, stepped toward the witch. She dropped the fabric, her mouth moving. Moire Ain knew what the witch was doing. Hedge-Witch was casting a curse on the knight. If he was lucky, it wouldn't kill him, but if he wasn't lucky . . . .

Moire Ain held her breath, trying to think of how to help. But her skin turned to a coat of ice butterflies when the old witch stopped muttering and said, "You will regret this disrespect." Hedge-Witch skulked down the road, turning again and again to stare at the horse and rider. Something was very wrong. Hedge-Witch never just walked away.

CHAPTER 5

It wasn't until the old crone had hobbled so far down the road that she was nothing but a bobbing shadow that Moire Ain was able to slow her pounding heart. She turned her attention to the knight. Who was he that Hedge-Witch didn't try to kill him after he was rude? He was as tall as the shadowy visitor who had made the deal to kill a king.

Moire Ain had not seen more than the back of the stranger who had bargained with Hedge-Witch. Even if she had seen his face, the knight below her was covered in haphazard bits of armor, including his face. She tried to think if she had heard the clank of armor from the stranger. But she was sure she had not.

She was certain the knight and the stranger couldn't be the same person. Hedge-Witch would have acted like she knew the knight if they were the same. Even if the knight was not the evil stranger, there was something about him. The prickling that broke out on her neck around things magick was going strong.

But maybe the bad feeling was left over from Hedge-Witch. Morie Ain tried to clear away all the frightening thoughts crowding her head. She hated it when her excellent imagination made her worry that the world was full of dark things like Hedge-Witch instead of good ones like Goodwife Greenfield.

But sometimes she was right. Like the time she'd read Hedge-Witch's intention to feed poison to a sick pig to get even with a villager who had not bowed to her. Moire Ain had gasped at the dark aura over Hedge-Witch and her potion. Hedge Witch had turned on Moire Ain in a flash. Hate and punishment shone out of her eyes when Hedge-Witch said, "What is it, girl?"

Moire Ain had made up an excuse about pinching her fingers in the mortar she was using to grind herbs. Hedge-Witch seemed to believe her, but Moire Ain was so panicked she'd used fennel seeds in the pig's potion instead of the monkshood. The neighbor's animal had thrown up bulbous plants for an hour, burped, and promptly went back to eating normally. Hedge-Witch had beaten Moire Ain when they got home and refused to feed her for three days.

Moire Ain reminded herself that those days were gone. She had *Magicks Mysteries,* and she had escaped. But she hadn't learned its magick yet, and she didn't feel good about the knight.

Moire Ain stared at him. Did he have a murderer's

aura? She watched the knight slashing his sword at the fabric that trailed his horse. Finally he grabbed the material and sawed and tugged; at the same time, the horse whirled. The cloth twisted around the knight's feet and on up to his knees. With an angry oath, the knight let go of the fabric but kept a tight grip on the horse's reins.

He hopped up, eye to eye with the blood-eyed beast. "Remember your place. Goblin steed or not, you are under my command. Stand still."

The horse froze like a statue. The knight shoved off the material wrapped around his legs and walked to the horse's rear. With both hands curled around his sword's hilt, he slashed off the cloth, along with half the horse's tail. The knight kicked the pale fabric out of the road and pulled himself up on his goblin horse's back. "You need no padding under your saddle. Find the dr'gon," he ordered.

Moire Ain had heard that only knights with a great deal of magick hunted dr'gons. If a knight had magick, even if he didn't seem to be a wizard, he had to be someone she would like to know. But something stopped her from calling out to him. She couldn't bring herself to feel good about asking him for help. What if Hedge-Witch came back and did something horrible to the knight?

Moire Ain leaned a little out of the cave shadows to look harder. "I never saw a goblin horse," she whispered.

For a second, she thought the steed stared straight at her. His eyes flared so hot a red, Moire Ain was afraid any second he'd burst into flames and set the whole forest on fire. She shrank back.

Before the horse's eyes could explode, the sky filled with squawking so loud the trees' leaves shook. The goblin horse galloped off, with the knight barely holding onto his saddle's pommel. Behind them they left the pile of cloth and the hunk of horse tail.

Overhead, Raspberries soared out of a flock of ravens. The birds called so loudly, Moire Ain no longer heard the horse's metal hooves. The ravens circled above the woods. Raspberries cawed to them, and the other ravens flew off in the same direction the knight and Hedge-Witch had gone.

His wings extended like a shining feather sail, Raspberries glided until he hovered over the cave's entrance. In his talons, he carried a small pail that sloshed something green. Carefully, he placed it on their ledge, then landed and cocked his head down at the clearing. He turned back and eyed Moire Ain. "Rsssppppbbb," he said, nudging the pot toward her.

Until a year ago, Raspberries had been no more than a pet raven she'd raised from an abandoned baby bird. At the same time Moire Ain started reading the dark intentions of Hedge-Witch, the bird had begun to do things that were exceptional. Sometimes he'd brought Moire Ain a bowl or an herb before she asked. Moire Ain kept his specialness from Hedge-Witch.

She peered into the pot, then followed Raspberries's gaze to the clearing and the fabric sticking to the bushes. She touched the rim of the pot and came away with a thick green liquid on her fingers. "Cloth and paint. We have everything to make those banners to find a wizard to help me learn. Thank you!"

Moire Ain climbed down the low cliff face, careful to keep the pot from sloshing out its contents. Raspberries flew ahead. He was pulling the cloth free of the bushes before she got to flat ground. The raven tugged and stretched the cloth flat while Moire Ain gathered up the horsetail strands.

Raspberries, head cocked to one side, stared at her as she stood with the horse hair gripped in one hand. He flew to her shoulder and cawed his approval when she said, "A paintbrush, I think." Then she said more surely, "Definitely a paint brush!"

Raspberries snorted. Sometimes the raven treated Moire Ain like she was not the smartest of the two of them. She thought sometimes he was right. An old suspicion flew off her tongue, and she blurted out, "Are you an enchanted prince?" He occasionally acted so human-like, she thought it was possible. But as usual, he gave her a hard look, snorted, and flew up to a creeper vine climbing a tree. He tugged it loose and dragged it over to Moire Ain.

"No one talks to me. Just like my book. You know it

talked to me once, but now, nothing." Moire Ain snapped off pieces of the vine and wrapped them around one end of a bunch of horse hair to make a brush.

Raspberries paced across the cloth, cocking his head one way and then the other. Moire Ain studied it too. "I was thinking. We have enough for only one great banner, so we have to make it really stand out. Different. The king uses long wide banners." She spread her arms out side to side. "But we'll be special. We'll make ours tall and narrow."

She tapped a foot and stared some more. "The trick is to think of the right words to get me a teacher." She paced around.

Since they only had a small bucket of paint and the one piece of cloth, she had to paint the right words the first time. No mistakes.

"How about this: *Wizard for Hire Wanted. Parsimonious Rates.*"

She stared at Raspberries, who stared back. "I like *parsimonious*, don't you? We haven't actually got anything to pay a teacher with, so we need one who won't ask for much, and who will barter down for even less." She decided to worry about paying a teacher later. Right now she had to find one, impress him, and get him to take her on as a pupil. And teach her before Hedge-Witch caught up.

Once she could use the book and do bigger magick,

she decided the first thing she could do to prove she was a good wizard was to stop Hedge-Witch. She'd use her new magick to figure out which of the five kings of Albion Hedge-Witch meant to assassinate. Moire Ain would warn him.

She scratched practice words in the dirt beside the poster cloth. "If I make the letters big enough for people to read from the ground once we've hung the banner in the trees, I won't have room for a lot of words. I really can't fit more than *Wizard for Hire Wanted Parsimonious Rates*. That will have to suffice." She nodded.

Raspberries landed on her shoulder and stared at the words. He grumbled but did nothing more.

"Good. Then we're agreed." Moire Ain took up one of the brushes she'd fashioned and dipped it in the pot of green paint. "Where'd you get this paint anyway? It kind of smells funny." While she stroked on the words, she tried not to think of how the paint reminded her of the smell of raven poop after Raspberries had eaten mulberries. *Wizard* was painted out before she realized that to fit the big letters, she would have to put her words in three lines instead of two. Since this still let her use the words she wanted, it would be okay.

Raspberries launched off her shoulder and hovered over the paint pot. He dunked his tail in and added some decorations along the long edges of the banner. His painting wasn't as precise as hers, but he was definitely creative, if you squinted your eyes and tried hard to believe the splotchy bits didn't look a lot like raven poop. When he'd finished, he squawked and perched on a branch. Before Moire Ain finished the next word, she heard snoring and looked up to see his head tucked into his shoulder.

Moire Ain painted, stretching the contents of the little pot of paint as best she could, but as she finished *for Hire,* she realized she still wouldn't have room for all the words. She decided to leave out the word *Wanted* to make the paint last. The pot was dry when she finished *Rates.* With the sun hovering, the banner would dry quickly.

She needed a short nap too. Tucking herself under a bush, she was soon dreaming of learning from her book, of doing great magick, and of never being hungry or afraid again. When she woke, Raspberries was stabbing his beak through one of the corners of the banner.

"Are you sure you're not an enchanted prince? Or artist?" She slid a look out of the corner of her eye, but Raspberries ignored her, now preening the length of one wing feather. "Raspberries. You're such a clever . . . bird."

Once the banner was threaded with the rest of the vines and ready to hang, Moire Ain folded it, tucking it under her arm. There was enough day left, so she and Raspberries took off hunting for the right tree on which to hang this important poster.

For the banner to be seen by lots of folks, they had to hang it on a tree along the roadway. Which was risky, and meant they had to keep watch to avoid Hedge-Witch. Moire Ain shushed Raspberries often to make sure they did not attract attention. She hoped Hedge-Witch had not changed her habit of skulking through the woods rather than using a main road. As long as they were out where travelers could see them, Moire Ain hoped they'd be safe from the old crone.

But still she worried about their voices carrying into the forest, along a creek, or in a hollow. If the old crone found them, she'd force Moire Ain to return to the village. At the very least, Hedge-Witch would punish Moire Ain horribly for her disobedience, but worse, Hedge-Witch would carry out her plan to use Moire Ain for the murder.

It only took minutes to get to a place along the road that Moire Ain was sure would be perfect for travelers to see her poster. Raspberries snagged the top of the banner and flew up into the tallest tree. He wound the vines from the top corners of the banner into high branches. Moire Ain tied the bottom tethers down to the base of the tree. Since the banner was tall instead of wide, Moire Ain's part was simple. She would have had to stretch the banners between trees and climb a lot if she'd gone with a wide banner. She felt pretty smart about her idea.

But it took almost an hour before Moire Ain was satisfied with how the banner hung. Raspberries grumbled as Moire Ain made him change branches so the top edges were even, but he kept at it until she smiled at him. Moire Ain and Raspberries turned and headed back toward the cave to rest again.

Things had gone so well, she started worrying. Her luck couldn't hold; it never had before. Still afraid they might run into Hedge-Witch, Moire Ain crept quietly through the woods' shadows, listening hard for the witch. Twice they detoured off to drink from a spring. After the second drink, Moire Ain recognized the rusty knight's screams. He was yelling at someone. This time his venom was not directed at his horse.

CHAPTER 6

"Get your slimy scaly cowardly green tail out of that tree, dr'gon!"

Cl'rnce's eyes snapped open; the scratchy bellow below him gobbled up his dreams of home and peanut-butter-topped-with-honey sandwiches. Faster than he could blink, the stench hit him, choking Cl'rnce on a gagging breath filled with the sour-soil reek of rotted rutabagas. He didn't have to look down through his nap-tree's branches. Nasty Sir George had found him again. That was twice since this Journey began.

Pacing under the tree, Nasty Sir George rattled and screeched in his rickety, hole-ridden, and mismatched armor. Cl'rnce was pretty sure Nasty Sir George's helmet was once a war horse's head armor. No matter how clownish Nasty Sir George might look, it was a mistake to think the knight wasn't dangerous.

This was the second nap Cl'rnce had missed in two days. The first time his exasperating twin sister had found him and awakened him to rail about the Journey and the duty he had to fulfill. She was impossible, mean, and rude. But unfortunately she had been right about how dangerous the Journey was turning out to be without a Wizard Partner.

Her nagging words still rang in Cl'rnce's head. It irritated him that she pretended to worry about him but had no problem kicking her twin into this situation without a Wizard Partner. Sisters!

She'd caught him as he left and hissed out one little tiny warning, her irritation-hot dr'gon breath nearly knocking him over.

"Word's out. Sir George is after you, and he's crazy. Mind you, he's not crazy funny like you try to be, Cl'rnce." Hazel'd smacked Cl'rnce behind the front horn to make him stop screwing his face up and giving her his famous crossed-eyes look. "Listen up; you get the Whisper Stone to the Council in the next five days. Are you paying attention?"

She'd paused and let a particularly long flame slide out of her left nostril. Cl'rnce stopped mimicking her and nodded. If she added flame from the right nostril, she'd fire it at Cl'rnce and fry him again. His sister had no sense of humor, not even a tiny bit.

"You'd better be listening, and you'd better get going," she'd continued. "Gaelyn scried the crystal waters. Even if he's not one of the expected obstacles for the Journey, Sir George is in the vicinity. He's killed dr'gons

69

from seventeen of the eighteen dr'gon tribes. He's bragged he'll add a River Dr'gon." She'd paused, made her prissy, tight-lipped face, and stared at him.

Like always, Cl'rnce filed his sister's fears away under *Crazy and Doesn't Have Enough to Do So She Makes My Life Miserable.* But to get rid of her without being assaulted again, he'd nodded enthusiastically. She finally let him go.

Unfortunately, Hazel had been right.

"Time's up, dr'gon. Come down, or I'll burn the whole forest." Nasty Sir George crouched at the base of Cl'rnce's tree. The knight began beating a small rock against another larger one. When he got a spark, he laughed. He stood and pulled up a handful of dried weeds, tossing them down on the big stone. "I'll have some roasted dr'gon if you don't climb down." He snickered, then smashed the rocks together harder. He blew at the sparks, sending them dancing over the dried leaves.

"Why?" Cl'rnce said. It was a good question, not just for Nasty Sir George but for Cl'rnce too. Why was he being diverted and irritated by this lunatic? He had only three more days to get the Whisper Stone to Ghost Mountain. If Hazel hadn't been scarier than this knight, Cl'rnce would have chucked his inheritance, run home to Dr'gon and Wizard Technological School and Knights Academy, and hidden in one of his nap places. At least until he could come up with an easy way to do the Journey or foist it off on Hazel.

His sister was plenty bossy enough to be the Primus; she could handle the Council. If life was fair, Hazel would be the one delivering the Whisper Stone. All-day napper was the kind of River Dr'gon Cl'rnce wanted to be. He shouldn't be running and hiding from a crazy killer knight or taking responsibility for the Whisper Stone.

Nasty Sir George ignored Cl'rnce. He pounded the rocks together in a rhythm and sang,

> *"Sir George will kill them all.*
> *Every dr'gon dies.*
> *Sir George will kill them all.*
> *Each nest of dr'gonelles will roast.*
> *Primacy will go.*
> *Every tribe will die.*
> *Dr'gon Slayer and I!"*

As he came to the last word, he dropped the rocks and drew out his overlong and rusty sword. Cl'rnce heard the knight murmur, "Dr'gon Slayer."

For a moment, Nasty Sir George stared down the length of his sword, smiling from his mostly-holes helmet with the long face plate that he wore backward. After a full minute, he blinked and looked around. "What was I doing?"

Cl'rnce clamped his lips together and hoped. Maybe the crazy knight had forgotten Cl'rnce and would wander off. But Nasty Sir George slowly looked up and grinned. "Kill the dr'gon!" he shouted, and swung to hurl his sword up at Cl'rnce.

But as his arm arced backward, a hand grabbed an edge of the knight's arm armor and jerked him down to the ground.

"No one dies today!" a small girl yelled. "No killers!" She kicked Nasty Sir George in the helmet, making his head rattle from side to side in the metal. Then she jumped back with one hand over her mouth like she was shocked at what she'd just done.

Nasty Sir George made growling noises, but like a turtle on his back, he couldn't quite swing himself upright. "I'll kill you next," he screamed, thrashing but not getting back up on his feet.

"You won't," the girl said calmly, and took a breath. She breathed again and muttered, "This time I have to make it work." She drew a short rowan tree branch out of her ragged sleeve and pointed it at the knight. "Stay until released!" she said slowly. She repeated it three times, until the twig cracked and fell out of her hand. She looked up at Cl'rnce. "Are you all right?"

"Fine." He dropped off his branch, unfurling his wings just enough to glide. Shifting his weight to the right, he managed to land on top of Nasty Sir George.

Cl'rnce settled on the squirming knight's face. "I think we'd better get out of here." He shifted his eyes to the trail to their right that he was pretty sure led in the direction of Ghost Mountain and the Dr'gon Council Chamber, the Uamha.

Staring at the knight beneath Cl'rnce, the girl smiled. "No hurry." The girl swept auburn curls behind her ears and smiled. "I enchanted that mean knight. He's not going anywhere. He can't move."

Underneath Cl'rnce, Nasty Sir George was anything but still. He rocked and squirmed, shoving at Cl'rnce's posterior and definitely saying things that he should have his mouth washed out for. Clearly the girl had *not* be-spelled the killer knight.

"Good job," Cl'rnce said, not in a hurry to insult someone who had possibly just saved his life. "But this knight is a tricky sort. I think we'd better get out of here before . . . uh . . . before your spell expires."

"Spells do that?" The girl reached into a worn leather pouch on her rope belt and pulled out a small book. "Spells expire. I didn't see that part." She thumbed through the book, then stopped. "I can't exactly read all the lessons, only some of it."

Cl'rnce leaned over to see the title of the book. *Magicks Mysteries.*

With the pressure off his face, Nasty Sir George screamed, "I'll kill you both."

"Ah," the girl said, "he seems not to be be-spelled any longer. Maybe we should go."

"Good thinking." Cl'rnce stood up, kicking Nasty Sir George in the helmet for good measure. The knight stopped screaming, and if Cl'rnce heard right, started snoring. "Shall we go, uh . . . I didn't catch your name."

The little girl tucked the book back in her pouch and wiggled one half of the broken twig up her robe's frayed sleeve. She held out her hand. "I'm Great and Mighty Wizard."

"Really?" Cl'rnce managed not to let his mouth drop open in what his sister would have called *Rude Surprise.*

"Actually, my name is Moire Ain, but I'm learning to be the world's greatest wizard. I've decided believing that I will succeed is important, right? So I've changed my name to Great and Mighty Wizard."

"Glad to meet you." Cl'rnce tapped her tiny hand with two of his long golden claws. "I'm Cl'rnce of the Merlin tribe of the River Dr'gons."

"That's a mouthful of a name," Great and Mighty Wizard/Moire Ain said.

"Well, actually it's Cl'rnce Merlin Clan Principus River Dr'gons. But you can call me Cl'rnce." He liked this perky little girl. She looked to be no more than maybe twelve or less in human years. Kind of skinny, but judging by her ragged clothes, she was thin because she came from a pretty poor family. Which unfortunately

74

meant that among the things she would not have in her pouch was food, like peanut butter and honey sandwiches. Cl'rnce's stomach growled.

"You can call me Great and Mighty. Okay?" The little want-to-be-wizard looked like saying yes to this was about the most important thing Cl'rnce could do.

"Great and Mighty it is. And thank you for saving me from Sir Nasty. Shall we?" He pointed down the dirt road and started walking. Cl'rnce was certain it would be a really good thing to get away fast, before Nasty Sir George woke up and rocked and rolled himself over onto his knees and came after them. No matter what this girl believed, she was not a for-real wizard. They had to run for it.

But no sooner did Cl'rnce urge her to leave than an overly large raven plummeted out of the sky and squeezed off a large dropping, which plopped smack on Cl'rnce's head just behind his left horn. With a satisfied squawk, the ebony bird landed on Great and Mighty's shoulder.

"Raspberries!" Great and Mighty said, scratching the mangy bird between the eyes. The little want-to-be wizard's mouth twitched at the corners like she fought to keep from smiling. "That wasn't a nice thing to do to Cl'rnce. He's our new friend. He's going to help me become a proper wizard. And I'm going to help him fly." She bent closer to the bird, whispering like Cl'rnce wouldn't hear. "In my book, proper dr'gons don't walk or glide. They fly. He needs our help. Don't you think?"

The raven grumbled but didn't move.

Cl'rnce wasn't overly pleased that the want-to-be wizard was excited about butting in and teaching him to fly, but he decided for now not to point out that she had not been invited to interfere. "Is that your rude bird?" Cl'rnce looked around for something to wipe his head with. He'd have demanded that the little wizard want-to-be give up her robe, but it was so worn he was afraid it would fall to pieces before he could rub the raven poop out from between his scales.

"Yes. This is my best friend, Raspberries." She ran a finger over the top of the bird's head. "You know, I've almost finished my *Magicks Mysteries* book." Great and Mighty patted her pouch. "I mean the parts I can read. So I don't think I can really do . . . ." She clamped her lips shut like there was a bad secret she didn't want to share. Then she pushed her lips into a tight smile. He hoped her secret wasn't that she doubted she could do *any magick.*

Looking at her pouch reminded Cl'rnce. He tapped the locket he wore around his neck. It still had the dull sound of being full. He hadn't lost the Whisper Stone. Which was good, since he'd spent the time after setting up his spell traps trying to find where to stash it safely so he could raid Dr'gon Wiz's kitchen for a "Going on a hero's journey" lunch. And then he'd spent precious time remembering where he'd hidden it before he finally ran from the angry school.

It wasn't putting out the vibrations any longer, but he figured that was okay. Since Hazel had given it to Cl'rnce, it would probably start nagging instead of vibrating sooner or later.

"There's a diploma in the back of my book," Great and Mighty rattled on.

"Sorry. But I'm kind of in a rush." With just three days left to finish his Journey, for once he really did need to hurry. He definitely did not want to think about what would happen if he failed. It wasn't the Geilt clan he feared, but his formidable sister. Which meant really big-time mean. If he messed up, she'd make his life not worth living. She knew a thousand ways to torture him.

Thinking about all of Hazel's rules and instructions finally reminded Cl'rnce. Hazel had said something about him having to read a message in . . . . He tapped his small case's center. It opened, and cupping it, he used one talon to snag a piece of paper wedged next to the stone inside.

"What's that?" Great and Mighty's voice went up an octave to match how she stood on her tiptoes trying to see into his paws.

"Paper." Cl'rnce felt proud that he'd remembered Hazel had said to read it on maybe the fourth day. He didn't think he should wait until then. What would a day early matter? Especially if it meant he could ignore her orders. He unfolded the paper.

"No. I meant that shiny thing in your necklace." The little wizard want-to-be stretched higher on her toes.

"Male River Dr'gons do not wear necklaces. They wear chains with small cases for carrying important papers and things." He snapped the locket closed. "Like this paper."

"No. I mean the shiny thing. The thing that looked like it was on fire inside your lock... I mean, ornamental case."

Cl'rnce wrinkled his brow at her. The Whisper Stone was the only thing in his case, and it was just a dull, dingy old rock as silent as any pebble. Which it shouldn't be. It was almost like Hazel had switched the real one for something she picked up in a bathroom pit, so she could send him on the Journey and drive him crazy.

Tricking him made more sense than so easily giving in to sending him off to become Primus. The sister he'd grown up with would never give away the chance to be Primus to Cl'rnce. She was probably busy getting a waiver so she could become the next Primus while he was on this wild snark chase. It didn't matter so much. Just for the chance to get away from her and school, Cl'rnce was willing to make the trip. Who wanted to be Primus anyway? Not him. After he got back, he'd tell on Hazel to their mother. No matter how important Hazel thought she was, she would never cross an Elder, especially their mother, who was very good friends with

Thomas, the current Primus.

Cl'rnce decided the sun was in the little wizard's eyes. The pebble he carried was definitely not shiny, not special. He ignored her question and read his paper, which oddly was written in Albion instead of Modern Dr'gon:

> *Dear Lout of a Brother who does not deserve anything,*
>
> *This is not a trick, which you've probably convinced yourself it is. You are definitely on the quest to return the Whisper Stone to the Council Chamber and claim the Primacy.*
>
> *I know it's ridiculous to believe you'd be doing a good job, but I hope at least you've remembered to read this on the third day. If you'd put any effort in, you could have flown straight to Ghost Mountain and delivered the stone in one day and completed the Journey required of every Primus to be. But I know you. You're fooling around doing stupid stuff.*

"Then why didn't she just do it herself?" Cl'rnce muttered. He read on.

I know you're asking why I didn't do the job myself. Why I didn't usurp you. Believe me, if I were allowed, I would have. But you, you lout, have to be the one. Just believe me on this.

Now get your rear in gear and get to Ghost Mountain. And if, as I'm sure, you're still nowhere near it, you know time's up and you HAVE to GET a Wizard Partner and get help with the toad-swallow spell to unleash your ability to fly. It's an embarrassment to this family and all River Dr'gons that you've scared off all possible Wizard Partners, and for River Sakes, never bothered to learn to fly. HONESTLY!

Cl'rnce turned the paper over looking for a map or anything more. But the back was blank. "I don't think she meant I have to swallow a toad," he muttered. "She was just being angry Hazel, I think."

"Yeah. Whoever wrote that was really snarky," Great and Mighty said from where she'd climbed on a rock to read over his shoulder. "You need my help. It says you need a Wizard Partner. I'm coming with you."

"Didn't you say you were just learning to be a wizard?" He looked up at her. A beginner wizard who really didn't know how to throw a spell? She thought he needed her? He needed to get the troll's-breath-rotted rock delivered to the Council so he could appoint someone to do the work, then go back to Dr'gon Wiz and skip class and nap by the river. Instead he was doing Hazel's bidding while running from Nasty Sir George.

Cl'rnce shuddered from snout to tail-tip. Nasty Sir George wanted to nail Cl'rnce's extremely attractive green and purple hide to his knight's hovel's walls. Hazel told the truth about the knight. Nasty Sir George had shouted at Cl'rnce and bragged that he'd slain every genus of dr'gon on Albion except one, and that one was Cl'rnce's, the River Dr'gon.

Cl'rnce was maybe fifty percent sure Nasty Sir George might be smarter than he looked. Dressed in armor that was at least as much rusted holes as metal, he wore two left boots. Which seemed really dumb but had been very helpful to Cl'rnce in keeping ahead of the knight. Apparently the boot on Nasty Sir George's right foot hurt a lot, and the knight had stopped to take it off and complain so often the first day Cl'rnce had finally gained enough time for a nap today. Knowing where the knight was by his loud whining—Nasty Sir George spoke in nothing but a loud voice—and the extra time Cl'rnce gained while Nasty Sir George took off and put back on his boot, had given Cl'rnce a head start twice.

Today, Cl'rnce had been certain his escape would

be permanent. He'd made that amazingly clever fake map to River Dr'gon Territory and dropped it where the knight couldn't help but find it. The map should have sent Nasty Sir George in the wrong direction. In fact, he should have ended up in Killer Dr'gon lands. Those guys didn't mess around with tricks and running away. They would have just eaten Nasty Sir George.

Cl'rnce was proud of the exceptional job he'd done making the map look authentic. He'd crumpled the parchment and rubbed it with mud to make it look old and real. But either Nasty Sir George had been too smart to fall for the ruse, which was doubtful, or he couldn't read. "Probably can't read," Cl'rnce muttered.

"Yes, I can," Great and Mighty said.

"Didn't mean you." Cl'rnce checked over his shoulder. "I think we should hurry. Run!"

CHAPTER 7

Moire Ain sent Raspberries into the air and sprinted to catch up. Behind them, Nasty Sir George's snores grew louder and louder.

"Dr'gons are supposed to fly," she called to Cl'rnce's wide rear. "Why don't you take to the air to get away from that knight?" She flapped her arms as she ran.

Cl'rnce turned and shot her a glance that was both sad and mad at the same time. "Don't ask me that. Unless you're some kind of mean person, stay away from the flying. It's enough that Hazel heckles me about not flying almost as much as she makes fun of me for walking and running on my back feet. She even has Mother sighing at me about 'her odd son.' And I get lectured at Dr'gon Wiz. If I wanted to fly, I would have passed *Aviation for Dr'gons* and been the most popular dr'gon at Dr'gon Wiz. I'd already have a Wizard Partner, and I wouldn't need you. I. Do. Not. Fly. So leave me alone."

"Sorry," Moire Ain said, swallowing the harsh words about not needing her.

Cl'rnce walked backward as quickly as Moire Ain could jog forward. He kept droning on, "I like being different. I like walking. And I'm very good at it. I can walk very fast or very slow." He stuck up one and then the other of his well-muscled back legs. "I'm quite a bit faster at walking and running than any other dr'gon."

"Okay. And I'm sorry. You are fast." She looked back over her shoulder. "Oh, oh. Do you see how that taller tree is shaking behind us? I bet Sir George is awake and pulling on that tree to get upright." She turned to Cl'rnce. "How fast would you say he can run in that armor?"

Cl'rnce looked over her head. "Good question. He's been chasing me for two days, and I'm mystified at how he keeps catching up. Wait. Come to think on it, he did have a horse or two. Did you happen to see a horse or anything he could ride?"

Moire Ain was impressed. Cl'rnce wasn't just bragging about being a fast runner. If he could keep ahead of a horse and rider, he really was. Which made a new problem for Moire Ain. Her legs were pretty short, and she couldn't run fast enough to keep up.

She thought of page 125 in her book. There had been a picture of a flying wizard. Moire Ain could do that, couldn't she? She'd made a rope out of her belt and crossed the river.

"I can fly," she said.

"Huh?"

"See the picture of the flying wizard?" She pulled the book out of her pouch and flipped it open.

Cl'rnce leaned close to the page. He ducked his head, peering underneath the book and then staring at the front cover. He said, "Just curious. But how far along are you in your *Magicks Mysteries* book?"

Moire Ain pointed again at the picture, trying to picture herself in the air like she had pictured her river crossing. "Flying!"

"You've done this spell?" Cl'rnce looked skeptical. He was probably thinking about how her spell on Sir George had expired.

She couldn't lie. "Well, not yet. The words. I can't—" Moire Ain started to say.

"So you can't fly." Cl'rnce turned and strode away like he was going to leave her behind. "We need to get out of here."

"I can too fly." She couldn't let him decide he didn't need her, didn't want her along. She ran and caught up with him. Jumping in front of him, she waved her arms to make him stop. "I can do spells, which means I can fly. It's just another spell."

"I hate to bring this up. But your spell to make Nasty Sir George stay still didn't really work. Are you sure you can do spells?"

Moire Ain's shoulders drooped, and her chin dropped nearly to her skinny chest. She couldn't lie to him, even if it meant this dr'gon was going to abandon her. "Not exactly."

"Well, then. Let's do it my way and *RUN!*" He scooped her up and sped faster than Moire Ain had ever seen anything run.

In no time they were so far down the road and past the forest that they were racing through fields. "Can you see him?" Cl'rnce panted.

Moire Ain, from her position slung over his shoulder, answered, "Nope. No sign of him. You really are some runner. No wonder you don't fly. Or are you some species of non-flying dr'gon?"

"Too many questions. There's a village up ahead. I'm going to put you down. You're going to walk into the village and scout for a place for us to spend the night."

"Why am I going alone? Why are we looking for a place for the night so soon? It's still daytime."

Cl'rnce groaned. "Are you as naggy as my sister?" He slowed and stopped behind a very tall haystack. As Moire Ain slid to the ground, he sighed as if he was expecting her to keep on berating him.

But she knew what it was like to hear nothing but negatives, so she cocked her head to one side and asked quietly, "Why is Sir George chasing you?"

"Because he kills dr'gons. According to my sister, he's looking to kill a River Dr'gon, which I am. So he's after me."

Moire Ain plopped down in the shade of the hay-stack. "I hate killers. Why you? Why not your sister? Pardon me. I didn't mean anything against your sister. But why you?"

"No problem. My sister should be the one he's hunting, if he wants a real mean dr'gon to slay. Come to think of it, I don't know why me and not my sister. Good question. Unless . . . ." But he didn't continue. He sat down next to her.

"There must be something special about you." Moire Ain straightened her too short robe so that it pulled as far over her outstretched legs as possible. It didn't reach her ankles as a proper robe would but made it halfway down her shins.

Cl'rnce stared at her again like she'd said something she shouldn't have, or maybe it was just that he disapproved of her. She blushed to think what he was seeing. Besides being raggedy, she was only a five-foot-tall human with reddish curly hair that was always falling across her round face. She wasn't pretty, although she thought her green eyes were okay. And of course she had freckles, which Hedge-Witch said were the sign of low-class people who didn't know enough to wear a hat in the sun. Not that she had a hat.

She was stunned when Cl'rnce finally spoke. "I like your freckles."

Moire Ain's heart swelled at hearing a compliment.

There she sat in a robe so faded its color could have been anything to start out with, from brown to blue. With the holes here and there, she thought it looked more like it was made of dust than cloth. And the shoes she'd fashioned out of leaves tied with vines were already falling apart. He had to be seeing the poorest of peasants, and yet he said something nice about her freckles.

"You said you can read?" Cl'rnce asked.

Moire Ain nodded proudly but didn't get a chance to tell about Goodwife Greenfield and the lessons. He went on, "Hazel claims human peasants cannot. Not that there's anything wrong with being a peasant. You're different since you can read, and you're teaching yourself magick!" He laughed like the next part was a joke. One that stung Moire Ain. "Hazel even said peasants need a team of wizards to teach them to come in from the rain. She says wizards may look human, but they aren't." Cl'rnce stopped and blinked at Moire Ain. His voice took on an apologetic note. "I think she's wrong. Look at you. Wizards had to come from someplace before there were wizard families. Which means the first wizard learned magick all on his own, like you." He smiled like he'd paid her a huge compliment.

Moire Ain shook off the sting under his words and asked, "You know who the first wizard was? I do."

Cl'rnce pulled a piece of straw from the haystack and ran it through his fangs like he was cleaning his teeth. "Really?"

"Did you know that the first wizard was a dr'gon?" Moire Ain held up her book, pointing to a picture of a dr'gon who had clearly just made a banquet table of food appear.

"Can't be," he said. Drool gathered in the corners of his muzzle. "I ran out of food the first day out. I need food." He held out his paws for the book.

But Moire Ain couldn't let go of her treasure. She was afraid he'd eat the book. He was licking his lips like he would. She pulled it to her.

"If dr'gons were the first wizards, why would I need a partner? I would be able to do it all myself. I can't." Cl'rnce snorted.

"Yep. Things have changed, and you said you need a Wizard Partner." Moire Ain jumped to her feet. "I need a teacher, and since dr'gons were the first . . . ."

"Don't say wizards. It's just not so. I don't think you can trust your book."

"Of course I can. It's a *very* good book!" But Moire Ain dropped it into her pouch. She needed the dr'gon. She was sure. And he needed her. Even if he denied it, a proper dr'gon should fly. If he didn't want to be her friend, at least they could trade helping each other.

Cl'rnce's head jerked up. "Did you say *trade*?"

Moire Ain was startled. She hadn't said 'trade' out loud. How did he know? It didn't matter; she was going to make this partnership work. He seemed to waver one way and the other. She'd do a little of what his sister did and push him to be her partner.

She put her hands on her hips. "Do you need a wizard or not?" She tried to make her eyes slitty and demanding, like she thought his bossy sister would.

Cl'rnce sighed. "I suppose. As fast as I can run, I only have three days to get to the mountain, and Nasty Sir George is a real nuisance. Truth is that I'm a little turned around on the directions to Ghost Mountain. I guess I need help."

"Maybe with your flying?" Moire Ain said. "I was just thinking if I could help with that, you could avoid Sir George and get to your mountain fast."

He looked a little irritated, but he said, "Maybe. Do you know Ghost Mountain?"

She shook her head.

"Well, they say one side looks like a scary face. But I think the only way you can see that face is if you're up in the air. And we have to find the entrance to the inside of the mountain where the Dr'gon Council Chamber, the Uamha, is."

The list of what she'd need to learn and do was getting long. And according to Cl'rnce, they didn't have much time.

"It's inescapable. I need to fly, and I need magick to fly." Cl'rnce sighed and looked at her again as if he wanted to get her book and eat it, or something.

Moire Ain hoped he wasn't convincing himself she was too raw and new at magick and he'd be better off just stealing her book.

"Yeah. I need a partner," he said. But Cl'rnce looked away from her.

She knew a lie when she heard one. Something about what he'd said was not true. The way he'd stared at her book made her believe he thought he could find something to help himself if he had the book. She wondered why he didn't just take it from her. Hedge-Witch would have. But he wasn't Hedge-Witch. Moire Ain didn't want to believe he was anything like the old crone.

"Say the magick word?" Moire Ain gave him her biggest smile.

"Huh? I thought you were the wizard with the magick."

"Honestly, you're rude." She couldn't help frowning at him, even though she was trying to get him in a better mood.

"That's what Hazel says."

"Really? I'd like to meet her."

"No, you wouldn't. Trust me." He eyed her pouch, and she quickly tightened the string closing it.

"The magick word is . . . ." She waited for him to say it. She wanted him to be that special dr'gon she needed.

Cl'rnce laughed. "Abracadabra!" He smiled.

It wasn't what she hoped for, but his smile made her feel better. "No. It's *please*."

Raspberries flew overhead cawing. She craned her head around the haystack. "Rotten frog farts!" she said as she scrambled to her feet. "Run!" And she took off in the direction of the village ahead.

CHAPTER 8

For once Cl'rnce didn't argue. He got up and ran after the already speeding Great and Mighty. In five paces he'd caught up with her, grabbed her by the back of the raggedy robe, and tucked her under one arm. Then he sped up to what he liked to call Ultimate Speed but his sister called Layabout-Brother-Sniffed-Out-Food-and-Is-Headed-for-It-Speed. Hazel wasn't completely wrong. He could locate and get to food very efficiently and quickly. Admittedly this journey was the first time he'd used his running ability for anything but food gathering or escaping school or avoiding sister punishment.

"Is Nasty Sir George close behind us?" Cl'rnce huffed.

"He's coming fast!" Great and Mighty's voice slid to him, backward over her legs.

Without thinking, he'd stuck her under his arm, facing to the rear. Which was pretty smart, but then he was exceptionally intelligent, with or without Dr'gon Wiz schooling or books in general. Which reminded

Cl'rnce. "You still have your book?" he asked.

"Of course I . . . ."

Cl'rnce felt Great and Mighty wiggle, hopefully so she could reassure them both about the book still being in her pouch.

"Uh-oh!"

"What do you mean, uh-oh?"

"My book. It's gone. No. I see it. It's back behind us in the middle of the road. When you grabbed me, you turned me upside down; somehow it fell out of my pouch. Quick. Go back for it."

Cl'rnce slowed slightly. He had to think. She'd said Nasty Sir George was close. How had the knight caught up? If Cl'rnce turned around and ran back for the book, Nasty Sir George could catch him. The miserable knight had a big rusty sword and a really bad temper. As a rabid dr'gon slayer, he'd do his best to make mincemeat of Cl'rnce. Great and Mighty wanted that book, and admittedly so did Cl'rnce. But maybe he could find another wizard who didn't need a book. Maybe Hazel was wrong, and these villages were full of peasants with magick and books.

And then Great and Mighty ruined everything. "Please, Cl'rnce. Please, go back and get my book. It's the only thing I have."

Cl'rnce stopped. This was crazy. She was crazy. He couldn't do this. He should just dump her and run away, but . . . he couldn't. Gently, he put the little want-to-be wizard down on the dusty road. He couldn't look at her. He knew from the sniffling that she was getting all soppy. He just couldn't allow that.

Cl'rnce took a deep breath, pushed his shoulders back so he stood his full twelve feet. "Stay here. I'll get your book." He sucked in a second, not-as-steady breath and said in a slightly shaky voice, "And I'll take care of that dratted knight."

"Roar at him!" Great and Mighty shouted.

"Roar?" Cl'rnce stared at the figure moving blurringly fast toward them. From the way the sun reflected off different areas of the figure, Cl'rnce was certain it couldn't be anyone but Nasty Sir George and his slapped-together armor. How could the knight have run fast enough to almost catch up, especially in all his clunkiness?

"Yeah, roar. Like a really angry and powerful dr'gon. That should scare Sir George."

Cl'rnce glanced at Great and Mighty. She wiped muddy streaks off her face, which once wiped didn't have quite as many freckles as it had before. A smile jerked at her mouth. "You can do it, Cl'rnce," she said.

No one in his whole life had said that to him. No one had needed him like she did. No one had believed in him. This was getting complicated. Cl'rnce tried to remind himself that he was just a selfish lout who wanted the book and not the wizard. He only wanted that book so he could get rid of the Whisper Stone, do his duty and order everybody else to do the Primus work, get Hazel off his back, and return to sleeping the afternoons away by the riverside.

But it wasn't working. He wasn't thinking about the book or naps when he started to run down the road at the knight and the book. He wasn't thinking about going back to being alone with no friends to worry about when he sped up to Ultimate Speed. He wasn't thinking about dumping Great and Mighty for one flying spell in the book when he drew in a huge breath and roared as loudly as he'd ever roared. Louder than the time Hazel snuck up on him and clamped a super angry and tenacious crocodile onto Cl'rnce's tail.

What he was thinking was seeing a smile on Great and Mighty's freckles-and-smudge face. He was thinking how it would make her happy if she really became a wizard. He was thinking how he'd never made a friend before, and how it wouldn't be so bad if she became his partner. Not that he needed one, but maybe.

Cl'rnce charged at Nasty Sir George, sucking hotter and hotter breath and roaring louder and louder. Cl'rnce was almost up to the book when he saw why Nasty Sir George had traveled so fast. The mismatched knight was riding a goblin horse. Faster than any dr'gon, goblin horses were made of fury and wind. They were warriors so feared that even dr'gons would rather fly away than fight them. Which Cl'rnce couldn't do. He skidded to a stop. "Rotten frog farts! Now what?" There was no way he was going to tangle with the goblin steed.

But Nasty Sir George and his horse never slowed. The goblin mount charged ahead, its bare, smoking head ducked down like a bull bent on goring Cl'rnce. One scratch from a goblin horse's horns could immobilize a dr'gon. Which would give Nasty Sir George plenty of time to capture Cl'rnce and behead him.

Cl'rnce stood his ground, counting the pounding hoofbeats of the horse. At the rate it raced ahead, it would be on him in ten, nine, eight . . . . At the last second, Cl'rnce danced to one side, and horse and rider rushed past. Cl'rnce had gotten particularly good at this maneuver when dodging his vengeful sister. His timing was honed by years of practice. He really should thank Hazel for the training.

Cl'rnce laughed when he turned to watch the horse and rider. But instead of turning to challenge him again, they continued in a straight line leading to Great and Mighty. "Run!" Cl'rnce screamed in a voice that was more panic and less bravado.

But the little wizard-to-be stood as still as a statue. It was as if she was paralyzed in fear. Cl'rnce sucked in an angry hot breath and took off to catch up with the goblin horse and Nasty Sir George.

As fast as Cl'rnce could run, he was no match for the

horse. This certainly explained how Nasty Sir George had kept up with Cl'rnce over the last two days. Cl'rnce wasn't going to get to Great and Mighty in time. If only he could fly. For no good reason, since he'd only just met this little Great and Mighty, he wanted the power to get her out of danger.

For the first time in his life, Cl'rnce's eyes got blurry. Probably an allergy to all the dust the horse kicked up with its burnt iron hooves. Cl'rnce had never cried, so that wasn't it. He snorted up his runny nose and wiped at his leaky eyes, still racing as fast as he could go. The horse and knight were almost on top of Great and Mighty. "Run! Please, *RUN!*" Cl'rnce screamed again.

But Great and Mighty did not move.

When the horse was only fifty paces away, she raised her arms and chanted. Cl'rnce could only see her lips move. He couldn't hear her words over his own screaming. She had failed with her Be-Still spell before. How could she think she could do anything now? Why didn't she escape? Maybe she'd dart out of the way at the last minute like he had. Cl'rnce hoped.

The horse was only twenty-five paces from the little wizard-to-be. Cl'rnce roared. He'd never roared so deep and loud. His own horns shook. He felt out-of-control anger so big he wanted to stop that horse and rider, to kill them if he had to. Everyone thought Hazel was right when she said he was afraid of his own shadow and couldn't hurt a fly. Cl'rnce didn't argue. Then again, he'd never been angry enough to hurt a fly before.

For no good reason, because really and truly he'd just met this girl, and really and truly he didn't need her slowing him down and tagging along, Cl'rnce roared out lava hot, booming. To his roar he added what he'd known in his heart of hearts was sleeping deep inside him. Fire. He'd never spit anything but sparks before. He felt he was too clever to resort to brutality when he could irritate and infuriate Hazel and anyone else without much effort by just using his wits. But for no good reason, really and truly, Cl'rnce spit a flame so large it was taller than the knight sitting atop the horse, and wider than the horse.

Cl'rnce couldn't scream and flame at the same time, so he hoped Great and Mighty would know to dodge out of the way. Too late to stop the fire, he prayed she would not be caught up in the flame with which he intended to crisp Nasty Sir George and his goblin horse.

The inferno engulfed the horse and rider. At the last second, Cl'rnce tried to suck it all backward toward him, but he couldn't stop it from reaching Great and Mighty and the mangy raven perched on her shoulder.

CHAPTER 9

Raspberries' wings beat Moire Ain's face, breaking her concentration. She grabbed him and held him to her chest. But the next moment, she dropped him and threw her hands back up. A huge ball of fire galloped at her. Sir George's face resembled a flaming jack-o-lantern, and his burning horse and sword were aimed straight at her.

"I need protection," she breathed to Raspberries, now silently huddled on her shoulder. "Like that shield bouncing at Sir George's side." And she knew what to do.

Her hands steady in front of her, she pictured a huge shield and sent it flying at the oncoming knight. He hit the invisible shield and flew backward, falling off his horse. But he was still on fire. Since she'd managed to get this spell right, Moire Ain flipped another one on him quickly, covering him with dirt.

The fire died in a column of smoke and dust. Moire Ain heard Sir George choking on the thick, dirty air. Before she could take a step to inspect her triumphant spells, Cl'rnce rushed at her. His arms pinwheeled through the smog. When he got to her, he stopped, staring first at her and then down at soot-and-dirt-covered Sir George.

Sir George's goblin horse pawed at the dirt, then head down, it butted Sir George over onto his back. Moire Ain tried not to laugh at the knight once again doing an imitation of a turtle unable to flip off its shell and back onto its feet. The horse snorted, turned, and cantered away.

Cl'rnce shot a look after the horse. "He's headed for the Elf Mountains." He gave Sir George a shove, making him spin on his back. "In case you were thinking of riding that horse again, you better head east. And leave us alone."

Brushing ashes off her robe, Moire Ain smiled to herself. Raspberries shook himself so hard, he almost fell off her shoulder. Soot sprayed everywhere, and Moire Ain had to dust herself off again.

Cl'rnce asked, "What did you do? You're not a bit burned. Dirty thanks to your ratty bird, but how did you get away from Sir George? Did his horse throw him?"

Moire Ain smiled. "It wasn't his horse! I watched the knight with his shield nearly bouncing off him. It came to me that shields were good defenses, even if Sir George didn't use his to avoid your fire. So just like that, I pictured a shield spell. He ran into it and bounced off. I'm not sure if he fell off the horse or was thrown. But the important thing is—that makes two!" She held up her pointer fingers on both hands. "That's two enchantments I've cast." When Cl'rnce didn't smile back at her right away, she added, "I know. You're thinking this one was the only one that's worked so far." He didn't say anything snarky about her magick, so she went on. "You surprised me when you breathed fire at Sir George. Good thing I put that shield up, huh?"

"Yeah." Cl'rnce stared at her, looked down at the knight and then up at the rapidly disappearing horse. "But what happened to my fire?"

Something in his voice sounded a lot like how she felt about her spells when they went wrong. He was worried his flaming had gone wrong. Maybe they had something in common. "Was that your first flaming?" she asked.

Cl'rnce shrugged. "Maybe I was only trying to make him smoky." He flicked another glance at the thrashing knight. "Maybe that's all I need to stop him. Smoke."

Not wanting to say anything that made him feel bad that his flame had gone out so easily, Moire Ain shook her head, letting more ashes fly. Her hair seemed to want to stick to her face. She pulled everything into a stubby ponytail and stood holding it behind her head. "I need something to hold my hair up. Do you have a ribbon?"

Cl'rnce choked. "Pardon? We just got through escaping death, and you think I carry around *accoutrement* for hair?"

She smiled. "I guess not." Letting her fistful of hair

drop, she peered down her filthy robe and stuck out an ash-smothered foot. "I guess I should have left the shield up a little longer. Like until the wind blew this cloud away. Maybe that's a flaw to my shield spell. It didn't last long enough." She went on, "Or maybe it was that extra I put on the spell. It sounded pretty impressive, but . . . ."

"Okay. What extra did you say? Do to my fire?" Cl'rnce sounded more irritated than anything. He didn't sound like he cared about her spell but only wanted to know what went wrong with his flame.

"Fog of war, shield me now." Moire Ain lifted her chin. She was sorry he felt bad, but she'd done something she hadn't been so sure she could do. She wanted him to be proud of her. "Pretty fancy, huh?"

Cl'rnce finally looked her in the face. It took a full minute before his mouth curled up in a smile. "You bumbled it."

Moire Ain felt like she'd been slapped.

He reached out and touched her lightly. "Wait. That's a technical term in magick. It means . . . ." His muzzle screwed up like he was trying hard to think of some way to get out of insulting her. "It means . . . you fancied it up. Yeah, it's Dr'gon for fancied-up spell." His eyes pled with her to be happy again.

Moire Ain had had enough of unhappy. If he cared how she felt, that was good enough. "I think I like that.

I'm a Bumblespells wizard! Fancy." Her smile slipped into place as she slapped again at the dirt on her robe. "I need a bath."

Cl'rnce chuckled and said, "You're not the only dirty one." Using a back talon, he shoved Nasty Sir George, which made the snarky knight curse even louder. "I think your fog addition maybe put out my fire. That's very interesting. You're sure you didn't see Nasty Sir George counteract my flames?"

Moire Ain covered her mouth so she wouldn't laugh at the knight. She tried to keep her voice serious like she was being very logical and not critical of a knight who was flailing harder as he spun on his back turtle-like in his overturned shell.

"I don't think he does magick." She tucked her hair behind her ears, but being curly the hair sprang forward again. Moire Ain sighed. "As for your flame, he looked like he was covered in it, but you know he wasn't burning. I think your blast went right over and all around Sir George and his horse, then bounced off my shield. That's when it got interesting."

She waved her hands to demonstrate. "When the bounced-back fire hit Sir George, I'm pretty sure his horse bucked Sir George into the air toward me. Then there was this loud bang. For a second it looked like Sir George was really on fire, but then the fire floated around like a cloud, sort of licked at Sir George, then drew into itself until it was a tiny little speck. Next I heard a second burp, and ashes blew out along with dust when he hit the ground."

Before she could finish, Raspberries rocketed off her shoulder, flying back the way they had come. "Come back!" Moire Ain called. But the raven cawed and swooped low. He snatched something off the road and flew back to her.

"My book!" she said as he plopped on her shoulder, dropping the book in her grubby hands. Moire Ain felt so good having her book, she wanted everybody to feel happy too.

She leaned close to Cl'rnce and whispered, "I don't want to hurt his feelings, but I think Sir George was so filthy and rusty his dirt caught fire and sort of became smog or something."

"Bumbled spell," Cl'rnce muttered. "At least it looks like my blast pretty much worked. Even if it was my first attempt, it would be catastrophic for a dr'gon to fail at flame throwing." He looked up as if startled to realize he'd said all that aloud. "So I guess now he's mad about being set on fire."

Moire Ain cocked her head to one side and watched Sir George flail and curse. "I think you're right that he's angry about the fire, but he didn't start cursing until his horse ran off. He's been saying some pretty interesting things about the horse. Listen."

Sir George threw his arms and legs this way and that, clearly trying to fling himself back onto his feet. "Dratted rotten goblin horse. Should never have trusted them. The next better not run away like a coward." In his struggles, he spun faster, like an out-of-control merry-go-round. His eyes found Cl'rnce's. "Don't think this is over. I will kill you, dr'gon. I will. It'll be different next time," he said, his voice rising and falling as he spun faster.

Cl'rnce took Moire Ain by the arm. "Time to go. I know a pond where you can get cleaned up. It's on my way to . . . ." He glanced at Sir George, who had quieted down and seemed to be listening. Cl'rnce leaned close to her and whispered, "To Ghost Mountain. Let's go get you cleaned up."

At once Moire Ain understood that they couldn't let the knight know where they were going. With one finger to her lips, she nodded, and she and Cl'rnce strolled away from Sir George. Raspberries rode on her shoulder, muttering a low growl.

"Where are you going? You miserable dratted dr'gon and your ratty friend, get back here!" Sir George screamed.

"The Albion Sea! I can wash up properly when we get to the ocean. Salt water takes out soot, right?" Moire Ain asked in a loud voice, winking at Cl'rnce.

He smiled back at her. "You're a smart one, even if

you are human," he whispered.

As they walked away, every few seconds either Cl'rnce or Moire Ain turned and looked behind them, making sure Sir George was still incapacitated.

After they had traveled a while, Cl'rnce slowed and stood with his neck stretched up high. "Finally, the village. They must have food!" His stomach growled, making Moire Ain remember how long it had been since she had eaten.

Pointing at the same village, now a big smudge on the horizon, Moire Ain asked, "When we get there, we can ask someone to go back and help him out, right?" The knight might be their enemy, but Moire Ain couldn't stand leaving him helpless.

"It wouldn't be my first choice, but okay." Cl'rnce sighed. "But we'll ask them to wait an hour, so we can get far ahead of him." Cl'rnce rubbed his stomach. "I wonder if there's lots of food? Got any ideas on how to convince the villagers to give us some?"

Moire Ain thought of the poor villagers where she came from. As hungry as she was, she wasn't sure she wanted strangers to give what little food they had to her. She hoped Cl'rnce wasn't thinking of threatening them with fire or anything.

They walked through the outskirts and on into the center of the village without seeing a single person, not even a dog on the road.

"Where is everybody?" Cl'rnce wondered.

"Maybe they're afraid of you," Moire Ain said. Raspberries swooped off her shoulder and perched on the top of one of the huts. She hoped they could walk through the village and keep on their journey.

Cl'rnce laughed. "Nobody is afraid of dr'gons. Be serious."

"Well, they're not afraid of me." Moire Ain pointed to the ten rickety stick huts lined along the dirt road. Not one of the shacks seemed big enough to house a flock of chickens, let alone a family of peasants. "These are a lot like the huts in my village. This is a very poor village." She frowned, hoping Cl'rnce would get the point and keep traveling.

"What's this?" Cl'rnce kicked at a pile of straw and feathers squatting in the middle of the village's one road. The center of the mess was dabbed with huge, dried-mud footprints. He circled the pile, then bent over one footprint for a long time. Moire Ain paced around him. At last Cl'rnce stuck one of his back paws out next to the footprint. His large paw was tiny compared to the print.

Moire Ain leaned over. "Rotten frog farts! That's from the world's biggest dr'gon. Can you believe the size of his paw prints?" She was amazed and a little afraid. Cl'rnce had been kind to her, but he had thrown fire at a knight. What would a really huge dr'gon do to a village?

"No, I don't believe it, not for a second," Cl'rnce said.

"This is a fake."

"What do you mean? Like as in not real dr'gon paw prints? What else could they be? They look real. See how detailed, even the muddy bits where the claws and chicken feathers are stuck together." Moire Ain bent, using her fingers to try to measure the huge prints. "It's twenty finger-lengths long! Wait. Do you mean these are some other kind of monster prints?" she asked.

Cl'rnce looked up at the huts. "No. I mean these aren't real anything footprints. Somebody faked 'em." Cl'rnce pointed. "Look where the smallest claw is on each print. Notice it's always on the same side. They're all right paws. No left paw prints. Unless this was a one-legged dr'gon, hopping all over the place . . . ."

Moire Ain clapped her hands, relieved that this wasn't a fast, dangerous dr'gon. "You figured it out. It's a one-legged dr'gon. He hopped on chickens to catch them. And probably flattened them." She took a step back from the mounds of mud and feathers. "It was an accident."

Cl'rnce shook his head. "That would be a pretty good trick, and it would mean the paw prints should be really deep from the weight of such a big dr'gon jumping up and down. These prints look like they were kind of painted on top of the straw. See? The straw pieces aren't even broken. If something heavy had trod here, the straw would be in tiny pieces."

"Why would anyone make fake prints?" Moire Ain asked.

"It was the chicken-stomping dr'gon! No food here. Pass on down the road," a voice yelled from the nearest hut. Raspberries sat on the hovel's top, pecking through the straw roofing.

Moire Ain understood and headed down the road. But Cl'rnce called her back. "Great and Mighty, look at this! The peasant's sitting in the middle of a pile of bald chickens." Cl'rnce had his head stuck into the opening of one of the huts.

Moire Ain doubled back and peered over his shoulder. The peasant inside pointed to Moire Ain and Cl'rnce. "Get out of my home. You're too big, and you'll pull it down, big, fat dr'gon." She squinted angry eyes at them.

"Am not fat. I'm perfect; my mother said so," Cl'rnce muttered as he backed out of the hut's opening. "Everybody's in a foul mood." He tapped Moire Ain's arm as she backed away. "You do notice the peasant's not afraid of me. Told you so."

The peasant bustled out of her hut, brushing chicken feathers off her robe. "Get out, you big, hungry dr'gon! We are not sharing our chickens!" The peasant punched him in the leg. "You're fat, and you're soft. Lazy."

She turned to Moire Ain, catching hold of one of the little wizard's hands and running a finger over the calluses. "This little one is a hard worker. Why are you hanging around with him?" She jerked her thumb backward at Cl'rnce.

"He's my friend," Moire Ain said.

"Hrumph." The peasant spit out of the corner of her mouth, just missing Cl'rnce's foot. "I don't care what you saw in the hut, you need to move on. We only have enough chickens for our village. Especially after that big, snarky dr'gon blew through here yesterday. Go away!"

"Was it a one-legged dr'gon?" Moire Ain pointed to the tracks.

"Of course not. Dr'gons all have two hind legs to run and steal chickens on. But this one didn't bother to run after our birds; he just swooped and scooped, and sort of skipped, coming back three times." She slapped a hand over her mouth. "I mean, another dr'gon hopped by and took all the rest of our chickens, so if you're from the king looking for tax-chickens, we're out."

"Of course!" Moire Ain said.

But Cl'rnce looked puzzled. "Dr'gons don't eat chickens. Dr'gons are vegetarians."

"Tell that to that nasty dr'gon." She snorted. "Haven't you ever heard of Killer Dr'gons? They eat all kinds of animals. Even dr'gons, especially fat, lazy ones like you!"

Cl'rnce choked. "We have to go." He grabbed Moire Ain's arm and pulled her away and down the road.

"What's wrong?" Moire Ain asked.

But Cl'rnce just shook his head. "We're leaving. I'm

not that hungry. We need to get to Ghost Mountain."

The peasant turned to one of the villagers, who had slowly gathered behind her. After a few words, she turned back to Cl'rnce and Moire Ain. "Easy. A day's flight." she pointed through the collection of huts to a low purple range of mountains. "See the big white peak? That's the one."

Before Cl'rnce could answer, Moire Ain said, "Oh, he can't fly. We'll have to walk. How far would that be?"

"Can't fly?" the peasant frowned. "I've never heard of a dr'gon who couldn't fly."

"It's okay. Once I become a mighty wizard, I'll teach him to fly," Moire Ain said.

"Oh, you're a wizardry student," the peasant said. "I could use a good spell for chicken food that never runs out." She raised her eyebrows like she was hoping Moire Ain would spit a spell out for her right then and there.

"Oh, uh. . . ." Moire Ain dug her toes into the dirt. Even if her last spell had gone well, she was nervous about a failure like the one before it.

"She's still in the training phase," Cl'rnce said quickly. "You know, where they only let her do a spell in front of her instructor. Very important that she learns everything exactly right during the first few months."

"Of course," the peasant said. "No chance of a simple spell to ensure rain every other night? Keep the crops growing?"

Cl'rnce shook his head. "Sorry, not until she's through probation."

"Too bad," the peasant said. "So why are you going to Ghost Mountain?"

Cl'rnce cleared his throat. "I need to pay a courtesy call on an old friend."

"Good bye," Moire Ain said, holding up her arm. Raspberries flew from the hut roof, landing lightly on her shoulder. But before she followed Cl'rnce, she bent over one of the naked chickens, who had waddled out of the hut and into the road, and whispered. The chicken bobbed its head and shook a stubby wing. A last white feather drifted into her outstretched hand. "Thank you," she said, and tucked the feather into the pouch with her book.

When Cl'rnce and Moire Ain had marched beyond the last hut, Cl'rnce asked, "Why did you ask for a feather from the chicken?"

"It's for your flying spell," she said, patting the pouch.

"Oh."

Moire Ain was surprised to see his eyes go a little watery. She had this feeling Cl'rnce didn't know what to do when someone wanted to be nice to him, be his friend. She felt sad for him, and happy that she wanted to be his friend, and she was sure he wanted to be hers.

CHAPTER 10

"I don't need a flying spell," Cl'rnce grumbled.

Moire Ain looked hard at the dr'gon. She hoped he was just being a grump, protecting his own embarrassed feelings. She didn't want to believe he was too lazy to learn flying so he could finish his hero's journey.

Raspberries squawked and squinted at Cl'rnce. He took off and circled over the dr'gon. Cl'rnce's head followed Moire Ain's pet. She tried not to laugh; she was pretty sure this big dr'gon was afraid of little Raspberries—or at least of his bad habit of pooping on the dr'gon.

"Come, Raspberries," Moire Ain called, holding out an arm. "Be nice to Cl'rnce. He's our new friend. He's going to help me become a proper wizard. And I'm going to help him fly."

"Rude bird!" Cl'rnce snorted at the bird. He turned to Moire Ain, "Who says I'm going to help you? I don't fly because I don't want to."

Raspberries flew off so fast, Moire Ain didn't have

time to feel hurt by Cl'rnce's selfish words. She was too amazed at her pet, who had rarely moved at anything but a leisurely pace.

When she looked back at Cl'rnce, she decided she had to persuade him to help. She would never be a great and mighty wizard if she couldn't be positive about learning. "Sure you are—going to help me that is. You're a dr'gon. I need a dr'gon. Dr'gons help. And as for flying, I saw it in my book. You know you want to fly. All dr'gons do." Moire Ain smiled, then pointed ahead. "Look! Raspberries has it. My banner. I don't need it anymore since you can teach me magick."

She watched the tiny, far-off banner rippling on the winds. "It sure is a good banner. Very eye catching. OH! Eye catching. Hedge-Witch. We have to get rid of it, or she'll find me." She clamped her mouth shut. She didn't want to scare Cl'rnce off with the old witch. Moire Ain swallowed hard and said, "We have to get it from Raspberries."

The raven flew in front of them, dragging the poster in the dusty road.

"We?" Cl'rnce grumbled. "What did you say about a hedgehog?"

Moire Ain inhaled a cool breath of relief. Cl'rnce hadn't heard 'witch'. She ran after the raven, grabbing for the end of the banner. Raspberries jerked the cloth out of reach just as she got close.

Cl'rnce jogged past her and snatched at the cloth, catching it in his claws. With a pretty hard tug, he jerked it out of Raspberries talons. The raven squawked, circled, and dumped a greenish poop on Cl'rnce's head. But Cl'rnce didn't flinch. He held the cloth stretched between his paws. "Parsimonious wizard? You want to be a cheap wizard?" He squinted at her.

"No!" she said. "How silly. I need to hire a cheap wizard. I mean ...." Her face went bright red. She grabbed for the banner, but Cl'rnce kept hold.

He read, "'Wizard for Hire, Parsimonious Rates.'"

His scaly eye ridges climbed nearly to his horns. "The wording is a little confusing, but I'm pretty sure this says you're for hire, and you're cheap."

"No. It doesn't. That's not what I meant. No one would think I was a cheap wizard for hire." Moire Ain grabbed the banner, wadded it up, and tucked it under her arm. "This was to find a wizard teacher who doesn't cost much. Parsimonious. Inexpensive." With her arms full, she stuck her chin out trying to look sure of herself.

"Bad wording, and does too mean you're a cheap wizard," Cl'rnce mumbled. He stared up at her raven, as if expecting it to defend her and splat him again for arguing with Moire Ain.

But Raspberries cocked his head to one side and seemed to shrug. Moire Ain waited for Cl'rnce to point out that even her raven agreed that the banner was bumbled, like her magick. She tried not to let the dump of hurt make her weep. She was not a crier! Moire Ain wiped her nose on her sleeve.

"Oh, for rivers' sakes, don't cry," Cl'rnce said. "It's no big thing. It's not like you left your address on banners all over Albion. Nobody's going to hound you about the misunderstanding."

"I forgot that too! No one could even find me!" Moire Ain sobbed. "It doesn't matter what it said. Don't you see? I can't do anything right. I can't even get a teacher." Moire Ain blinked to try and stop the fall of tears that betrayed her.

Cl'rnce looked alarmed and puzzled all at the same time. "We can fix this," he finally said. "Look. I think you're making too much of the banner. You don't need a teacher. You just need practice. I think you're getting better with your spells."

Moire Ain's eyes filled all over again. He believed in her.

His eyes got purpler and bigger. "Please don't cry. I'm not good with crying. I tried to comfort my sister once with a pat, right after a snake bit her on the snout. She turned and snapped at me, biting so hard Mother sent for a hedge-witch to pry her off and sew up my arm."

"Hedge-Witch?" Moire Ain snuffled out. He knew about witches; did he know how evil her foster mother, Hedge-Witch, was?

His face straightened like he'd found a way to make her stop crying, which he had. "Yep. This hedge witch was an extremely cranky old hag who spent most of the time complaining about her worthless assistant who kept disappearing for hours when she was supposed to be herb hunting. When the old crone ran out of whining and snarling, she spit on a leaf, smacked it on my arm, and said, 'You'll live.'"

Moire Ain started to smile around her leaky face. Cl'rnce's tone of outrage at how he'd been treated made her picture Hedge-Witch and her foster mother's fear of only one creature—dr'gons.

Cl'rnce continued, "It got worse. Mother refused to discipline Hazel. Instead, Mother just shook her head at me and sighed. The whole thing was very painful." He held out his paws. "You can see why I'm not taking any chances on another bite from anyone. So, you okay?"

Moire Ain snuffled up, but the story wasn't enough to stop the cascade of tears. She could tell by the way he started pacing that she was causing him pain. After so many years of being the 'stupid girl' Hedge-Witch yelled at, Moire Ain was determined to be the best partner Cl'rnce could ever have. But already she had failed. She cried harder.

"I am worried about you. Crying too long can lead to very, very bad occurrences. You knew that, right?" He stopped pacing and looked at her.

Moire Ain hiccuped and shook her head.

"It's very bad for the scales. Rusts them, you know. And besides, any minute I expect frogs." Cl'rnce said, adding a smile.

She sniffled to a stop and asked, "What did you say?"

"The way you're pouring water, I thought a frog would swim out of your nose or something," Cl'rnce said, grinning bigger.

"I—I—I wish I could conjure a frog!" She started crying louder all over again. "I can't do any magick right!"

Cl'rnce stomped down the road, turning around a wooded curve before Moire Ain could catch up. She was still crying when she nearly ran into him.

"Yipes stripes! Look over there. Is that a king pacing on that castle wall?" Cl'rnce yelled over the wailing.

"Huh?" Moire Ain snorted a stop to the tears. "I wonder if he's the one." She looked around. She didn't know what king Hedge-Witch meant her to kill. Could this be the one?

"Do you want to see a king?" Cl'rnce said. He took a deep breath, like he was making an offer he didn't want to. "Now, mind I have to get to Ghost Mountain quickly, but for you . . . . We can detour so you can see one."

Moire Ain stared down the road. She didn't see any kings or anyone else. If this was the one, she could warn him. "Thank you." She scrubbed her face with one

119

sleeve. "Do you think I could offer to do magick for him? So I could talk to him? Warn him." She said the last bit in a whisper, because she wasn't ready to tell Cl'rnce or anyone that she was supposed to be an assassin.

Cl'rnce stared at her. "I have exceptional hearing, you know. Warn him about what? Chicken-covered peasants and chicken-stealing dr'gons?" Cl'rnce snorted. "Kings never mess with dr'gons. The peasants are on their own."

Moire Ain muttered a promise that if she had to, she'd go see this king alone. Even standing on tiptoes she couldn't see the king, but if Cl'rnce saw him, then she would go warn him. She squared her shoulders and marched ahead.

Surprisingly, Cl'rnce didn't argue anymore. Instead he followed, whistling a tune that was short and repeated over and over. Pretty soon it played in Moire Ain's head, and she couldn't stop it. She whistled along with him as they got to a rise in the road. At the top, they looked down into a very green valley. In the center of the valley, a wide river circled a village and castle on three sides before it meandered off toward the mountains again. An hour more, and they stood before the gates.

Moire Ain checked the sun and thought about how she could warn the king without getting herself and Cl'rnce into trouble. It would be tricky, but she thought about questions she could use to find out if he was the king Hedge-Witch was after. If he was, she'd warn him and get away quickly. After all, Cl'rnce had to get to Ghost Mountain. She could hear him grumble about her ignoring his quest. She wouldn't do that, but she had to do this.

"I want to help you, Cl'rnce. What can I do? You haven't said."

He shook his head. "I'm not sure. Well, yes. As Hazel said, I need a Wizard Partner. Every dr'gon has to have one. It's important, like getting to Ghost Mountain. And getting to Ghost Mountain is critical." He slid a look out of the side of his eyes at Moire Ain.

She felt like he'd just given her a present. He really needed her!

"But you're not exactly an official wizard, right?" His eyes weren't as friendly as Moire Ain wanted, but still . . . .

Moire Ain shook her head. "I'm not a wizard, not yet."

"I have to get to Ghost Mountain in three days. Which is impossible, because we are so far away. Especially since my snarky twin sister didn't even warn me until too late." He tapped his chin with one claw. "Then again, Hazel is a tricky one. Maybe I don't need an official powerful wizard."

Moire Ain swallowed and tried to keep the smile on her face. She didn't want him to know how badly his words hurt about how he knew how un-powerful, how un-wizardly she was.

He went on, "Maybe Hazel wanted me to waste time

getting a powerful wizard I don't need. Maybe even an untrained wizard is enough. I certainly don't have time to train you. And you might be the wrong wizard." He shook his head like he'd just talked himself into and then out of believing in Moire Ain. "Maybe an untrained wizard who bumbles her spells will be a bigger disaster.

"Maybe I should do this alone. Fast. I could leave you with the king and hurry to the mountain. You can practice magick while I finish my delivery. I might come back and help you later."

Moire Ain's throat felt like she'd swallowed something big and stuffy. She was so disappointed to be left behind that she couldn't speak. She just nodded her head and walked on.

High on the castle ramparts, Moire Ain saw a figure lean so far over the wall she thought he would fall off. The short, fat man in long, sky-blue robes clamped one hand on a crown and put the other over his eyes like he was staring at them, then ran to a tower. Next, he sped back to the edge of the wall with a drum and beat it frantically. All the villagers milling in the town below ran this way and that, scattering into the buildings below the castle.

Moire Ain stood up straighter and walked forward. This was it.

Cl'rnce grabbed her arm. "Whoa! I don't think this is a friendly kind of king," he said. He pointed to the row of archers lining up along the castle ramparts. The short, fat man clutched at his dingy yellow crown while he waddled back and forth past the archers. The way his mouth worked and the way his skin went from chalk white to tomato red, he seemed to be yelling orders, but Moire Ain couldn't hear them.

"Do you think we're far enough away not to get shot?" Moire Ain asked. Staring at the king and the archers, she reached back and wrapped her fingers around the edge of one of Cl'rnce's folded wings.

At her touch, Cl'rnce jerked. "What?" He looked at his wing. "Look at that! Where you touched me, you left marks." He stared.

But when she looked, the only difference in his wings was that they'd taken on a slightly golden color, instead of their usual grassy green.

Cl'rnce wiggled them a little. "They feel different, heavier. And scratchy." He wiggled like he was being attacked by itchy worms. His wings snapped out straight and wide. "I never used them for anything but gliding before. And even then only for short distances from low heights, because they're usually so limp, like ornaments, not real dr'gon appendages." He clamped his lips together like he'd said too much.

"Did I do that?" Moire Ain asked, but her attention jerked away from him. "Do you see what I see?"

"What?"

"There in the moat on the front side of the castle. Is that Sir George riding on a kelpie?" Moire Ain was on her tiptoes pointing at the moat. Her stomach tightened. The water creature had four legs like a horse but with gills along its long neck, and a truly hideous scaled face with rubbery lips that drew back over shark-like teeth. For an instant Moire Ain thought the kelpie looked like Hedge-Witch.

She glanced at Cl'rnce, wanting to tell him about Hedge-Witch, but he was examining his wings. "They don't look normal. They're better." He looked up at her. "You did that."

But Moire Ain didn't have time to revel in the compliment or wonder how; she was too rattled. "Cl'rnce? Are you listening? That's Sir George again. And I think . . . ."

When she glanced back at the kelpie, it no longer looked like Hedge-Witch. Moire Ain went on, "He's riding out of the moat on a kelpie. I know why he's here. He's going to keep us from seeing the king, or worse."

Moire Ain was sure Sir George was connected to Hedge-Witch, even if he'd seemed before to not know her. Maybe he didn't know Hedge-Witch was his kelpie. Maybe only Moire Ain could see the old witch. Maybe, maybe this, maybe that. It didn't make sense though, for a witch who hated water to disguise herself as a water monster.

Moire Ain shook her head in confusion and paced,

kicking dusty pebbles on the road. Looking up, she watched the king pacing almost in a twin to her agitation. Moire Ain stopped. If Sir George had come with the witch to kill the king, Moire Ain had to prevent it. The king had archers. If Moire Ain could get him to fire on Sir George and the kelpie, the knight and his monster would run away and leave the king alone.

But Moire Ain's plan fell apart when the king leaned over the moat and yelled at Sir George. With a nod, the rusty knight whipped his river horse. The kelpie sprang out of the moat and charged after a small child still sitting in the road between the village and the inner castle walls. As the kelpie snapped at the child's head, Sir George jerked on his reins. The kelpie raised up on its hind legs, missing the child and bucking Sir George. The knight managed to hang on, but it was clear he was losing control of the killer river-horse.

Warning the king would have to wait.

"Quick, we have to get that kid!" Moire Ain yelled, already running for the moat. She scooped up the child as Sir George was thrown through the air. He landed in a pile of dented armor, cursing loudly. The kelpie's head snapped to one side and then the other, as if it was trying to decide if it wanted the knight or the more tender child and Moire Ain, who hugged the little girl close.

Before Sir George could rock to his feet, Cl'rnce was there. He stood between the kelpie and Moire Ain.

Moire Ain's heart soared. He was a hero!

But she heard him mutter to himself, "This is not me. I've never done anything brave before. I probably shouldn't be doing this. If I get killed, Hazel will string my brains for a room decoration. But I'm here, and since I'm taller than the kelpie by at least two feet, I should be able to get out a good roar and startle it into running. At least I can distract the monster long enough for Sir George to get up and get out his sword to defend himself and the child, and hopefully the archers will fire on it."

Cl'rnce cleared his throat. Turning its head slowly, the kelpie's eyes went to Cl'rnce. Between thin, snarling lips, its sharp teeth dripped more than moat water. Moire Ain thought she saw small bones of fish and maybe birds drop through its lips. The kelpie held still, as if deciding what to do next.

Moire Ain glanced at the archers, willing them to shoot the kelpie, but the king held his hand in the air to halt any firing. She understood. The king did not want to risk killing a peasant child. Moire Ain turned back to the kelpie, who now watched the king. Darting another glance up, Moire Ain saw the king signal the archers to move their positions. The way they realigned themselves, Moire Ain saw, put them in a direct line to fire at her and Cl'rnce. The king didn't care about the child.

Moire Ain held up the little girl. "Save her!" she

yelled at the archers. The men lowered their bows an inch, but the king screamed for them to prepare to fire. The archers looked at each other as if unsure.

Then the kelpie roared and charged Cl'rnce. "Shoot your arrows! Get the monster!" Moire Ain screamed.

But the king yelled, "Hold. Do not harm my pet. Shoot those others. Now!"

The kelpie and the king were allies. This was not the king Hedge-Witch was after but possibly her ally or her boss. The king would not save them from the monster. He wanted them all dead, all but the kelpie.

Since Moire Ain suspected the kelpie was really Hedge-Witch, and she knew Hedge-Witch feared dr'gons, Moire Ain was stunned when the monstrous water-horse snapped at Cl'rnce. Cl'rnce dodged the blade-sharp poisoned teeth. He ran, headed away from Moire Ain, the child, and even Sir George. The kelpie chased him.

"If I had working wings, now would be a good time," Moire Ain heard Cl'rnce say, as he jumped, catching hold of a massive oak branch. He tucked his feet and pulled himself up. The kelpie snapped, just missing him. Moire Ain knew kelpies were great swimmers and runners but not climbers or jumpers. Cl'rnce hung from the branch and kicked at the kelpie's head as it tried again and again to bite him.

The dr'gon's digits were slipping. A claw came loose

just as Raspberries flew down low and dropped a huge load of bird excrement in the river-horse's eyes. The kelpie screamed and shook its head, trying to toss the poop off. It ran in circles, seeming to have forgotten Cl'rnce, Moire Ain, the child, and Sir George.

Shaking its head, it raced at Sir George as he finally stood, holding his rusty sword. As the monster came even with the knight, it dove for the moat. Sir George swung and sliced off its head. With a hiss of black steam jetting into the sky, the head and carcass dropped to the ground short of the moat's brackish waters.

Cl'rnce took a deep breath.

"Thank you," he said as he dropped from the branch he'd clung to.

"Thank you, Sir George," Moire Ain said. She handed the child to a hysterical peasant.

Sir George nodded. He took off his helmet and wiped his grimy face. "That didn't go the way it was supposed to."

"Tell me about it," Cl'rnce said.

Moire Ain stood next to Cl'rnce, not certain how close they should get to Sir George. Just because the knight had killed the kelpie didn't mean he was their friend. He was saving his own life, not theirs.

"Kick the kelpie into the moat," the king yelled from where he leaned over his tower parapet.

"It seems only right," Sir George said. "Like a burial

for a knight."

"No!" Cl'rnce and Moire Ain yelled at the same time.

But they were too late. No sooner had Sir George kicked the two pieces of the kelpie into the moat than the scummy waters began to boil. The kelpie's bellow rang out from the volcano of water that spouted skyward.

Moire Ain froze when she saw Hedge-Witch's face in the tower of water.

"Run!" Cl'rnce yelled. He scooped up Moire Ain and raced up the road toward the chicken stomping village.

"Don't lead it back to the villagers!" Moire Ain screamed.

Grumbling about how soft-hearted she was and how she was complicating his life, Cl'rnce took the *Y* in the road and headed away from the chicken stomping village and the castle.

"Not bad. We're actually headed the right way. We are going to the mountains," Cl'rnce said. "I have to get there."

CHAPTER 11

"That Sir George sure does ride some bad-tempered horses, but how did he end up on a kelpie? I thought he was chasing you. Why would he be in a moat on a hedge—I mean monster?" Great and Mighty asked as Cl'rnce trotted down the road.

Cl'rnce slowed. He would have set her down, but he was a fast runner, and she was a short, slow human.

It was a good question. How did Nasty Sir George come up with his steeds? Cl'rnce had never heard of a knight on anything but a regular warhorse. Somewhere, this knight had gotten magickal creatures. Cl'rnce was pretty sure the raggedy knight wasn't a sorcerer or anything magickal himself.

If Cl'rnce had been Nasty Sir George and knew enough magick to call up a goblin steed or a kelpie, he would have also given himself a really shiny set of armor with matching parts, instead of the rusted stuff Nasty Sir George wore. It didn't make sense for Nasty Sir George to be able to conjure up these mounts and still keep his ragged armor. Even if he had magick, both the goblin horse and the water-horse had thrown Nasty Sir George. They sure looked like they'd rather kill him than keep letting him ride them. If he had any, Nasty Sir George's magick was pretty poor—dangerous, but poor. Something was not normal about the knight.

"And how did he get to the king's city ahead of us? He couldn't have ridden a water-horse all the way. No rivers," Cl'rnce said. "Good questions. I think he's getting help."

"From the king, or—who?" Great and Mighty stumbled over the 'who.' "He's not a nice guy."

Cl'rnce slowed and stopped. He looked behind them down the road. Not a speck moved. No one was following. It was about time for some good luck, like the kelpie snagging Nasty Sir George and dragging him back into the moat to eat. That would certainly keep the kelpie busy, what with the armor to bite through and all. "Didn't look to me like the king was helping Nasty Sir George, just ordering around the kelpie. That means someone else is helping him get these magickal steeds, or he's good at hunting them down and crazy enough to try to tame these horses himself. I go with crazy." Cl'rnce put Great and Mighty down. "I'm thirsty. All this talk of the moat, you know."

The little want-to-be wizard looked like she wanted to say something, but instead she studied her pouch, then pulled her little book out of it. She flipped the book open. "I really should be learning this from the beginning to end. But I saw something in the pictures. This page—no, wait." She flipped backward a page and stared, her finger tracing a picture Cl'rnce couldn't see, and her forehead wrinkled. "I'm pretty sure he's not the one," she muttered.

"What's all the muttering? Do you need help reading your book?" Cl'rnce was an indifferent student at the Dr'gon Wiz Academy, except in a few courses, one being literature. Anytime you could learn something that went well with napping, like reading yourself to sleep, or practical jokes, or reading all kinds of books to come up with all kinds of practical jokes, he was ready to learn. Cl'rnce worked hard to pull off truly creative and original practical jokes. He not only could read any book he got his paws on, but he'd learned to read every language ever written. He was always ready to find the smelliest recipe for a stink bomb in the whole world.

"I can read just fine," Great and Mighty snapped, then apologized, "I'm sorry. I can only read a few words here and there in my book. Most of it is written in some magick language that does weird things." She flipped forward a page.

Cl'rnce was intrigued. He hadn't really paid attention. Could this be a language he hadn't learned? "May I?" He held out a paw, and she handed him the book. "Oh, no problem. That's Old Dr'gon. I know this one."

"You do?" Great and Mighty grabbed his arm and squeezed it. "Teach it to me, please."

"Sure. But not now. My Journey. I have to get to Ghost Mountain in the next three days. Of all the languages I've learned, Old Dr'gon is the hardest. It took me a month to learn it. That's twice as long as any other language."

"Oh." Great and Mighty's body seemed to shrink with her disappointment.

Cl'rnce knew he shouldn't say it as soon as he formed the words, but he did. "I'll teach you the whole thing as soon as we get my Journey done. Okay?" He reread the passage, then looked at the little wizard want-to-be. "Have you ever done any big magick?"

Great and Mighty blushed. "You mean successfully?"

He nodded.

"Well, so far I haven't really done so much with the spells from this book, but I can cure anybody anywhere with herbs. Of course, I haven't had a chance to really learn *magick* magick. After I escaped, I was going to go through the book and learn it from front to back." She peered up at him through lowered lashes. "You saw how that first spell I tried on Sir George went."

Cl'rnce cleared his throat, for no good reason he choked down his usual snarky retort. Instead of assuring her she had failed, he found himself saying, "Don't worry about it. Everything was happening at once, and it was really confusing. Besides, you got that shield spell to work. If you haven't worked on a formal spell before . . . . They aren't easy. Which is why I don't mess with magick." He smiled, pleased with himself for being so kind, even if he'd lied a little.

Great and Mighty giggled. "No offense, but you are just a little on the lazy side for such a learned dr'gon."

Instead of marking her down on his list of those deserving a practical joke played on them in the near future, Cl'rnce did what he had never done before. He laughed at himself. "Yep. I am the nap king at Dr'gon Wiz. And I hold the skipping-class record five years running."

Great and Mighty grinned, shaking her head. "Naps. I've never had time for one. But I attended class, sort of." She lowered her voice as if afraid someone was listening in. "I hid in the trees and listened when Goodwife Greenfield taught her children. I thought it was a big secret, but it turned out she knew I was spying and learning the whole time."

Cl'rnce didn't know what to say. He'd never had to do a thing to get his education. He'd been sent to the right school by his mother. He'd always had everything he wanted no matter how badly he acted or how little he did to appreciate or earn it, simply because he was the last male River Dr'gon heir. Even though Cl'rnce would rather it was Hazel who inherited. This whole journey was about Hazel saying it was time for Cl'rnce to step up to rule the clan of River Dr'gons and all the rest of the tribes of the Dr'gon Nations. While River Dr'gons had a paucity of males, the clan was well populated with females. Cl'rnce wouldn't be surprised if they all were mean like Hazel, who had yapped all her life about how she should be the next ruler but couldn't. But that was how it went with River Dr'gons. Cl'rnce was tired of thinking about it.

"Uh-oh," Cl'rnce said.

"What?" Great and Mighty had her finger on a page of her book.

"Paucity of males." He raised his eyebrows. "Big trouble."

"Huh? What's a paucity?"

"Paucity means not many, not many at all. My River Dr'gons are down to one male qualified to inherit the Nations' Primacy. Being down to only one inheritor happens just before the change in rulers." He raised his eyebrow ridge to let her know she should understand what he was saying.

"I don't get it."

"Primus Thomas. Hazel was telling the truth." Cl'rnce took a deep breath. It was time to let Great and Mighty know just what she was involved in. "Whether by age, or battle, or even Clause Two Retirement, which has never happened, the change in rulers always happens when there is only one heir, one male in the direct line. It's always the same. Everybody knows now that I'm the only candidate, and the Whisper Stone has shown up to be presented and restored, it means the current ruler of all the Dr'gon nations will . . . you know . . . ."

"Die?"

"Yep. Big nap in the dr'gon sky. It's why I'm on this errand. The Council of all the Dr'gon tribes meets, I have to bring them the Whisper Stone, and it declares the Primus." He removed the little pebble from his locket and pointed to it. "Which is always a River Dr'gon. I'm the one delivering the Whisper Stone to Ghost Mountain and the Council Chamber."

"You're some kind of royal herald? You're supposed to deliver the news, and Sir George is trying to stop you? If you don't deliver it, the wrong dr'gon will take over and be Primus?"

"Sort of," Cl'rnce said. "I'm not so much delivering the stone, as I might be the new guy. If I don't get to Ghost Mountain, to the Council, in three days, then . . . I might be failing to do what needs to be done to become the Primus of the Dr'gon Nations."

When Great and Mighty didn't look overwhelmed to be in his presence, he asked, "Do you know what a Primus is?"

"No."

"It's the Dr'gon Nations' king." He waited for her to

bow or curtsey.

"King? You? You're supposed to become a king?" Great and Mighty's eyes were wide, but she didn't look impressed. She looked scared.

"What's wrong? Don't you think I should be the Primus?" Cl'rnce was annoyed, even though he didn't really want the responsibility, and down deep thought if everything were fair, Hazel would be the one.

"It's not that. I don't know what kind of king you'd be. Maybe you'd be the best. But could someone be out to . . . kill you?" She swallowed and stared at him, her hands gripped together like she was pleading with him.

"You mean other than Sir George who is just out to kill a dr'gon from every nation?" Cl'rnce was about to say everybody else loved him, but there were more than a few former and current students at Dr'gon Wiz Academy who definitely bore a grudge because of his brilliant practical jokes. "The Killer Dr'gon tribe is always after the Primus." Cold fear prickled the scales on the back of his head. He'd been so busy snarking about his bossy sister, he hadn't let himself dwell on how truly dangerous his journey might be. More than snarky Hazel, more than clumsy Nasty Sir George. Hazel had warned him about the Geilts.

"Would they hire a hedge-witch to use magick against you?"

"Wouldn't need to. Killer Dr'gons don't need magick.

They're big and mean and lethal." Cl'rnce swallowed. "The Primus is always protected. Well, that happens after coronation. I wasn't thinking about this being a big deal to anyone but snarky Hazel. And come to think of it, I haven't heard a word from Mother that Primus Thomas is dead. This could be one of Hazel's tricks. Maybe I really don't know what's going on, and there's another River Dr'gon. And she's using me to attract killers. No, that doesn't make sense. This whole 'appearing Whisper Stone' thing is only supposed to happen when the heirs are down to one, and . . . ARGH! I don't want to think about it."

He pulled out the Whisper Stone and stared at it. "I'm not even 100 percent sure this errand of Hazel's means anything other than getting on her good side so she'll stop black-mailing me and torturing me. I think she switched the stone. Does this even look like some special stone? It looks like a garden pebble to me. And it's not vibrating.

"And now that I think of it, the last I heard from Mother, the Primus wasn't sick or anything. He'll be in charge for centuries. Yep. This is a trick, and besides, I'm not in any hurry to be king of anything. I'd have to work. Ruling is every-day, all-day, no-naps work. Yuck. Not to mention how cranky Hazel will be when she has to bow to me." Cl'rnce laughed and held out a paw for the book. Great and Mighty handed it to him.

"I'm glad you're not about to be king." Great and Mighty looked relieved more than happy. Odd little girl. "And you're sure it's a trick?"

She started to add something, but Cl'rnce shook his head and held up one digit. "I know what you're thinking. You think maybe our journey is for real, and what happens if I don't become the next ruler? Don't worry. I'm impossible to kill, and I have a plan. If Hazel thinks I'm on her side now, when the real time comes, not this stupid test of hers, and she can't inherit because of the Laws but I do, she'll still be on my side. Because she's my sister. See? Simple." He hoped he sounded convincing.

He pointed to Great and Mighty's book. "I think this spell is what we need right now. Let's find some good drinking water, hopefully on the way to Ghost Mountain." He sighed. No matter what he'd told Great and Mighty, if he delivered Hazel's stone, he had an itching feeling he might indeed be accepting the job of Primus. Not only did he not want Primus Thomas to be dead, but he did not want to be ruling dr'gons that included a sister who was irrational about being excluded. She had friends, angry friends, and none of them agreed with automatically passing the Primacy of all dr'gons to a male. Would Hazel and her allies become his enemy, start a civil war? Nah. Mother wouldn't allow it.

Cl'rnce yawned. And besides, he was opposed to fighting through naps.

He read the magick words aloud, first in the rolling Old D'rgon tongue that included a lot of clicking of back teeth. Then he translated it. "It's a simple spell. Just close your eyes and say the words three times. While you're saying the words, keep picturing the kind of water you want. Make it clean and drinkable, please. No bumblespell embellishments. Don't end up with muddy garden water, okay?"

Great and Mighty nodded her head.

"Here we go:

> *Nourisher of the earth*
> *Drink of the Goddess Aquariana*
> *Show me."*

Great and Mighty took a breath and opened her mouth.

"Wait!" Cl'rnce said. "You have to get the words exactly right. And I cannot repeat them more than one more time. Do you need me to say them again?"

"No. I have a really good memory." The little want-to-be wizard took a deep breath and started.

> *"Nourisher of the earth*
> *Drink of the Goddess Aquariana*
> *Show me."*

She stopped. Cl'rnce hoped she wasn't messing up the envisioning part. He suspected that was where her bumblespell-additions came from. He circled a claw in the air to encourage her to repeat again. She did. After the second time, Cl'rnce smiled, circled his claw, and nodded, holding up one digit. She said the spell the third time.

And they waited.

"Uh," Great and Mighty said. "I don't see any water."

"Oh, right. Close your eyes and tell me what you see. Remember, think clear, drinkable water we can get to."

She squeezed her eyes and told Cl'rnce what she saw: a cliff with crystal water. The water fell into a small pool and disappeared. The pool was surrounded by trees and boulders. She tried harder and said, "I can't figure out where it is. Show me where."

Her shoulders hunched as she seemed to gather herself into a tight ball to get the whole picture. "I see it. It feels like I'm Raspberries. I'm flying above a dusty road. I see you and me on the trail. The king's castle and the chicken-stomping village are far away. We're alone on the road. And . . . we're close. We're almost at the water right now! We're maybe half a mile through . . . ." She opened her eyes and pointed at a group of trees. "Through there. There's a pond. This way." She took off running.

Cl'rnce scooped up the book she'd forgotten and followed her. He called to Raspberries, who flew circles around his head, "If she's right, there's hope she can really do magick. She might be my Wizard Partner. I think I might just need her to get to Ghost Mountain." He hadn't meant to say his hopes about Great and Mighty out loud, but it was true. He felt like maybe she could help him, really help, like a real wizard.

Raspberries cawed one sharp note and landed on Cl'rnce's shoulder. The dr'gon winced, expecting an attack, but the raven sat quietly. Something was wrong. Cl'rnce stood where he was, not running after the little wizard. It was too quiet, and her suddenly "seeing" was too easy. Too many things were very wrong. If this was really his journey to become the Primus, why would Hazel help him get to the Council? She had never supported him before. Even if she made it impossible by waiting until he almost didn't have enough time, she still gave him the rock and the locket. As badly as she wanted to be Primus, would she trick him? Would she send him to the wrong place? If he missed the appointed time . . . what would happen? Had she figured out a way to become the Primus? Would her scheme cause a war?

"Cl'rnce! HELP!"

CHAPTER 12

Moire Ain shook her head. "Sir George, you are more trouble than a herd of cats! How did you get in this predicament? I'll get help." She turned around on the boulder that hung over the clear pond and yelled again, "Cl'rnce! HELP!"

When she finished, she turned back to watch Sir George sink a third time, then splash his way back up to the surface. "Help me, girl!"

Moire Ain crept to the edge of the rock. "Help is coming." She heard Cl'rnce thrashing his way through the thick bushes and trees. And she heard him cursing. This time the words he used to curse were very interesting. Not like "stupid pigsty dummy head" or "rotten frog farts," like she would have said. But he said something about cursing a branch into growing backward and up into someone's—

Cl'rnce emerged from the forest. A branch from his right smacked him in the snout as he batted away a thicker one on his left side.

Moire Ain said, "I knew you could do magick! You cast a spell on that branch! It's like it's alive."

Cl'rnce rolled his eyes. "Everything on a tree is alive. No magick. I broke the branch, which will go very hard with the wood elves. Pooped-on-dr'gon scales, I'll have to pay them a fine. And for what? You're perfectly okay. Why did you call me like you were being killed by Nasty Sir George?"

"Not me. Sir George." She pointed to the bobbing knight. His nose and mouth were barely above water, but he wasn't splashing much. "I think he's drowning. We have to help him."

Cl'rnce edged to the tip of the boulder and stared down. "Yep. Hi there, Nasty Sir George. Nice day for a bath. Save some for us." He turned away, smiling.

Raspberries landed on Cl'rnce's shoulder, croaking like he was laughing along with the dr'gon. Moire Ain held out her arm. "Come here, Raspberries! It's not funny to let someone drown. We have to help." She used her best serious stare. Raspberries quit croaking, fluttered to her arm, and muttered softly. She turned to Cl'rnce. "Hurry. Go get him out of there."

Cl'rnce shook his head. "Nope. He tried to kill me. At least once today, and if he'd been able to stay on that kelpie, twice. All in one day, I'd like to remind you. Let him swim out on his own."

"Cl'rnce, please. He's drowning. You can't let him

die. Dr'gons are the guardian angels of humans. I saw it in the pictures in my book. You are one of the good guys."

"Not all dr'gons are good guys," Cl'rnce muttered. "Take Philomena Flannach of the Geilt clan. I'm pretty sure she killed my father. Maybe I'm one of those Killer Dr'gons."

"Don't be ridiculous," Moire Ain said as she tugged on a long vine. She leaned all her weight into her tug and almost pulled it free of the tree it climbed around. If Cl'rnce refused to help, she'd throw the vine to Sir George and drag him out herself.

Cl'rnce plucked the vine out of her hands. When he began to tie a noose in one end, she started to protest. "You aren't going to try to hang him while he's drowning?" she asked. If only she could do un-bumblespelled and reliable magick, she could raise Sir George up out of the water and float him over to the pond's bank. She reached for her pouch to get her book. But her pouch was gone. "*NO!*" she screamed.

"*Yes!*" Cl'rnce said. "I'm going to pull him out, if he'll hang on." He threw the looped vine at Sir George. The frantic knight grabbed at the noose but missed as he sank again. "Suppose he'll float back up?" Cl'rnce peered into the water.

"Come on. We have to go after him." Moire Ain felt the stupid tears start to build up again. In her whole life, she'd never all-out cried, never before today. It was like she was falling apart. And maybe she was. She'd run away believing she could learn magick to protect herself, lead a life she'd be proud of, and not be a pawn used to kill a king. But the book she needed was gone. She couldn't do magick without it. And Cl'rnce didn't care that a human being was about to die. He was no better than Hedge-Witch.

"Oh, for poopy dr'gon scales' sake, don't cry," Cl'rnce said. Paw over paw, he pulled the vine back in and threw it back at the spot where Sir George's armored hand was visible just below the surface. "If he doesn't grab it this time, I'll go in."

"You can swim?" She sniffled, relieved that at least this time she hadn't started bawling. She willed Sir George to bob up one more time and grab the vine.

"Of course I can swim. I'm a River Dr'gon. I'm an expert. Really." He stared down. "Hmm. I guess he's not coming back up. You think he's still alive?"

"Please! Save him!" Moire Ain couldn't stand to see anything die. Once, she'd nursed a spider that had foolishly set up its web in the corner of Hedge-Witch's hut, near the poisonous plants. The fumes had nearly killed the creature.

"I think he's floating back up," Cl'rnce said.

Sir George's hand twitched a bit but didn't rise.

The dr'gon sighed and waited another second, like

he was hoping Moire Ain would tell him to forget it. When she just stared at him, he said, "Fine. Here I go." Cl'rnce handed Moire Ain her book, stepped back, and started to take a running jump into the pool. But as he neared the edge of the boulder, he tripped on the rest of the vine and skidded backward, landing on his back. His head hit the boulder hard. His eyes closed, and he began to snore.

"My book!" Moire Ain hugged it to her. She would have thanked Cl'rnce, but when he began to snore, she realized she was all on her own. The knight was drowning, and she wasn't strong enough to swim out and carry an armor-covered knight back to shore. There wasn't time to search the book for a picture of a spell she could try to figure out. She did the only thing she could think of. She put together the first words that came to mind. "Float like a cloud, Sir George. Rise NOW!" She repeated it three times, as quickly as she could spit out the words, picturing the knight dripping water but floating over the pond's surface like a big, rusty cloud.

No sooner did she finish the last repetition than Sir George's limp body lifted out of the water. It hung face down in the air, raining water just like the cloud she had imagined. Moire Ain held her breath. Was it too late? Had he drowned?

Raspberries took off from her shoulder and buzzed over the knight, pecking at his helmet. Flying by again, the raven pecked two more times. The third time, the rusty knight groaned.

"Hurray, you're alive!" Moire Ain cheered. "You're okay."

Sir George raised his dangling chin enough to peer at her through the slit in his helmet. "I'm not okay. I'm hanging over a pond that tried to drown me. Get me out of here."

"You really are rude," Moire Ain spat back at him. "I saved your life, and you're not a bit grateful."

"Get me out of here, and I won't kill you," Sir George said. "Is that grateful enough?"

"Or you could just hang in the air until you figure your own way out, and I could leave. You can't kill me if I'm not here," Moire Ain snapped back at the mean knight. She didn't want to tell him she had no clue how to move him. She started to picture how winds moved clouds, but stopped when he jetted to the far end of the pool, flipped over, and jetted back. Focusing hard, Moire Ain pictured him just floating again. "I guess that counts as a bumblespell," she said. "I added a bit more than I should have."

Since she had her book back, she considered finding a book spell. But then she wondered: what would happen if she freed Sir George completely? Cl'rnce was still out cold and helpless. The knight wasn't very nice, and something made her suspect a trick; plus, he might be working with Hedge-Witch. Would he take advantage and kill Cl'rnce? If the knight gave her his knight's word, she might trust him. "If I move you to firm ground, will you go away and leave Cl'rnce and me alone? Give me your Knight's Honor oath that you will?" she asked.

"Maybe," Sir George said.

"Wrong answer." Moire Ain sat down next to Cl'rnce. She opened her book, then looked at Cl'rnce. He needed to wake up before the knight figured out on his own how to get out of hovering over the pond. She pushed on Cl'rnce's shoulder. He groaned and rolled to his side. "Come on, Cl'rnce, get up. Sir George is out of the pond, and we need to get out of here."

"Get me down!" Sir George yelled.

"No," Moire Ain said. "You'll hurt Cl'rnce. I won't let you do that." The cursing knight was definitely mean enough to be working with the old witch.

"It's my job to hurt Cl'rnce, just like it's your job to do magick. Now get me onto the land!" Sir George yelled louder. He thrashed around.

Moire Ain held her breath, not sure if she hoped he would thrash himself back into the water or keep floating. He was her enemy, but she was not a killer.

He managed to flip again in the air.

She turned the pages of her book while Sir George cursed in far more colorful and common language than Cl'rnce had used. She found pictures of levitation spells, which even without the Old Dr'gon translation didn't look much like the one she'd used to float Sir George. She skipped further into the book and found a picture of a spell for waking a sleeping princess. Moire Ain glanced over at Cl'rnce. He was drooling now, quite a pool of sticky, slightly purple dr'gon goo forming under his muzzle. His snores sounded a lot like a landslide and a pig snort wound together. He definitely didn't look like any princess she'd ever heard about. But he had said something about becoming the next Primus of the River Dr'gons. That was royalty, a king. Princess, king, royalty.

She shrugged and studied the several pictures on the princess-waking spell. Scattered on the page were words, maybe a third of which were in her language. Since Cl'rnce wasn't a princess, maybe all she needed was those few words. Maybe the part she could read would be enough. "Wake Sleeping Beauty," she repeated three times.

Sir George stopped cursing and started laughing. "Beauty? Are you talking to the dr'gon? Cl'rnce of the River Dr'gons? He may be the most arrogant and conceited dr'gon, but he's the only one who thinks he's beautiful."

Raspberries croaked out a laugh. Moire Ain snickered and covered her mouth. She couldn't help herself. Cl'rnce really was about the vainest being she'd ever run into. Although he thought she didn't see him doing it, he took every opportunity to admire himself in anything that reflected his face. She didn't know what made a beautiful dr'gon, but Cl'rnce certainly would say it started and ended with him.

Cl'rnce's snores stopped, and he sat up. "What happened? Why is everybody laughing?"

CHAPTER 13

Nasty Sir George swallowed a laugh, coughed, spit, and grumbled. "Get me down. Now!"

Cl'rnce growled back. "No way. I like you helpless." He got up and looked from the water to the floating knight. Cl'rnce shot a look at Great and Mighty and pointed at her and back at the knight. "You did this?"

She nodded and smiled.

It was a bit of a surprise that the little wizard want-to-be had been so successful at saving Nasty Sir George, but then the knight was caught in the air, so maybe she was still a bit of a bumblespells wizard.

While Nasty Sir George was helpless, Cl'rnce decided to get information from him. "You tell me why you're trying to kill me."

Cl'rnce wanted the knight to say it was just for a River Dr'gon trophy. But when George shook his head, Cl'rnce knew it was bigger. Nasty Sir George wouldn't miss a chance to brag unless someone else bigger and nastier was involved. Cl'rnce stabbed a sharp claw at the knight and added, "And where did you get the goblin horse and the kelpie?"

Nasty Sir George shook his head again. "Get me down," he said, not yelling this time but with a discouraged droop in his voice.

"Answer me." Cl'rnce wasn't buying the poor sad knight act. He strode to the edge of the pond and leaned out. With all his claws out and taking a swipe at Nasty Sir George, he only missed the knight by a few inches. "I'm going to catch you and drown you myself," Cl'rnce said.

"*NO!*" Great and Mighty threw herself in front of Cl'rnce. "You can't hurt anyone. That's not right." She inched closer to Cl'rnce on the mossy rock, but her foot slipped on a wet spot, and she slid toward the water.

Cl'rnce grabbed for her as she skidded off the ledge. He snagged a bit of her robe, and for a moment, she hung angled backward over the pond, her arms pinwheeling as she grabbed at a sapling growing out of the boulder. But her fingers missed, her robe ripped, and she fell into the pond.

"Oh, great," Cl'rnce said. "I'm coming." This would be easy. He was the best swimmer of all the River Dr'gons. He squatted to push himself off the rock ledge into one of his elegant dives. This was his most graceful—head down and arms, legs, and tail spread wide until just before he hit the water. He called it the Dying Swan. Before he broke the pond's surface, he would bring his ever so graceful arms over his head and cut the water without so much as a splash.

"I wouldn't do that, if I were you," Nasty Sir George said, then slapped a gloved hand over his mouth.

Cl'rnce straightened up, first shooting a look at the knight, then staring at the water. The little wizard had gone under and not come up. "Where is she? I have to get her. She should have bobbed up by now."

Nasty Sir George sounded like he really regretted helping, but he said, "I told you. The pond tried to kill me. If I hadn't been covered in iron, I would have been eaten alive."

"What? You mean the kelpie is in there?" Cl'rnce looked for the tell-tale whirlpool of a kelpie on a circle-hunt.

"No. Or maybe. I don't know," said Nasty Sir George. "If you get me to dry land, I'll help you save the little wizard."

Cl'rnce looked at the knight who had been trying to kill him for two days. "Why would I believe you? I'm going in after her."

"Hold it! Before you do something stupid!"

Cl'rnce raised a scaly eye ridge and snapped his claws to hurry Nasty Sir George on.

The knight quickly spit out, "There's no reason you should believe me, except I did warn you. I could have let you jump in to your death, but I didn't."

"You just want to get free and kill me yourself,"

Cl'rnce said, watching a trail of bubbles heading for the waterfall. He thought he could make out legs kicking beneath the water. He hoped he was watching Great and Mighty swim. Or it could be a kelpie headed to an underwater cavern. It might be too late to save the little want-to-be wizard. Which would leave him on his own with a killer knight and a journey to make without a Wizard Partner. Alone was how he liked it. Or used to. Now, he wanted . . . Great and Mighty.

Nasty Sir George sighed. "I admit it. I was paid to kill you, and I will. But no one paid me to kill the girl. She saved me. I am not a murderer, just a dr'gon slaying knight for hire. I have principles, you know."

"How do I know?" Cl'rnce thought he saw a second, wider and denser set of bubbles following the first. "That has to be her in front, on her way to the waterfall." He pointed to the first set of bubbles.

Nasty Sir George said, "Two bubble trails, huh? My attacker is following her. We're running out of time. Do you want my help?"

The second set of bubbles was closing in on the first. Cl'rnce was ready to jump in and rescue Great and Mighty, but he really wanted to know what was in the pond. "It's a kelpie, right? Is that what's following her?"

"No. The kelpie I was riding only lives in the moat. That's something else." Cl'rnce heard a rattling of armor that might have been Nasty Sir George shivering.

Now mad and concerned for how long the little want-to-be wizard had been underwater and for what was following her, Cl'rnce stared into the water. "You claim you don't know what it is. Before, you were screaming for help. You're lying. You can't help. You don't know how to kill it. I should kill you before I save her."

"Okay! It's a giant frog. I ignored it when I got here, but then I fell into the pond. It jumped after me and started trying to eat me."

Cl'rnce stared harder. The kick of both watery blobs swimming below the surface did resemble a frog stroke. But the knight was a killer, a villain; Cl'rnce couldn't believe him. "I never heard anything so stupid. A giant frog? There's no such thing. You're lying again. And besides, why didn't you fight it? You have a sword."

"Fine. I'm lying, and meanwhile it's almost on top of your friend."

The bubble trails were only a few feet apart. It seemed like the smaller one in front had slowed. Maybe Great and Mighty was tiring, or drowning.

"What can you do?" Cl'rnce asked. His flames wouldn't work underwater. If it really was a frog, it would be too slippery to catch. Cl'rnce was an excellent swimmer, but not a fast one. Wing drag slowed him down.

Nasty Sir George sighed. "Drop me in the water. It will come after me. My sword fell out over by those bushes when I slid in. You'll have to grab it and kill the frog before it eats me."

The bubbles were almost on top of Great and Mighty. Cl'rnce didn't have time to worry over why the knight would suddenly help instead of attack.

"Done. You're lucky I know a little magick. The one for dropping things, like water balloons, will work." Cl'rnce had dropped five water balloons over a line of professors while he watched from behind a bush. But he couldn't picture that now. The bubble trails had almost merged. "Gravity take over," he repeated three times as fast as he could, envisioning the balloons and Nasty Sir George dropping.

The knight dropped into the water. The bubble trails parted, and the smaller one headed for the knight.

"How long can she hold her breath? And why is she swimming back to the knight?" Cl'rnce muttered as he searched for the sword in the bush nearest the edge of the rock. "Got it." He stood up, holding the sword, and scanned the pond. Nothing, not a ripple, on the water. Not a wizard, not a knight, not a frog.

His heart felt like a boulder had been tied to it and dropped into the deepest, coldest sea. Great and Mighty and Nasty Sir George had drowned. And worse, there was no sign of the monster frog to wreak any revenge on. A single tear slid out of Cl'rnce's eye. He batted it away, but the drop plopped on the pond's surface. Where the tear hit, the water began to churn and whirl. A second later, Nasty Sir George and Great and Mighty bobbed up, coughing and spitting water.

"Huh?" Cl'rnce said, forgetting his usual smarter-than-anybody elegant speech. He had no idea why his tear had made the pond spit back the little wizard and the rusty knight, but it had.

Nasty Sir George and Great and Mighty swirled in the water as if caught in a whirlpool that was sucking up the top of the pond, and then Great and Mighty spun off, landing in the bush next to Cl'rnce. Right behind her, the knight jetted past Cl'rnce, crashing into a tree at the edge of the rocky ledge.

Great and Mighty picked her way out of the brush. "You should see what's down there!"

"Killer frogs?" Cl'rnce asked.

"No. A mermaid! Can you believe it? A real, honest-to-goodness mermaid. And they're a lot smaller than you think." She held her hands close together.

Cl'rnce grunted and turned on Nasty Sir George. Holding the knight's sword in one paw, he said, "You want to tell me again about that killer frog?"

"No!" Sir George said, kicking his legs in the air to try to right himself. He had landed on his head, both feet in the air, one leg stuck in a branch that seemed to be gripping him with its twigs.

"You're a liar. You knew she was never in danger. You tricked me!" Cl'rnce looked down at the sword he held. It would be so easy to lop this knight's head right off. No more problems from him. Cl'rnce and Great and Mighty could get going to Ghost Mountain and not worry about this jerk.

"Maybe I'm a liar, but it bit me," Nasty Sir George grunted. He almost had one leg free.

"Allow me." With the knight's sword, Cl'rnce took a long, hard swing at the knight, the broad side of the sword definitely not aimed at the branch, definitely aimed at the knight's head. He deserved a good headache.

"Arrestama!" a high-pitched voice screamed.

Cl'rnce's swing missed the knight, the branch, and the tree. The force of his powerful move pulled the sword out of his paws. It landed point down in the rock right behind where Nasty Sir George was still entangled in the limbs.

Cl'rnce turned to yell at Great and Mighty for stopping him from eliminating a dangerous evil knight. "What?"

Right behind the little wizard, floating on a funnel of water atop the pond, was a tiny woman with a fish tail and large purple eyes. The tiny woman said, "You, River Dr'gon, I am ashamed of you. On behalf of all the river folk, I grieve that you are such a cruel dr'gon." She dove off the fountain into the pond.

"Oh, boy," Great and Mighty said. "That was a mistake. I think from now on you're going to have a hard time swimming without being pinched and nipped."

"I was only defending myself and you. That cranky mermaid must know my sister, Hazel." Cl'rnce wasn't sure if he was ashamed of wanting to kill the helpless knight, but he sure hated being yelled at.

"She said her name is Sweetgrass, and I think you made a big mistake, Cl'rnce. The mermaid has a lot of relatives and water folk friends." Great and Mighty shook her head. "She's right. You shouldn't go around killing people, you know."

But it wasn't the little wizard or the mermaid's criticism that caught Cl'rnce's attention. It was what Nasty Sir George asked next.

"Hazel is your sister?" the knight asked. "Your sister?" He pointed at Cl'rnce.

Great and Mighty untangled the knight from the small branches and long vines and helped him get on his feet. "You know Cl'rnce's sister?" she asked.

"She hired me." His eyes shifted away from Great and Mighty's, and then quickly back.

CHAPTER 14

Moire Ain dropped the corner of Sir George's rusty shoulder armor she'd been pulling on. The knight rocked back onto his rear, but for once he didn't say a thing. She watched the knight's eyes flash from her to Cl'rnce.

Behind her, she heard a rumble and a click. She smelled something that had just caught fire. Moire Ain whirled around. A lick of flame slid out of Cl'rnce's nose. His eyes were angry slits, and he was definitely growling.

He held up a paw when she started to talk and shook his head at her. "You, knight. You liar! You insult my family thinking you can make me so angry I'll do something foolish that might turn me into a Killer Dr'gon. Not going to happen, liar. I don't know who hired you to slay me, if anyone did, but I know it wasn't my sister." Cl'rnce took a step closer to the knight, a longer slick of flame darting out of the corner of his mouth and slapping at the top of Sir George's helmet.

"I'm not—" Sir George started to say.

But Moire Ain stepped between Cl'rnce and the

knight and snapped at Sir George. "Shut up!" She didn't know where the axe-hard edges in her voice came from. In all her life, she'd tried never to be mean to anyone. For fear of her life, she hadn't dared to be cross with Hedge-Witch, and Moire Ain had tried to treat everyone else in the village as nicely as possible to make up for Hedge-Witch's cruelty. But right now, in this moment, she didn't care if anything bad happened to Sir George. She cared about protecting Cl'rnce. She couldn't let him do anything bad that would make him sorry or get him in trouble. She wouldn't let Sir George goad Cl'rnce into being a killer.

"Listen, Cl'rnce." She stared into the dr'gon's eyes, stepping side to side as he tried to avoid her gaze. She made him keep his focus on her instead of Sir George. "I think we need to get out of here. The knight is not a good guy. You were right. Don't listen to his drivel. Let's get back to the important stuff. We have an errand to run. Let's get going."

"He said—he said—" Cl'rnce couldn't seem to catch his breath with fire sliding out the sides of his mouth. He looked down at the rusty sword in his paw. He looked back up at Sir George.

A shrill, piercing whistle came from the river. Joined by another and another. So many that finally Cl'rnce clapped his paws over his ears, dropping the sword. Moire Ain, one arm cradled over her head and ears, started to lean down to take the sword, but Sir George had already crawled far enough to wrap his fingers around the hilt.

She lunged, dropping her arm from around her head, but the piercing whistles made her head swim, and she fell face first onto the rock. Moire Ain watched Sir George, apparently unfazed by the noise, grab the sword and get to his feet. For a moment, she thought he was going to swing at her, but he turned on Cl'rnce.

Moire Ain couldn't move her arms from her head; she couldn't get to her feet. All she could do was think. All she could think was that if Cl'rnce was in the pond, Sir George would not get near the dr'gon or the pond he feared. She managed to turn her head to Cl'rnce. His eyes were huge with pain. Moire Ain whispered, "Into the pond, Cl'rnce." It wasn't a spell, she was pretty sure. But she said it three times, just in case wanting something this badly could make a difference.

Cl'rnce stumbled backward two steps and fell off the rock into the water.

As soon as he hit the surface, the whistling ceased. Moire Ain's head stopped feeling like the knight was running it through with a red-hot sword. She turned to Sir George, afraid that he'd be so mad at losing Cl'rnce that he'd take it out on her. But the knight stood with the sword dangling from his fingers and his helmeted head bowed down to his chest. He said not a word but turned and marched off into the woods, loud clanking marking his passage. He looked ashamed.

Moire Ain got to her feet and ran to the border of the woods. She couldn't believe the knight would just give up, especially if he worked for Hedge-Witch. She expected to see him setting up an ambush in the trees. But he made it to the road, and kicking up dust, Sir George rattled away at a semi-run.

"I don't get it," she said.

"I feel great!" Cl'rnce called from the pond. "Come on in, Great and Mighty!"

"Huh?" she trudged over to the edge of the rock. She had hoped just to protect Cl'rnce. It never occurred to her he'd be happy about it.

"Water's fine." Cl'rnce shoved both forepaws forward, creating a big wave that broke over the ledge the little wizard stood on, soaking her all over again.

Moire Ain pushed her waterlogged hair out of her face. "Don't you want to know where Sir George is?"

"Who?" Cl'rnce splashed her again.

"What's the matter with you?" She sat on the rock, hanging her feet over the water and wringing out her robe's hem. "Is this some kind of joke?"

Cl'rnce smiled. "What doesn't kill us makes us stronger." He splashed her again. "And you did some pretty neat magick for someone who can't read Old Dr'gon and hasn't finished her *Magicks Mysteries* book."

"But you were so mad." She stared at him, open mouthed. "You had fire coming out of your—" She pointed to her nose and mouth.

"And somewhere else," He raised his eyebrow ridge and pointed to his tail. "So it's a good thing you shoved me in the pond. Apparently, when I get really angry, I spout fire out of everywhere." He rolled his eyes and grinned like he'd just made a big joke.

"But you're not mad anymore?" Moire Ain couldn't get over this. All her life, Moire Ain could not remember Hedge-Witch not being angry. And certainly the old crone had never been really angry and then become happy in a matter of seconds. Something was wrong with this dr'gon.

"I hope we never see Nasty Sir George again. I don't want to kill him. That would be bad." Cl'rnce sat down so only his eyes and horns were above water. He blew bubbles.

"Yes, yes. Killing is very bad," Moire Ain said. She remembered when Hedge-Witch had deliberately prepared a poisonous tea instead of a healing one for Goodman Fen. Hedge-Witch wanted the man's hut for her own. But Moire Ain had substituted healing herbs. Hedge-Witch had been so furious she had starved Moire Ain for a week.

"Well, yeah. Killing is bad, but for a dr'gon it's *really* bad. Did you know that? All it takes for a dr'gon to risk becoming a soulless Killer Dr'gon is to slay without extreme justification just once. Killers are outcast in the Dr'gon Nations. There are rumors that they have banded together to execute our leaders and take over the Primacy of the Dr'gon Nations. No way am I ever going to become one of them. Hazel would kill me! Mainly because one day I'm supposed to become the Primus." He grinned, but his smile was loopy, like he was drugged by the water.

Moire Ain tried to remember what she'd seen in her book that might be about Dr'gons and their Primacy. But there was nothing. Things were getting complicated. "So you're really supposed to become this Primus?" she asked, trying to think what questions he'd be able to answer clearly so she could figure out what was going on, and what she could do. A knot in her stomach said Cl'rnce was the king Hedge-Witch was after.

"Well, yeah. Hazel sent me on this errand. She hopes I'll fail. I know she'd like to become the Primus, but there's never been a female ruler of the Dr'gon Nations. She's crazy."

"Wait! You say she wants you to fail?" Moire Ain felt chills jumping up and down inside her stomach. He hadn't said that to her before. Could his sister be working with Hedge-Witch? "Don't get mad, but, Cl'rnce, do you think Sir George was telling the truth? Could your sister have hired him to get rid of you?"

Cl'rnce disappeared under the water. Moire Ain waited, counting the seconds, getting worried when she had counted to sixty and there was still no sign of Cl'rnce. She leaned over the water. Below, she spotted his big green body in a darker green shadow. He wasn't moving.

"Cl'rnce!" she yelled.

He didn't move.

"Cl'rnce!" She stood ready to dive into the water. Would she be able to drag someone as big as him up into the air? Could a River Dr'gon drown just by sitting down in a pond? Had she made him so sad at the thought that Hazel could be behind the killer knight that he just wanted to die?

Moire Ain felt like her heart was being squeezed into a tiny wad of nothing. She'd tried all her life to be a good person, but by asking if Cl'rnce's sister could be his enemy, she'd hurt another being so much, he was trying to hurt himself. She couldn't allow that.

She jumped high into the air and out over the pond. She looked down, hoping to land in the water right beside Cl'rnce. As her feet pierced the surface, she felt a soft thrumming along her skin. Sinking down beside the dr'gon, she felt the water shaking ever so slightly. At last, she floated even with Cl'rnce. His eyes were open.

Her heart contracted into a seed. He was dead. That fast. She'd really killed a dr'gon. Tears leaked into the water surrounding her face, but not because the dr'gon was the one who could read Old Dr'gon and help her become a real wizard. The old crone had been right all along. She was right to tell that stranger that Moire Ain would be the perfect tool to assassinate the king. It didn't make any difference that Moire Ain had run away with her book and her plans as soon as she'd overheard the plot. It didn't make any difference that Moire Ain wanted to be a powerful and good wizard. Moire Ain was only good for helping to do evil. Moire Ain should be the one drowned in the pool, not Cl'rnce.

CHAPTER 15

When bubbles tickled his snout, Cl'rnce opened his eyes. The first thing he saw was the little wizard floating in front of him. Her face was all big scared eyes, like she'd done or seen something truly awful. He sighed. This had been an extra busy day; he'd missed all his naps, not eaten, and he wasn't even a third of the way to Ghost Mountain. Now what?

With the tips of his long talons, he caught hold of the neck of Great and Mighty's robe. Cl'rnce pushed off from the bottom of the shallow pond, where he'd settled for the smallest of small naps and tried to not think about how empty his tummy was. The little wizard want-to-be's eyes went from scared to blinking surprise.

When Cl'rnce and Great and Mighty broke the water's surface, she coughed and choked out a titanic amount of water. Cl'rnce gave her a smack on the back to expel the rest, then tucked her under one arm and climbed out of the pool at the end with the waterfall. He ducked behind the cascading water curtain, stepping up on a dry ledge.

"You okay?" he asked, gently depositing her on the rock.

Great and Mighty choked again, spit, and said, "I thought . . . I thought you were dead." Water drained off her freckly skin, through her curly hair, and out of her eyes.

"You're *not* crying again, are you?" Cl'rnce said. "Don't do that." Using his back left paw, he scratched behind his left horn, a bad habit he fell into whenever he was exasperated and unable to control a situation.

"No." She swiped at her eyes. "Well, maybe a little. Sorry."

"Just stop. Please," Cl'rnce said.

"O—o—okay." Great and Mighty pressed her robe to her face. "I can't," she wailed. "I made you try to kill yourself. I'm the worst person ever!"

"Huh? No you didn't. Where did you get that idea?" Until today, he'd thought female dr'gons were confusing, but this female human was a puzzle wrapped in a mystery wrapped in a riddle wrapped in . . . .

"I saw you. Your face . . . you looked like you were dead." She let her robe drop and snorted up another sniffle.

"Want me to dry that stuff off your face?" Cl'rnce offered. If he could be helpful, maybe she'd quit the bawling.

"What stuff?" She snuffled again.

"The uh, uh . . . ." He never knew what would set Hazel off. He was pretty sure if he ever mentioned nose mucous to his sister, she'd rip his horns off for embarrassing her. Great and Mighty wasn't nearly as prissy as Hazel, so maybe she'd think he was being thoughtful to dry her nose leakage so she didn't have to use her ragged robe to wipe it up. Maybe. Then again none of his dealings with his sister or her friends had ever gone smoothly. He had a feeling there was no way this was going to go well. "The snot," he said fast, hoping she might not hear him correctly but that he'd get points for answering anyway.

"What?"

Yep. She was mad. But there was such a long drip off the end of her nose. He couldn't help himself. He pointed to her nose and made a wiggly motion with one claw to show her the long dribble. "I could flame it off. Just one second's worth, and it would disappear. All gone!" He held his paws palms up to show how simple.

She grimaced. "If you need a reason to spit fire at me, to get even for me saying such a mean thing about your sister, go ahead." She closed her eyes and threw her shoulders back.

"Argh," Cl'rnce muttered. He'd almost never used his flame, so he hoped he could control it. He spit a tiny particle ball of fire at the snot drop. The blob burst into smoke and disappeared. "All gone."

Great and Mighty slowly opened her eyes. "That was it? That's my punishment?"

"Punishment? You are weird. Do you really think, because you worried Hazel might hire a hit man, that I would do something bad to you?"

"But you were ready to kill Sir George when he said the same thing. And then it looked like you dove in the pond to kill yourself or something." She shook her head and held up her hands like she was really confused.

"First, I was busy cogitating, you know, thinking in the pond, not hurting myself." He wasn't about to admit anything about the tiny nap. "And second, I was trying to get rid of Nasty Sir George. That's why I got mad at him." Cl'rnce shook his head. "You worry a lot."

"No. I don't. You were leaking fire and talking about killing. I know you're upset about Hazel." She clamped her hand over her mouth.

"You know so little about dr'gons. I know Hazel didn't hire anyone. For one thing, she doesn't have any money. No dr'gons possess money. Knights like Nasty Sir George always work for money." He snapped his digits to show Great and Mighty how simple it was.

She took a step closer. "That's it? You're sure, because Hazel doesn't have money? What if she promised him something besides money?"

Cl'rnce was about to dismiss such a notion when

he thought of something. "Oh, you mean like if she can get to be the Primus, she'd be able to give him valuable stuff he'd want." Cl'rnce glanced over at the waterfall pounding into the pool. Maybe he needed a real thinking session. Cogitating underwater was his specialty, but this time he needed to not be interrupted. He was beginning to feel itchy-around-the-horns uneasy about Hazel and this Primus thing.

The little wizard tapped his arm. "Cl'rnce, I have an idea. You said if you get to Ghost Mountain on time with the Whisper Stone you're carrying, you'll have completed your errand. Are you sure about what kind of errand? Could this be more than you think? Could it be the for-real big one where you become the Primus on the spot, or could it be for something else?"

Cl'rnce shook his head. "I'm not so sure. It could be for real, but Mother would have said something, gotten all teary and packed me five lunches for something that important. Hazel wants me to return the Whisper Stone. But something's wrong with the rock she gave me. When I first got it, I knew it was real from the vibrations. But it's not doing that anymore. Maybe Hazel stole it back. Knowing Hazel, it might be a trick."

He heard himself saying words the lazy side of him wanted to believe. "One of the things the Primus can do that no one else can is communicate with the Whisper Stone. If this is the real one, and I'm supposed to be the Primus, which I someday am, it's not working. I can't talk to it, and it can't talk to me. Taking it back to the Council Chamber won't change that. It's like me reading the Old Dr'gon spells to you in your language doesn't make you able to read Old Dr'gon." He felt a little better. That made sense. A practical joke from Hazel. It would be over soon. He'd get back to naps. His future as Primus was not yet here.

"Are you sure?" Great and Mighty asked, staring at him intently.

"Pretty sure." Cl'rnce thought back to his classes at Dr'gon Wiz. "Well, maybe. Then again, maybe not. I might have missed maybe a little something when I sort of played hooky the entire semester of Dr'gon History 101. I mean why should I have to go to that class? I'm a dr'gon; I know about my kind. That should have been a class just for wizards."

"There are classes just for wizards?" Her face turned dreamy, like she'd heard something impossibly wonderful.

"Sure, at Dr'gon Wiz. The point is, I may have missed the part about the step-by-step process to become the Primus for the Dr'gon Nations. It's sort of possible I don't know everything." Cl'rnce kicked some loose gravel through the waterfall's curtain.

"What if you missed an important part about the Whisper Stone?" she asked.

Cl'rnce stared through the waterfall, thinking how he'd like to sit in this water, or any water anywhere, right now and not think, just nap. But Great and Mighty wasn't going to let him goof off. He could tell by the way she'd started pacing. He wanted her to calm down.

"Look, Hazel just sent me on another one of her endless errands." When Great and Mighty shook her head and kept pacing, he went on, "Fine, let's say taking the Whisper Stone to Ghost Mountain is really a step toward becoming the Primus. If Hazel was trying to sabotage me, why would she even give me the stone in the first place? Why not take it there herself? We're letting liar Nasty George confuse us."

"I don't know. It doesn't make sense. Unless she was testing to see if you're the real Primus. You know, finding out if you could communicate with the stone and all. Would she do that?" Great and Mighty sat on a small boulder and twisted her hair, wringing water out of it. At least she wasn't dripping tears anymore.

"I don't think so." Cl'rnce ducked down to look into Great and Mighty's eyes. "What if she's truly doing her sisterly duty, even if she has no choice but to send me on this errand, because the Primus *has* to be me?" Cl'rnce felt proud of his reasoning.

"Why does the Primus have to be you?" Great and Mighty asked.

"I thought I said a gazillion times. It's always been

the law. One of the male Merlin Clan River Dr'gons at the time of change is it. And I'm the last male of the clan." He smiled. This was easy. Hazel couldn't possibly undermine him. There was nothing she could do about him becoming the Primus, no matter how often she nagged him about what a lazy, no-good slacker he was and how she'd be twice the Primus he would. And how it just wasn't fair.

"What happens if the River Dr'gons run out of males?" Great and Mighty walked to the falling water and cupped a hand. She captured a palmful of water, turned, and offered it to him.

"Thanks, not thirsty. I had plenty while I was napping—I mean thinking underwater." Cl'rnce watched the little wizard drink. Run out of males? He'd never thought of that. What *would* happen, really? Hazel and he were twins. She was seven minutes and seven seconds older than him by birth. Eldest or not, she was still a girl. But if there were no males, like he was dead, could she be the Primus? Did his clever sister have a plan to foil the Geilt clan's claim?

"Do you have an idea how to find out if the rules would let her become the Primus?" Cl'rnce asked. He hoped Great and Mighty wouldn't think of going back to Dr'gon Wiz Academy. He had an errand to do, no matter what. But it really made his hungry tummy knot to think there was even the smallest chance his snarky sister might try to have him killed. On the other hand, he had to admire a plan where she had someone else do it. She was one clever dr'gon to figure out how to prevent herself from morphing into a Killer Dr'gon. Cl'rnce shook his head to make the traitorous thoughts go away. Hazel wouldn't do that.

Great and Mighty rubbed her hands on her robe. But her clothes, like her hair, were still soaking wet. She shook her head, and then waved her hands as if to air-dry them. "I might have seen something in my book to help us. A lot of the stuff I skimmed through looked like history. There's got to be a chapter on dr'gons and, well, you know . . . ways to get rid of . . . ." Great and Mighty shivered, wrapping her arms around herself for a moment.

Cl'rnce drank in a deep breath and held it for a second, until it warmed in the hot spot next to his stomach, his fire chamber. Then he flexed his claws at Great and Mighty to signal her to come near. She stepped up. He took hold of her hands and blew a warm breeze into them.

She stood still while the warmth rushed to her, then she twirled on tiptoes in his long, hot breath. When he ran out of air, she smiled. "All dry." She pulled her book out of her pouch. But the leather pouch was not waterproof, and neither was the book. It was a soggy mess. "Oh."

"No book. So we're on our own," Cl'rnce said. "We need a plan." The only plans he'd ever worked on in his life were his practical jokes (the best in the world) and his patented plan for skipping class and napping undisturbed by the river.

The class-skipping-napping plan utilized a number of rather complicated practical jokes to keep Dr'gon Wiz Academy students and faculty busy. It also required an entirely new plan each time he wanted to skip class, so that no one was sure who was responsible. Cl'rnce loved his own cleverness. If he could concoct such complicated schemes, he could definitely work out how to get to Ghost Mountain no matter who was chasing them.

He was counting on one of the Council being in the mountain when they arrived so his questions could be answered. If Great and Mighty was correct, once they got to the mountain, he'd really, truly be officially in line for the Primus. His mission was not a joke, and it was dangerous. Not that he wanted to be the Primus, but he sure didn't want Hazel to win. Especially if by some weird chance she was actually trying to get him killed.

He and Great and Mighty needed to start by getting away from the pool and on the road to Ghost Mountain. Night was falling. Less than three days left.

CHAPTER 16

Moire Ain couldn't believe she'd ruined *Magicks Mysteries*. She laid her book on the rock. With the tips of her fingers, she tried to pry the soggy leather cover away from the soaked pages. But the cover wouldn't budge. She sat back on her heels and stared at the mess.

"I don't suppose your breath could dry my book?" She looked up at Cl'rnce, who wore a big smile on his face and was kind of jittering up and down on his back paws. "What's up with you?" she asked.

"I can't wait to get going. We'll get to Ghost Mountain. I'll finish my errand no matter what Hazel is up to. She's a sneaky one, but I . . . well, I just can't see her facing Mother if Hazel managed to get me assassinated. See? Hazel can't be behind Nasty Sir George." His eye ridges rose as if he was trying to convince himself as much as her.

"I can help with that. You said we had to be there soon. We need to travel faster. If I could learn a spell, I could help you fly." She stopped.

Cl'rnce stood statue still. His face settled into a frown,

then went blank. "We do have to get to the mountain in less than three days, but *forget* the flying stuff." When Moire Ain started to tell him how she was sure he could learn to fly, he waved a paw and said, "No. I don't want to talk about flying. Forget it. What else do you have?"

She shrugged. "If I could look through the magick book, I might find some kind of spell to get us to that mountain real fast." She looked down and patted the waterlogged book. "But it's too wet to open. Can you dry it out?" she asked again.

Cl'rnce took a deep breath. She heard rumbling from his upper chest. Then he bent over the book and blew a gentle sip of warm air over it. He repeated this until at last she could pry apart the book. Careful not to rip the paper, she turned the pages. On one blurry leaf, there was a picture of a dr'gon flying, but the words below were all run together and some were even washed away.

Cl'rnce shook his head. "Too dangerous to try a spell unless you have all the correct words. You could end up blowing me away or something. Now will you give up on the flying thing?" He decided to not mention how many of her spells had been bumbled.

Moire Ain nodded, but she continued to turn the pages. Some were partially ruined. Some were partly okay, and the diploma at the back was fine. But how on earth was she going to earn a wizarding diploma and become an official wizard when so much of her book was . . . an unreadable mess?

Having gotten to the end of the book, she turned back, desperately hoping there was some spell in the book that she'd missed. She had to become a real wizard. The book was a bit of a disaster until halfway through she realized the middle two pages were undamaged. "Why didn't I notice that before?" she whispered to herself.

The damaged page before the middle was the flying dr'gon picture, and the damaged page after was something about creating a big hole. But these two middle pages had pictures of a mountain with caves in the side that made it look like a skull, and fog curling out of the 'eyeholes' like escaping ghosts.

There was also a smaller picture of a group of six dr'gons sitting around a big stone table. Each of the dr'gons looked very different from the others. One was orange with two horns behind its ears and a third on its forehead. One was a dark purple with large ears lined with bright pink feathers, and wide pink wings were folded on its back. The third was a dark brown with glowing green spots and the happiest golden eyes. The fourth was glittery red and much smaller than the other five. The fifth was a washed-out gray with scarlet eyes and black wings edged in red. Something about this one made Moire Ain shiver. But the sixth was a handsome green and purple dr'gon with beautiful jade wings. It looked a lot like Cl'rnce. Probably a relative.

"Is this Ghost Mountain?" she asked. "Is that the Dr'gon Council?"

Cl'rnce studied the page. "Yep. The ugly green one doing all the talking is Hazel." He dug a claw into his nostril and flicked his nose contents at the page. The snot bounced off the book and splashed back onto his muzzle. "Figures."

Moire Ain smothered a giggle. "I think your sister is quite beautiful. Her wings are the largest and prettiest." She was only a little surprised when the picture came alive. The dr'gons in the picture all stood and stretched their wings, then bowed to each other, and all the rest nodded to Hazel.

"Stop about the wings," Cl'rnce said.

"Why?" Moire Ain would have let it drop, but there was so much pain in Cl'rnce's tone. She had always wanted to heal anyone in need, whether it was sickness or unhappiness. She couldn't stand Cl'rnce's pain about not being able to fly.

"I can't fly because my wings are too small," Cl'rnce hissed, and turned away from her.

Moire Ain looked at his back where his wings were folded. They didn't seem any smaller than any of the dr'gons in the picture. "Are you sure?"

Cl'rnce did not turn around to her. Instead he slipped around the curtain of the waterfall. Moire Ain followed him. He stepped off the rock, over the pond's bank, and stood on the road. He didn't look at her when he said, "Of course I'm sure about my wings. Hazel measured them when I turned one hundred eight. She told me the bad news: I would never fly. She did it in front of Mother, so I know it's true." He glared at Moire Ain. "Satisfied? Now can we start walking so I can get to that dratted mountain and do what Hazel thinks I can't do?"

"How long ago was that? That you measured your wings?" Moire Ain put her book back in her pouch, but she had a feeling that there was a lot more to this wing thing. She stood in front of Cl'rnce, blocking his way.

"Three-hundred-plus years ago." He nodded his head toward the road leading away from the pool, as if to point the route they needed to take.

"But they could have grown since then," she said.

"No. They couldn't have. I'd know. And Hazel wouldn't keep nagging about curing me. There's no point to this. Can we just get going?" He began to walk.

Moire Ain paced beside Cl'rnce. After only a few minutes, she yawned. She'd gotten an inspiration, and she wanted to try it. "I'm awfully tired. Do you think we could get some sleep? I promise I'll run faster than a deer tomorrow and make up the time." She yawned again and made her eyes into sleepy slits.

"Oh. Yeah. We could do that," Cl'rnce said, yawning along with her. He looked around. "Since we don't know if Nasty Sir George is coming back, I think we should sleep in a tree. So we can see and hear him coming."

"Good idea." Moire Ain looked around at the forest until she spotted an old oak that she was sure would hold Cl'rnce's weight. It had thick branches halfway up and higher. "That one?"

"Nice choice." Cl'rnce bent down, his digits intertwined into a kind of stepping stirrup.

She put her foot on Cl'rnce's paw, and he lifted her up. But she was too short to reach the first branch. He tossed her, and she flew up to the branch, grabbing hold. "But how will you get up? It's way over your head," she called down. She hoped he'd forget and try to fly.

But Cl'rnce sank all four paws' claws into the tree's bark, and faster than she could say, "Cl'rnce!" he climbed the tree and was on the branch above her. He held a paw down to pull her up with him, but Moire Ain shook her head. "That's okay. I'll sleep on this branch. No offense, but we don't know how strong these are. I don't want to put too much weight on them."

Cl'rnce nodded and curled up, his tail twined around his branch. She wedged herself into a fork on hers and closed her eyes. She waited until she heard Cl'rnce begin to snore, then took *Magicks Mysteries* out of her pouch and opened it to the middle pages. While there was still light, she found some text in her own Common Language, with a lot about the Dr'gon Council. What she learned made her heart beat harder. She had to get

Cl'rnce to that mountain, and fast.

He was wrong about his wings. Male River Dr'gons didn't develop until they hit their first teens, four hundred and older. Either Hazel had lied to him, or he'd spent too much time napping and not enough time learning about his own kind. It was true that up until now only a male River Dr'gon had ruled the Dr'gon Nation. And it seemed Cl'rnce was the hereditary designee. Also it was true that if Cl'rnce did not complete his errand, another dr'gon could be elected. *Or* if he had a twin . . . and this was where the book was vague. It said twins were rare in River Dr'gons, and it said nothing about a female twin being unacceptable as the heir if the male could not serve.

The book said that the eldest twin of a rare pair of River Dr'gons would serve as Primus. There were no recorded male and female twins, so nothing in the book addressed Hazel. If Cl'rnce didn't get that Whisper Stone to the Council, Moire Ain was sure Hazel could take the Primacy. But if Hazel wanted the Primacy, why didn't she just forget to tell Cl'rnce about the Whisper Stone delivery? Why didn't she do it herself and claim her right by birth order? Cl'rnce had said something about her being seven minutes and seven seconds older. Moire Ain thought the rules were fuzzy enough that Hazel had a claim.

CHAPTER 17

Moire Ain couldn't continue reading history. Her mind wouldn't let go of trying to find a way to get Cl'rnce to try to fly. First, of course, she'd have to get him to open his wings and see if they'd grown. She peered up through the leaves. Cl'rnce's belly hung over his branch, but she couldn't see his wings. They were probably folded across his back, as usual. Quietly, she tucked her book back in her pouch. Balancing on her branch, she slowly stood. The wood beneath her feet creaked but didn't crack. She held still, waiting for the noise to wake Cl'rnce.

He continued to snore. "So far so good," she whispered. She edged around until her nose was inches from the trunk. She placed her stretched fingers on the bark. With her digits splayed, she noticed her nubby nails, worn down from digging herbs and doing all the hard work Hedge-Witch ordered. Moire Ain hoped her torn nails would be long enough to help her climb.

She squinted up the tree's trunk, but there weren't any small branches to grab. The first branch above her was the one on which Cl'rnce lay stretched out and around. Moire Ain reached up and was just able to grip the branch. Kicking with both feet, she managed to swing herself up onto it.

She froze, hoping the branch wouldn't creak or move and wake Cl'rnce. But she'd done it correctly. Since she had landed close to the tree trunk, she was on the most stable part. But when she stepped toward Cl'rnce, the branch gave a sharp *crack*. Moire Ain wobbled and almost lost her balance as the limb dipped.

"Uh-oh." She backed up to the tree's trunk.

Cl'rnce snorted in his sleep and mumbled. It sounded like he said, "Need a wizard to unlock the spell. Could fly if called."

The branch cracked again. His eyes popped open, and he shrieked.

Moire Ain jumped away from him and fell out of the tree.

As she dropped, Cl'rnce's paw swooped toward her. Snatching at her robe collar, he caught her. For half a second, Moire Ain's heart slowed its panicked pounding. Thirty feet below her lurked the forest floor, but Cl'rnce had her.

And then her robe tore.

"Great and Mighty!" Cl'rnce screamed as she fell.

There was nothing she could do. Her brain couldn't even pretend to come up with a spell or a plan to stop her fall. The only thing she could think of was how handy Cl'rnce's wings would have been. "I wish I had wings," she chanted over and over. Before she finished the fourth repeat, Cl'rnce dropped beside her. He grabbed her arm and pulled her next to him. But Moire Ain was furious. Not only had she caused this accident, but now Cl'rnce would fall to his death along with her. It was all her fault. She should have figured a way to make Cl'rnce fly before the book was damaged, before they were both about to die.

Picturing him with wide wings, she wished with all her heart that he could fly. "Fly dr'gon, fly dr'gon, fly dr'gon." She whispered the chant she hoped would work.

She glanced down. The ground was not coming at them as fast as it had been a second before. She turned to Cl'rnce. Behind him, enormous wings stretched, catching the last of the setting sun's rays slithering between the fading forest light. His wings were a deep jade, and the dusky sunlight reflected a thousand shivers of light. It was like green stars were caught in his membranes. His supposedly stubby wings were at least twice as wide as he was long.

They glided to the ground. At the last moment, Cl'rnce's wings folded. Moire Ain and the dr'gon made a hard Cl'rnce's-butt-first landing.

"You have amazing wings! They're not a bit stunted."

Cl'rnce started hiccuping. "They are? Honest to River Water! You are going to be the death of me. What if my wings had not been big and beautiful? Before, I only used them to glide a little. I didn't really know . . . Hazel said there was a painful spell . . . ." Cl'rnce shook his hiccup-bouncing head. "What if we both had fallen and broken our necks?" With each hiccup, he bounced a little where he sat.

Moire Ain couldn't hold in her giggles. "But we landed on our butts. My butt's not broken; is yours?"

Cl'rnce's hiccups folded into a deep laugh, like boulders rubbing together or thunder getting ready to grumble. "We landed on *my* butt, and no, I'm not broken. This time. You can't sneak up on me."

"Aren't you happy to know your wings are perfect? You can fly, I know you can. Well, if I can learn to be a for-real wizard and unlock the spell, then you'll be able to fly, not just glide."

Cl'rnce grumbled, but before he could say anything, Raspberries streaked through the trees, dropping a large poop on Cl'rnce's head, and settling on Moire Ain's arm.

"You mangy little bag of feathers! Now you show up, you little river waters-infested. . . . I'm going to teach you to dump on me!" Cl'rnce jumped to his feet. His eyes were wide, rimmed in hot red. A bit of flame leaked out of his muzzle. As he stood breathing hard, his wings unfurled and stretched to fill the empty space between the trees. "Nobody poops on me! Come here, birdie, birdie." He crooked a claw at Raspberries, rolling his lips back from his sharp fangs.

"Leave Raspberries alone." Moire Ain scrambled away from the out-of-control dr'gon.

"*No!* That miserable flying poop-fest has defecated on me for the last time!" Cl'rnce vibrated where he stood, but he did not move closer to Moire Ain and the perching bird.

Raspberries made the famous spitting noise he was named for and flew at Cl'rnce. The bird zoomed past the dr'gon, bombing Cl'rnce with another big splotch, this time on the dr'gon's wings. The dr'gon's reddening eyes focused on the bird. Cl'rnce turned, and his wings beat one down-stroke, lifting him just above the ground and settling him back down.

Moire Ain screamed. "No, Cl'rnce! Leave him alone. You can't fly yet. You'll hurt yourself and Raspberries. Don't try." She wasn't sure who she was more worried about, or why Raspberries was picking a fight with Cl'rnce.

"Seems I can. Somebody lied about flying," Cl'rnce said, his wings taking another beat down. His feet left the ground.

Raspberries jetted through the woods, back in the direction of the pool. Cl'rnce launched himself upward, his wings taking huge digs at the air. He took off after the raven. Moire Ain raced through the forest after them. Dodging sticking vines and leaping over logs and boulders, she ran as hard as she could. She kept an eye on Cl'rnce high above her. She couldn't believe how well he flew. How could he have been so sure he couldn't?

She was so intent on watching Cl'rnce that she didn't see the sword held across her path. Tripping over the weapon, she fell face first into a soft mound of mushrooms. The fungi exploded, and spores flew into her nose and face. She choked and swiped at her eyes.

"Well, well. The little wizard." Moire Ain recognized Sir George's voice. "You'll come with me."

"*No!*" she yelled as a cold, iron hand grabbed her hair and pulled. She screamed "No!" over and over, trying to keep on her feet, still blinded by the spores. She managed to pull away for a second, but then a rusty arm knocked her back down. Before she could stand again, Sir George tied a rope around her wrists.

Moire Ain feared he would bind her feet next, so she tried to kick, but he was too close. When he stepped back without tying her feet, she struggled again to get up and run. But her legs wouldn't work. Nothing would. All she could do was lie where she was, tears gathering in her eyes from the spores. She tried to wiggle her hands, but even they wouldn't move. She was paralyzed.

It had happened so fast, her head whirled. All she knew was that if she couldn't run, at least she could scream. So she did. She had to warn Cl'rnce so he could escape from the rotten knight.

"Cl'rnce, run!" she screamed again and again.

Her eyes shut against the itching spores, she smelled Sir George's rotted rutabaga breath on her face. "Quiet! Or I'll silence you. You don't want me to silence you. There's this little hitch to silencing someone. When I do, they not only can't talk, but they can't swallow or breathe. It's not a good way to die. Want to die, want-to-be wizard?"

Moire Ain swallowed hard. She wanted to live, but she couldn't let Sir George get to Cl'rnce. So she screamed again, "Run, Cl'rnce!" The tears in her eyes made her vision blurry, but she made out Sir George digging something out of a saddlebag on a blood-red skeleton horse.

He held the wadded-up something and waggled his head at Moire Ain. "You asked for this." Clanking his way back to her, he shook the rag at her. When he got to her side, her tears had now washed her eyes clean enough so she could see. Sir George's eyes were red slits behind the opening in his helmet. For the first time, he looked like something out of a nightmare, like the nasty knight Cl'rnce kept saying he was, not an iota like the helpless knight she had rescued at the pool.

Sir George stuffed the rag into her mouth. Gagging, she waited for her breathing to stop, for her world to go black and end. But other than the rag smelling like it had recently cleaned out a skunk den, nothing happened. She couldn't scream again, but maybe she didn't have to.

Above Sir George, Moire Ain spotted a glowing Cl'rnce soaring through the sky, spitting fire at Raspberries, who flew just ahead of him. Would Cl'rnce see her on the ground? Or was he too focused on chasing the naughty raven?

Sir George leaned down closer to her, and then turned his head, following her gaze. "Ah, company," he said. He picked her up and threw her over the back of the skeleton horse. At least this horse was not trying to get away from Sir George. Moire Ain figured it took a dead horse to get one that didn't want to bolt from the knight.

Sir George jumped on the steed and kicked its sides. Quieter than a gentle spring rain on a newborn leaf, they raced through the trees.

As they slipped deeper into the rapidly darkening woods, Moire Ain heard Cl'rnce yell, "Great and Mighty, where are you?"

CHAPTER 18

"Which way did she go?" Cl'rnce yelled at Raspberries. Slowing his wingbeats so he didn't soar far ahead of the raven, Cl'rnce scanned the ground. He nearly spun out of the sky when Raspberries swooped onto his shoulder and pecked his head. Cl'rnce shook, trying to dislodge the pesky bird, but Raspberries grabbed his right horn and tugged. Cl'rnce tried to shake him off again, rolling his shoulders and bucking a bit like a bull with a burr in its backside.

Raspberries let go and flew in front of Cl'rnce and then darted upward. "Stop it, bird. I have to find Great and Mighty. I heard her scream. Where is she?"

Raspberries hovered in front of Cl'rnce and cawed, followed by the spitting noise that sounded a lot like a fair-sized dr'gon fart. Next, the raven took off and flew straight forward. Cl'rnce ignored the rude bird and continued to scan the forest below. If there hadn't been a moon, everything below would have looked like nothing more than a shadowy lump. He spotted owls asleep in trees and skunks patrolling for food, but no Great and Mighty.

When Raspberries returned and dumped a big hot steamy one on Cl'rnce's nose, the River Dr'gon lost patience and chased the raven. He flew after Raspberries for five deep wing-beats and was close enough to snap the bird up. But Raspberries plunged down, then lifted up, dropped down, then flew up. Cl'rnce slowed. "What is wrong with you?"

Raspberries flapped in a circle around Cl'rnce, then took off to the east. Looking closely to figure out why the bird was acting even stranger than usual, Cl'rnce finally saw it. Glowing with the new night's shine on the rider's armor, a figure on a flying skeleton horse raced across the face of the moon. They flew in a direct line with a mountain. The mountain they swept toward glared dead-bone white in the distance.

"Ghost Mountain," Cl'rnce breathed. "I didn't know we were so near. Well, close as the dr'gon flies. I'm not sure we would have made it in time walking, even with a week." Cl'rnce took a deep breath. "I smell his rotten rutabaga stench. That's got to be Nasty Sir George flying to Ghost Mountain. Why?"

A wingbeat later, he reached the answer. "He knows I'm headed there. He's trying to trap me. I need Great and Mighty. I saw something in her book that we could use against Nasty Sir George. A spell to rust him in place. Great and Mighty wouldn't want me to kill him, even though he deserves it." Cl'rnce shook his head and tucked his chin to check below again. "Where is the little wizard?"

Raspberries flew straight at Cl'rnce and landed on his muzzle, gripping so hard Cl'rnce was sure the rotten raven was drawing blood. "*GET OFF!*" he roared.

In answer, the raven pecked him between the eyes. Then Raspberries pushed off and flew ahead, as if following Nasty Sir George.

"Forget it. I'm not going after that killer knight without Great and Mighty's help, you stupid bird. I need her spells, or her book anyway." Cl'rnce got ready to tuck his wings and descend for a better look at the dark forest below. But as he did, Raspberries dove beneath him and attacked, all screaming caws, beak, and claws.

Cl'rnce spread his wings and stroked back upward. The bird left him alone, and flew ahead toward Nasty Sir George again. Cl'rnce took a harder look at the horse and rider. He made out a dark bundle on the back of the skeleton horse. "Great and Mighty?" Cl'rnce sucked in his breath.

It was bad enough the knight wanted to kill Cl'rnce, but there was no way Cl'rnce was going to allow Great and Mighty to die for being his friend. Cl'rnce pumped his massive wings and took off as fast as he could fly.

Raspberries screeched again and landed on Cl'rnce's

shoulder. This time he gripped hard but did not peck or otherwise torture Cl'rnce. So the dr'gon let him hitch the ride. Cl'rnce beat his newly working wings harder, trying to catch up to Nasty Sir George. But he had never labored this hard. Gliding and dropping rotted fruit on the student knights as they practiced jousting wasn't hard work, or even really flying. To avoid being punished for that joke, he'd carefully maintained Hazel's belief that he of all the dr'gons couldn't even glide.

Not being a flying dr'gon had gotten him out of so much work Hazel and his professors would have assigned. It was hard to admit that by being so lazy, he'd missed out on something that now made him feel so powerful.

Cl'rnce's shoulders ached, but he kept pulling through the dark night air. "I think we're getting closer, gaining on him," he whispered at Raspberries. "He looks bigger, not small and far away."

Raspberries cawed, but it was not a reassuring congratulations. Cl'rnce focused beyond the knight's flight and saw how close Nasty Sir George was to Ghost Mountain. Cl'rnce pumped his wings harder, flying faster. But a moment later, Nasty Sir George disappeared. One second he was a blot of armor and glowing bloodied horse bones against the ghostly phantasm whites and darkest Stygian glooms pock-marking Ghost Mountain, and the next the knight had vanished.

Cl'rnce flew faster, his shoulders, wings, and back groaning with pain, a feeling the lazy nap-dr'gon had never experienced. Then things got worse. Sharp flashes of electric torture burst around him, shot at, and nipped him. One jolt darted past his nose.

"Huh?" Cl'rnce backpedaled to avoid another hit. He steered to the right. Was someone shooting lightning at him? Nasty Sir George? But as quickly as Cl'rnce flew to the right, another flash veered straight at him. He dove to the left and down. A ball of light followed.

Cl'rnce had never seen anything like this before. It couldn't be lightning; the skies were clear. And no one could shoot balls of fire or whatever and have them actually chase him like they were alive, matching Cl'rnce's dodges. He flew a zigzag pattern to escape the newest fire bolt. After twenty turns, he somersaulted in the air. "I'm going to be too tired to get to the mountain. No more running away from this. I have to get to Great and Mighty." He back-beat his wings to stall in the air.

The ball of flame hovered in front of him. Then went out. For a moment, Cl'rnce was still blinded by the fire and couldn't see, so he tucked his wings and plunged to avoid whatever else might come for him. The sudden dive pulled the Whisper Stone out of his neck case. But Cl'rnce didn't care. If it was really his, he'd find it again easily. Right now he had to save Great and Mighty.

When his eyes adjusted three seconds later, he

heard a buzzing and looked up to see a smallish dr'gon diving at him.

"Stop!" Cl'rnce shouted. "I'm Cl'rnce River Dr'gon. In the name of the Council, I order you to stop." Cl'rnce hoped this was not a Geilt Clan dr'gon. He'd hate to have to fight to the death with one of those killers.

The dr'gon halted when it was eye level with Cl'rnce. He was relieved to see the signature green inner and outer rings in the large purple eyes. This little guy was a River Dr'gon, but not one he'd ever met before. It was a male by the scarlet plume under its chin, and young by the double pink feathers at the base of the plume, just a dr'gonelle, a baby. So how did a too-young dr'gon without a wizard have wings that worked? It was a male Merlin Clan River Dr'gon, younger than Cl'rnce. Why was he here? Was he a contender for the Primus too?

"Who are you?" Cl'rnce asked, trying on a friendly grin.

The dr'gon cocked its head to one side but said nothing. It spit a small flame that did not reach Cl'rnce, then flew a beat closer. It was all Cl'rnce could do not to backpedal away. He needed to get to Great and Mighty. He had no time for this dr'gon. He had to find Nasty Sir George and Great and Mighty.

"It's rude not to introduce yourself," Cl'rnce said, not feeling like even trying to be friendly, but this little guy was sticking too close. "I'm on a mission. I have to . . . ." He stopped to decide if he should tell the newcomer about his errand and the Whisper Stone and the Primacy. Maybe he'd skip that, ask the little guy what he knew about the Primacy later. "I have to save a small wizard from a dr'gon-slaying knight."

The little dr'gon stared but said nothing.

"Are you deaf?" Cl'rnce asked.

The little dr'gon moved his head, as if he understood Cl'rnce's words, but he still remained silent.

"Okay. Not a big talker. I get that. Around my sister, I'm quiet as a mouse." Cl'rnce made mouse ears by putting his front claws over his own ears. Then he put a paw over his own mouth and shook his head. The little dr'gon watched him intently but made not one sound.

He'd never heard of a mute and deaf dr'gon, but maybe this young River Dr'gon wasn't able to speak. So Cl'rnce decided to act out what he needed. First, he tried to pantomime a knight riding a horse, whipping its hind quarters, and trotting in midair. Then he acted out Sir George attacking with a sword. The little dr'gon watched silently, hovering up and down, following Cl'rnce as he acted out his story. Cl'rnce was pretty proud that he'd managed to stay airborne while he worked hard to communicate with the little dr'gon. "I have to find Nasty Sir George. He's kidnapped my friend," Cl'rnce finally said.

The little dr'gon raised his eyebrows, then shrugged

his shoulders.

Raspberries let go of Cl'rnce and flew to the little dr'gon. He cawed and clucked, sounding an awful lot like the noises Nasty Sir George made as he clunked around in his broken-down armor.

The little dr'gon's eyes grew wide and then became slits. Cl'rnce got ready to defend Great and Mighty's flea-bitten bird, but the little dr'gon flew past Cl'rnce and Raspberries, straight at the mountain. He looked back and jerked his chin as if urging them to follow. Cl'rnce sped behind him. Something about this little guy made Cl'rnce feel braver and stronger.

Just as they reached the side of the mountain, the little dr'gon dove down to a darker-than-dark spot on the mountainside and disappeared. Cl'rnce followed him, flying into a cave as shadowy as the inside of a lump of anthracite coal.

CHAPTER 19

At first the mountain tunnel was wide, so Cl'rnce followed easily, flying behind the little dr'gon. Slowing the beat of his wings to not pass the youngster, Cl'rnce kept an eye on the soft glow of the wisp of flame seeping out of the little dr'gon's muzzle. It reminded Cl'rnce of a baby drooling. Cl'rnce wondered where this little guy came from, and why he didn't speak. And why Cl'rnce didn't know any other male of the Merlin Clan existed.

The little guy was clearly a River Dr'gon and should have understood everything Cl'rnce said, but Cl'rnce was pretty sure he didn't. It was lucky the little dr'gon had figured out what Cl'rnce was trying to communicate with his clever pantomimes, or Raspberries' caws.

The whole mystery of where this dr'gon came from irked Cl'rnce. What if the little dr'gon was working with Nasty Sir George? Could Sir George really be part of some kind of plot to take over the Primacy? Cl'rnce slowed even more. He wanted to rescue Great and Mighty, but he couldn't, if he let himself get captured, tricked, or killed. The little dr'gon had to tell Cl'rnce what he knew.

Since Cl'rnce couldn't figure out how to get him to talk, Cl'rnce decided he'd follow for now, but stay on super alert and super paranoid like his sister Hazel. No matter what might be going on, the self-assured way the little dr'gon flew made it seem like the he knew how to find Great and Mighty.

The little guy disappeared around a bend. Cl'rnce backstroked and hovered when he got to the turn. He dropped to the cave floor and slowly craned his head around the corner to see what was down the tunnel. "ARGH!" he started to scream when purple eyes shone into his.

But a quick small paw slapped over his muzzle before Cl'rnce could get the whole scream out. The little dr'gon shook his head as if to tell Cl'rnce to be quiet. When Cl'rnce nodded and managed to make his slamming heart slow to a reasonable beat, the little dr'gon grinned and jerked his head over his shoulder.

Then the dr'gon pantomimed sneaking very quietly along the tunnel. Cl'rnce nodded and imitated taking a slow, careful step. The little guy nodded once and turned to creep down the passage. Cl'rnce wasn't sure why they were moving this way. This tunnel was no darker now than it had been when they first raced in, and he certainly didn't hear anything. The little dr'gon must know something. How did he know it? What was it? Was it more than where Great and Mighty was?

Cl'rnce bumped into the little guy when he stopped suddenly. Without turning to Cl'rnce, the little dr'gon pointed to his ears and leaned forward. "You hear something?" Cl'rnce whispered. The little dr'gon didn't respond and didn't move. His paw remained cupped to his ear, as if listening.

Cl'rnce held his breath and tried to listen. The quiet was so intense that all he could make out was the thump of his own heartbeats. Funny he hadn't noticed that before. He listened a little harder and made out a quicker, softer beat he was sure was the little dr'gon's heart. *Cool,* Cl'rnce thought. But then a fainter sound joined their hearts. Two slower beats, too slow to be dr'gon. They might be human; they might be Great and Mighty and Nasty Sir George.

"I hear them!" Cl'rnce was astounded. When the little dr'gon didn't respond to his whisper, Cl'rnce tapped him on the shoulder and waited for him to turn. When he did, Cl'rnce tapped his own ear, then tapped over his heart. Then he pointed to the little dr'gon's chest and tapped again over his own heart.

The little dr'gon nodded but jerked his head back at the tunnel and cupped his ear again, as if trying to tell Cl'rnce about the other heartbeats. Cl'rnce nodded furiously and held up two digits. The little guy smiled and held up three.

"Three?" Cl'rnce listened again concentrating as hard as he could, but aside from himself and the little dr'gon, he only heard two more, human. "Nope." He shook his head.

The little dr'gon nodded harder and held up three claws. A chill slid down Cl'rnce's back. No matter how he held his breath and tried, he only heard the two others, the humans. What else could be in the Dr'gon Council's sacred Ghost Mountain? This little dr'gon was wrong. He probably heard echoes. He was too young and didn't know what an echo was.

Cl'rnce shrugged. He was sure the little guy was wrong, but this was not the time to argue. They needed to track down Nasty Sir George and rescue Great and Mighty. Didn't they? "Or might this be a trap? Nasty Sir George set it to get me in here. But I was headed to this mountain anyway. Why would he lead me where I wanted to go?"

The little dr'gon ignored Cl'rnce's whispered chatter and went back to slowly edging down the tunnel.

Cl'rnce needed to think this out. He had to know why Nasty Sir George would come here. The killer knight had zoomed into the mountain. He knew his way around. Humans weren't even supposed to know Ghost Mountain existed. Or at least they weren't supposed to know about the entrances and the Dr'gon Council

Chambers deep inside. Or know about the treasures of the Dr'gon Nations that were stored there.

"That's it!" Cl'rnce hissed. "He's after the Dr'gon treasures, and he's taken Great and Mighty so I'll have to trade the location to free her. And then he's going to kill me. And her. And you."

The little dr'gon didn't turn back but just kept crawling forward. Cl'rnce followed, letting his imagination go wild. Although he liked the kidnapping and trade for treasure best, Cl'rnce's vivid imagination came up with a thousand other conspiracies to explain why the nasty knight had hunted Cl'rnce and now lured him into the mountain. Half his fantasies included the little dr'gon being a rogue who worked for the rotten knight. But Cl'rnce kept coming back to the knight saying something about working alone.

Cl'rnce grabbed the little dr'gon's shoulder and pulled him to a stop. The little guy turned around, his muzzle scrunched in irritation.

"Wait," Cl'rnce whispered. "This is mixed up. Why would Nasty Sir George try to kill me, then turn around and lead me here to get me to show him to the Dr'gon treasure? That doesn't make sense. It's backward."

The little dr'gon stared at Cl'rnce as if trying to figure out why Cl'rnce was pacing back and forth, hissing his whispers louder and louder. Finally, the little guy floated, without unfurling his wings, until he was even with Cl'rnce's face. He drew back an arm. Cl'rnce tried to dodge the blow that was coming.

But the little dr'gon was fast, and his paw smacked between Cl'rnce's eyes and stayed there, almost like it was glued. In two, almost three days of strange happenings, maybe the weirdest now happened.

Cl'rnce didn't hear the little guy speak, but he saw a picture hanging in the air between him and the dr'gonelle. Great and Mighty was tied up and laid on a big flat rock. Nasty Sir George stood beside the rock with his hand out to a dark, squatty shadow a few feet away.

"Give me my reward," the rusty knight said.

The shadow figure stayed in the corner of the cave. It spoke with a scratchy voice Cl'rnce had never heard before. "Reward? You bring me trouble, and you expect a reward?"

"I've played your game and brought what you demanded." Nasty Sir George rattled his extended hand.

"The dr'gon is still alive. What did I tell you about that?" The shadow figure moved around the walls but got no closer to Great and Mighty, Nasty Sir George, or the fire in the brazier beside the rock the limp want-to-be wizard lay on.

"That shadow guy hired Nasty Sir George to kill me. I knew it wasn't Hazel," Cl'rnce whispered, careful not to dislodge the little dr'gon's paw. "What is it doing with Great and Mighty? Where are they? Are they close?

Can we get to them?"

The little dr'gon still didn't speak, but the picture before Cl'rnce changed to a vision of where they currently stood in the tunnel, then zoomed straight ahead along the passage until it arrived in a cavern with Nasty Sir George, Great and Mighty, and the shadow figure.

"You don't talk, but you do understand. So they're down this tunnel, not that far. We need to get in there. I'll take care of that miserable knight and his skulking boss. This mountain is the Dr'gon Nation's holy ground. Nothing can defeat me here!" He waited for the little dr'gon to do something that might give him away as part of the knight's plot.

As if he knew Cl'rnce's suspicions, the little dr'gon dropped his paw, a discouraged look on his face. He rolled his eyes, then slapped Cl'rnce behind the horn, and stuck his paw back onto Cl'rnce's forehead again.

The picture changed. A knife glittering with killing ice hung in the air over Great and Mighty. Nasty Sir George backed away from the knife, the rock, and the shadow figure. "You promised me payment. That's all I ask." He gulped, sounding scared.

The knife seemed to grow bigger and drop lower over Great and Mighty's chest. It dipped until its point rested on her worn robe. Nasty Sir George breathed deeply, like he was less scared since the sword-sized knife was meant for Great and Mighty. He clunkily backed farther away from the rock and the shadow figure. But no sooner did he stumble back three paces, than the knife turned and flew at Nasty Sir George.

Dodging it, the knight tripped over his feet and fell to the rocky floor. Once again, his luck ran out, and he was trapped on his back, rocking once again like an up-ended turtle. "Just let me go!" he whined.

Cl'rnce pushed the little dr'gon's paw away and headed down the tunnel. "It'll be Great and Mighty next. No way."

The tunnel became too narrow to stretch his wings and fly, so he ran for all he was worth. Pounding down the rock halls as hard as he could, sure the cavern was just ahead like it had looked in the vision from the little dr'gon, he ran and ran, but the shadowy tunnel never got lighter from that brazier fire in the open cavern. He kept running. The tunnel didn't turn or offer more than one way to run, it just kept rolling on in front of him. Finally he ran through rock walls and out of the mountain.

Too shocked to unfurl his wings, he dropped like a boulder. Stunned to be suddenly falling, all Cl'rnce could do was stare down at the moon-silvered trees he was falling into. Before he could blink, there was an explosion of light, and the little dr'gon was beside him, pulling on Cl'rnce's wings to unfurl them and force Cl'rnce to save himself.

Shocked by the little dr'gon's strength, Cl'rnce felt

his wings spread out. He barely managed to glide to the earth just before he crashed. He looked up at Ghost Mountain. His eyes were runny wet, definitely only because of the wind that had blown into them. "How did I run through the mountain? I saw where she was. Why can't I get to her?"

CHAPTER 20

Moire Ain slammed her eyes shut again. She'd knocked her head hard against the skeleton horse's flank and blacked out. When she awoke, she was lying on cold stone in a creepy rock chamber with a prickly rope around her hands and ankles. She had seen Sir George but not his horse. She guessed the bloody stallion had bolted away from Sir George as soon as it could, just like his other two steeds. Too bad it hadn't fled before she ended up tied up on a flat rock in a cave.

Before she did anything that made the crazy knight angrier, she decided to listen and learn.

The first thing she realized was that she heard someone else in the cavern besides Sir George. By the footsteps, she could tell the horse hadn't returned. She slit her eyes to try and see, but the other presence was a darker spot in the shadows. Afraid to open her eyes wider and give away that she was awake, she continued to listen.

Moire Ain made out rough breathing and a hoarse voice with a familiar southern Albion accent. Someone she knew was here? Who? Moire Ain didn't know anybody important enough to know a knight, not even a rusty, clunky one. She listened as the shadow lectured Sir George about failing to accomplish what he'd been hired for.

Sir George complained, "For all my success, you treat me ill! You owe me more."

Despite echoes that bounced and distorted the voice, the haranguing shadow sounded too familiar. Cold suspicion wrapped her heart. Moire Ain barely kept her eyes from flying open or gasping when the argument took an ugly turn. She opened her eyes the tiniest bit. With a frozen hiss, a knife swept the air over her chest. Keeping her slitted eyes on the rimed weapon, she heard Sir George rattle away from her side. He too knew the double-death the iced knife could deal.

The knife slipped lower, and the knight whined to be let go. Moire Ain couldn't stop herself. Frozen dread making her breathe hard, she turned her head. There she was, the person Moire Ain dreaded most, the witch who had created the frightening slow freezing death that froze the victim in a slow, pain-filled final death—Hedge-Witch. Blocking Sir George from moving, the old crone swept her arm, and the sword-sized dagger flew away from Moire Ain. It stopped and hovered next to Sir George. She snapped her fingers, and the sword pressed against the knight's chest where he cowered on the rock floor.

Moire Ain struggled to yell at Hedge-Witch to leave the knight alone, but a drumming of thunder rocked the stone Moire Ain lay on and bounced the knight against the floor. The sword pierced his armor, and Sir George screamed. When no blood flowed, Great and Mighty was relieved that he hadn't actually been stabbed.

Hedge-Witch snapped her fingers again, and the sword shrank back to knife length and flew into her hand. Once she held it, she gave the blade a shake and let it grow to sword length again. "Do you know what that was? Do you know who broke the air and shook this mountain? It was the dr'gon you were supposed to kill, fool." Her eyes had that maniacal shine Moire Ain had learned to fear and to hide from.

Still trapped on his back, Sir George whimpered from the floor. "I did everything else you said. I acted like I didn't know you even when we were alone. I . . . ." Flailing his arms and legs backward, still upside down and turtle helpless, he tried to scoot away from the witch. He scrambled so hard his face was beet red. Hedge-Witch slammed the sword into the rock floor. The vibration made Sir George tumble a good three feet into the air. He came down on hands and knees. She tossed the sword to him and yelled, "Get that dr'gon. Kill him now!"

Sir George struggled to his feet and backed toward the cavern's entrance. But he ran into the skeleton horse as it stepped out of the shadows.

"Ride!" Hedge-Witch commanded. "Make sure that River Dr'gon dies. He's the obstacle." Red eyes glared from the depths of the hood she drew farther over her head.

Sir George threw himself up on the skeleton horse. Before he could grab the reins, the steed broke into a gallop, heading across the cavern straight for a wall. The knight screamed as they passed through the wall and disappeared.

"I know you are awake, Moire Ain," Hedge-Witch said in a voice so snowy Moire Ain felt her bones freeze. But the pain in her body was nothing like what came in the next moment. Icing mist poured out of Hedge-Witch's hood, encasing Moire Ain.

Refusing to say a word that might tell the old witch how petrified she was, the want-to-be wizard wiggled to get away from the fog, or at least loosen the restraints on her hands and ankles. This was not the first time Hedge-Witch had used icing mist in front of Moire Ain. It was the first time Moire Ain had been the victim. If Hedge-Witch did not counteract the spell quickly, her quarry died of the frost. Moire Ain remembered when Goodwife Oak would not pay Hedge-Witch to prevent the witch from releasing a fungus to kill the Oaks' crops. No one else in the village spoke about the goodwife's frigid death in the warm season, but Hedge-Witch had a fancy new silver chain a week later.

The cold crept along her skin, and Moire Ain felt her muscles go hard. If she'd learned to be a for-real wizard, she could cast a spell that kept a warm aura on her skin. She'd have armor to protect her from Hedge-Witch's favorite form of slow murder.

With her skin becoming ice inch by inch, Moire Ain imagined the words she'd use if she could call up a warm armor. "Like sunshine on my skin, armor to protect." But it was too late; the mist's cold drove her forward to the dark sleep. With the last of her strength, Moire Ain repeated the words two more times, just like a real wizard.

As the last word echoed in her clouding mind, her lips too frozen to move, she felt warm fingers race over her body. A cracking noise echoed through the cavern. Moire Ain forced her icy lashes apart, forced her hands wide, and kicked her feet. Another echoing pop and she was warm and freed from the restraints. She sat up.

"Nicely done, Moire Ain. I thought you'd never learn. When you found that book, I feared you'd be dependent on others and never find your own power." Hedge-Witch pulled down her hood. She appeared as she always did, a wrinkled old face with muddy brown eyes, and eyebrows as white as her thin hair. The only thing that didn't match was her smile. Although her teeth were a threatening pointy mouthful, her lips were soft and full like a young child. It was one of the many creepy things about her.

"Power?" Moire Ain was not about to admit anything about having done any magick. She'd run from the old crone when she heard the conspiracy to kill a king. Moire Ain had been glad to think she might have a future as a wizard, but she refused to help Hedge-Witch do evil. This friendly tone of the old crone's was a trick. Moire Ain knew there was some way the witch thought Moire Ain would be useful.

"Don't play stupid with me, girl. Why would I keep a miserable peasant like you unless you had power?"

Moire Ain almost laughed to see the evil old harridan go so fast from uncharacteristically nice to her usual nasty. "Power to clean your pig pen of a home? To feed your animals? To gather your herbs? To heal the people you would rather kill?" Moire Ain couldn't help herself. After years of this old horror, if she was going to die, she was going to stand up and say what was true.

"Granted. You make a very sufficient serf." Hedge-Witch shrugged and paced around the rock Moire Ain sat on. "But I could enslave a thousand elves to do such petty work. Think. Why would I, Themora, take in an orphan?"

The old crone had a name. Moire Ain almost laughed that she'd never thought Hedge-Witch had one. But Moire Ain held her tongue for a moment. All her life she'd seen Hedge-Witch do cruel little magicks, but Moire Ain had never seen a sign that the woman could do any kind of big magick, like the skeleton horse Sir George rode. Could the old witch really call up elves?

And what was this Old Language name, Themora? Moire Ain had never heard the word before. Despite the warmth clinging to Moire Ain's skin, she shivered. Hedge-Witch was something different from what Moire Ain had always thought, and that something felt even worse.

"I'm waiting for an answer, girl!" Hedge-Witch paced. "Never mind. You may have the power, but you are certainly not that bright. Clearly intelligence and power are two different entities with you. All the better for me." She stopped in front of Moire Ain. "What did you use?"

"Pardon?"

Hedge-Witch growled. "What did you use to counteract my freezing spell? Do not bother to pretend you didn't do it. Before I took you in, I tested you. If you did not have the potential to call power, then I would have been wrong about you." She shrugged and slit her eyes at Moire Ain. "But I am never wrong."

Moire Ain refused to speak, but an inferno broke loose in her brain. All this time she'd believed she couldn't do big, impressive magick but hoped somehow she might learn it. She'd managed the small bumblespelled magick she'd done with Cl'rnce, but something had changed.

Hedge-Witch was saying Moire Ain had released herself from the freezing spell. There was no one else here. That meant that even without believing she could, Moire Ain really had cast a big spell-breaking. A life and death spell-breaking. Without any bumblespelledness.

Moire Ain was astounded as she realized she had real magick. How much, and how fast could she access it? What was the key to getting to it? Was it as simple as not worrying and simply focusing on doing it? She needed to get away from Hedge-Witch and get to Cl'rnce before Sir George killed him.

Hedge-Witch stamped her foot, and a crystal staff grew from the cave floor. Gripping it in her left hand, the crone broke it loose from the ground and pounded it on the floor. A whisper of smoke formed, looking like a man, like the shadowy figure who had met Hedge-Witch in her hut. The smoke swirled and became a small dr'gon, black-brown instead of green like Cl'rnce, but with a growl twice as loud. Using the crystal rod, Hedge-Witch tapped the floor again, and the dr'gon began to grow. When it was twelve feet tall and its tail lashed about, knocking boulders loose, Hedge-Witch bowed to the dr'gon. "My lord, this is the girl. She is the key. She has the power you seek. I have seen it."

The dr'gon eyed Moire Ain, but not in the friendly or joking way Cl'rnce did. This dr'gon's eyes were black like anthracite, with a burning red fire in the center. He didn't speak, but he nodded to Hedge-Witch and took a step toward Moire Ain. His fangs dripped red.

Moire Ain swallowed a scream and tried to think. She felt the warmth-armor she'd made to repel the freezing spell. It was still on her skin, but dr'gons had their own fire. Fire and warmth would not protect her and keep this guy from eating her, or whatever he planned. She needed the opposite of warm. Cold. Moire Ain thought of the elements of warm that repelled the ice spell and turned them inside out.

Slowly, she sat up and focused cold in her fisted hands. She bowed her head, letting her hair drape over her face. Moire Ain concentrated and gathered from inside herself what she hoped she could use. A moment later, her hands felt like blocks of ice. She looked up. She hadn't heard him move, but the dr'gon's muzzle was only a foot away. Using all the strength she had, Moire Ain jumped up, slamming her iced hands onto the dr'gon's muzzle.

The creature bellowed and fell back far enough for Moire Ain to run past. But Hedge-Witch blocked her way, holding the crystal staff, pointing it at Moire Ain. Moire Ain didn't hesitate; she ran faster, straight at the witch. Moire Ain screamed, "To me!" She slammed a shoulder into Hedge-Witch. The rod flew to Moire Ain's extended hand.

She did not wait to see if Hedge-Witch followed, or

if the dr'gon was a frozen statue. Instead, she focused on the rod she held in front of her. Moire Ain ran for the wall and the spot Sir George had passed through.

Thinking *Escape in one piece* three times, she ran into the wall. And ran, and ran.

CHAPTER 21

Outside the mountain, Cl'rnce had hit the dirt, stumbled, rolled twice, and hopped to his feet. He didn't have time to check for injuries before the little dr'gon buzzed around his head. In a blur of black feathers and loud caws, Raspberries zoomed past the dr'gonelle and straight at Cl'rnce. The raven pecked Cl'rnce on the nose.

Cl'rnce looked up, ready to bat at the feathered fleabag, but he saw something more important. Nasty Sir George on his skeleton horse soared down the side of the mountain, headed straight at Cl'rnce. The killer knight screamed something so high pitched it hurt Cl'rnce's ears.

"That's not good," Cl'rnce said. He concentrated and sucked in a deep breath. The air went straight to his fire pit, fanning a blaze so hot it almost hurt Cl'rnce's chest. He muttered to himself, "At least Great and Mighty isn't here to tell me no. No matter what she thinks, I'm going to fry this knight until he helps me get to the little wizard!

And kill him after."

His throat roasty-hot from the gathered flame, Cl'rnce blew a long tongue of fire, scorching over the horse and rider. The horse went up in flames and ash. The knight fell from the sky, charred to a crisp. He landed with a spray of ash.

Cl'rnce edged over and kicked the burnt knight. He wasn't sure if he heard a whimper, but the knight didn't move. "Ah, river *rats!*" Cl'rnce said. "I didn't mean to do that. He's dead. Now how am I going to find Great and Mighty?" Cl'rnce looked back up at Ghost Mountain. "Why did Nasty Sir George leave her?"

The little dr'gon flew up to Cl'rnce's face, snorted a hot breath that clearly said Cl'rnce was an idiot, then smacked Cl'rnce in the chest with his tail.

"Ouch! That hurt. Are you crazy?" Cl'rnce patted his chest. "You might have broken the Whisper Stone. Hazel will have my hide if it gets damaged. I don't have time for repairs or finding a replacement. No, wait. I dropped it. It could be around here. I guess we should find it. I still have to get it into the Council Chamber."

He patted his pouch and was surprised to feel the locket he thought he had lost. Pulling it out, he checked it over quickly. It was dented but fine, and most importantly, not lost. He sighed in relief. "Weird, but lucky for me. Lucky for you, everything's okay." He raised his eye ridge at the little dr'gon. "I'd hate to have to tell on you to Hazel."

The dr'gonelle flew to Cl'rnce's face and snorted, then hovered over the little case in Cl'rnce's hand and spit on it.

"Stop that!" Cl'rnce said, gripping the locket and getting ready to stow it back in the pouch in the folds of his chest scales. But when he closed his paw, he noticed light leaking out. He opened his paw again. The locket glowed, spraying rays of purple and gold. "I'm pretty sure it's not supposed to do that."

Raspberries plopped on his shoulder, pecked him behind the horn, and said, "Nevermore."

Cl'rnce was too absorbed to push the raven off. He couldn't take his eyes off the light in his paw. The rays moved and danced, and then darker rays formed figures. Three images. At first blurry, the three became more distinct, and Cl'rnce was certain one of them was Great and Mighty. But he didn't know what the other figure was. Cold terror made his scales stand on end when he realized the third figure was a dr'gon, and Cl'rnce recognized him.

At Dr'gon-Wiz there was only one class Cl'rnce had attended faithfully and even done the homework for. It was *The History of Villains*. Cl'rnce wasn't convinced all the villains the professor lectured about were real. In particular, Cl'rnce had been sure the Killer Dr'gon of Ghost Mountain was a myth.

The myth said the Killer of Ghost Mountain was obsessed with hunting and destroying all the leaders of the Dr'gon nations. The Killer sought the day when the Dr'gon Nations were in chaos, without a true Primus, to take over everything, to rule humans as well as dr'gons. But that myth supposedly happened hundreds of years in the past. Some hero Cl'rnce couldn't remember had defeated the Killer, or maybe banished him. It didn't matter. No way the Dr'gon Council was stupid enough to set up in Ghost Mountain if this killer guy was real and still around.

Except right there in front of Cl'rnce was the image of the Killer Dr'gon straight from the illustrations in the *Book of Villains*. This was the only dr'gon ever to have four regular horns on his head, plus one the length of a sword on his muzzle. The muzzle horn was said not only to be sharper than any sword but to ooze poison as well. The myth of the Killer Dr'gon of Ghost Mountain said that centuries ago, when the dr'gon had been banished, the horn had been disabled.

Cl'rnce remembered that now. A spell was put on the Killer to deactivate the poison, a spell that a dr'gon could not counteract. It would take the blood of two dr'gons and a wizard to restore the poison and make the Killer Dr'gon of Ghost Mountain lethal enough to take power. Cold ran down Cl'rnce's spine. The Killer might just be there, imprisoned somewhere in Ghost

Mountain, not banished. Hopefully, he was jailed somewhere he couldn't escape from.

Cl'rnce couldn't look away from the figures sparking from the locket. The one he thought was Great and Mighty did something to the Killer Dr'gon, then grabbed a long pole and ran at a cave wall that Cl'rnce felt certain was the same one he and the little dr'gon, and Nasty Sir George and his horse, had come through. As the Great and Mighty figure neared the wall, the locket went dead dark.

Cl'rnce shook it. Rubbed it. Snorted hot breath on it. But it stayed dim. He looked up at the little dr'gon hovering near. "Great and Mighty, she . . . " He followed the dr'gonelle's upward gaze. "She's falling out of the mountain. Now!"

Cl'rnce raced to the spot under the plunging Great and Mighty. He ran back and forth as she dropped, holding his arms up to catch her.

Raspberries cawed, "Nevermore."

The little dr'gon flew in a circle around all of them.

For a moment, Cl'rnce stopped racing about and stared up at Great and Mighty. She had one arm out, and something long and sparkly extended from her hand. It seemed like she had slowed, but she still came plenty fast. Shooting past Cl'rnce, the little dr'gon continued to circle. Cl'rnce dismissed the little guy, who had clearly panicked and gone round-and-round crazy.

But Cl'rnce checked the little guy again when he saw the path of the dr'gon's circle lighting up. It looked like glowing fog. The dr'gonelle flew faster, snorting small flames at his path, which made it more solid. Cl'rnce took a deep breath and turned to follow the circle; he added his own flamed air on the little dr'gon's path. Immediately, the entire circle's glow thickened. It was flattening into a disk, like a big round blanket that might stop Great and Mighty from crashing. But the center where she would hit wasn't filling in fast enough.

Cl'rnce stretched up to catch the little wizard. A moment later, she crashed into his arms and bounced out. She hit the circle like it was made of a tight, stretched blanket and ricocheted back into Cl'rnce's arms. This time he closed them on her in a big hug.

"Where did you go?" he said.

Great and Mighty started laughing. "Well, I thought I'd visit with my old mistress, Hedge-Witch. So I let Sir George take me there. While we were at it, I thought why not meet a really scary dr'gon."

"Dr'gon!" Cl'rnce hissed at the reality. "Bad idea, that dr'gon. Do you know who that dr'gon is?"

Great and Mighty shook her head. "Who? And who is that?" She pointed to the little dr'gon. "He looks like the shiny thing in your locket."

Cl'rnce shook his head and grinned. "He didn't come out of my locket—I mean, storage device. I'd introduce you, but I don't know his name. He helped me find you, sort of. And he made the bouncy ring that helped you not crash to earth. But he doesn't talk."

"Thank you!" She smiled at the little dr'gon. Then she turned back to Cl'rnce. "You know about that scary dr'gon in the mountain?"

"Unfortunately, I think I do. I saw him in the Whisper Stone, or its lights." Great and Mighty looked blank, so he went on. "Seems the rock does tricks like show you to me, when you were in the mountain with the Killer Dr'gon and someone else."

"The someone else is Hedge-Witch. She used this staff to call up that scary dr'gon, Killer Dr'gon." Great and Mighty held up the rod she still gripped. "And she called him 'my lord.'"

Cl'rnce shivered. "That's not good." He held a paw out for the rod. At first Great and Mighty shook her head and gripped it harder, but then she passed it to him.

"What did she do with this?" Cl'rnce asked after he sniffed it, licked it, and pinched it. He handed it back to Great and Mighty.

"She slammed it into the ground like this!" Great and Mighty smacked the staff into the forest floor. "And swirly smoke appeared, like the man .... Then a tiny dr'gon appeared. She did it again, and the dr'gon grew into the big scary one."

Cl'rnce and Great and Mighty both shot looks over

to the little dr'gon who hovered over Sir George's burnt armor. Raspberries walked around the roasted knight, poking at the crispy metal. When the little dr'gon did not grow, they both heaved sighs of relief.

"The little guy is not another Killer Dr'gon, huh?" Great and Mighty asked.

"I guess not. I hope."

"Why are he and Raspberries so interested in that burned metal pile?" Great and Mighty started to walk over.

"Wait!" Cl'rnce grabbed for her arm. "Let me explain."

"Sir George," Great and Mighty said as she bent over the armor. "Talk to me. Right now. We want to know details—why Hedge-Witch wants Cl'rnce dead, and . . . what she planned on doing with me."

"He's dead. Burned. And I did it," Cl'rnce said. He watched her face, waiting for Great and Mighty to show how disappointed she was in him. "But it was him or me. I swear." He waited again for her to tell him he was as evil as Hedge-Witch.

"He's not dead." Great and Mighty looked up. "But his face is really red through the armor. I think you roasted him a bit." She kicked the armor. "Answer my questions."

"Don't know," Sir George muttered, still not moving. "I'm not talking to you two."

"Because you're afraid?" Cl'rnce joined Great and Mighty. "You're afraid of the dr'gon, aren't you?"

"You? I'm not afraid of you," Sir George said. "The old hag hired me to kill you. Plain and simple. I lied about your sister. Now let me go."

Cl'rnce poised a big back foot over the knight, like he was going to squash him like a bug.

Great and Mighty pushed him away. "Sir George wasn't there when Hedge-Witch made the dr'gon appear. I don't think he knows any more than he said. Hedge-Witch seemed all excited that I can do magick. I did do it, really big magick. No bumbled spells. Oh, yeah. She ordered Sir George to bring me to her."

"Yep," Sir George said.

"So Hedge-Witch calls forth a Killer Dr'gon she calls 'lord,' she wants me dead, and she wants you to have magick. I hate to say it, but I know about this. It sounds like the formula for unleashing the Killer D'rgon of Ghost Mountain and making him the Primus. All they need-ed was another dr'gon's blood plus—" Cl'rnce pointed to himself and then at Great and Mighty. "—you." They both turned to look at the little dr'gon. "And maybe him."

"What are we going to do?" Great and Mighty asked.

"They're in the mountain, and I have to get the Whisper Stone into the Council Chambers. We have no choice. We have to get into the mountain and put a stop to the Killer Dr'gon's plans." Cl'rnce stared up at the mountain. He felt a rush of optimism, because Great and Mighty could do magick now. They were going to need her power. Maybe she could start with finding the Council Chambers, so they could deliver the stone, fast. That done, they could work on finding Hedge-Witch and the Killer Dr'gon. Sounded like a plan.

CHAPTER 22

Magick power or not, Moire Ain hated the idea of going back in the mountain. Somewhere inside was the person she'd feared her whole life. Moire Ain's stomach clenched at the same time her heart beat so hard she put her hand over her chest in case her heart punched through. After years of doing whatever she could to keep from being hurt by Hedge-Witch, Moire Ain had finally escaped. She even had what she'd wished for most, magick power.

If she had to go back in, Moire Ain hoped she could defend herself with that magick. Really hoped. But she worried. How reliable was her magick? How powerful? Was it possible she'd used it all up? Would she have enough to keep everybody safe from the Killer Dr'gon? Even Hedge-Witch acted like she feared him a little.

Moire Ain was so immersed in worrying that she only heard a bit of what Cl'rnce was saying. "What?"

"I said, Nasty Sir George claims he doesn't know anything more. He's useless and a bad guy. I think we should throw him in the pond and be rid of him forever," Cl'rnce said.

"Drown him?" Moire Ain shook her head until her hair flew like it was caught in a tornado. "No! Killing makes us evil, like Hedge-Witch. It's what she'd do. It's what she wanted to force me to do. No evil!" She slammed her rod down and repeated "No evil!" two more times.

When she finished, Sir George yelled. Cl'rnce, Moire Ain, Raspberries, and the little dr'gon all whipped around to look at the knight.

Sir George had managed to right himself and get on his feet.

Moire Ain, Cl'rnce, and Raspberries gasped together.

Sir George's formerly dented, rusty, and mismatched armor, which had been charred and full of more holes than ever, now gleamed like new. It shone like a polished silver coin. There wasn't a single hole, and for the first time, his armor really fit him. The missing left lower leg plate had appeared. With arms extended, he stared at himself. He made a chugging noise like he wanted to put together words but couldn't.

"You're welcome," Moire Ain said.

"You did that?" Cl'rnce asked. "How? Why?"

Moire Ain leaned close to Cl'rnce and whispered, "I guess I did. I sort of only hoped to stop anything evil, like broken bones or us getting dead. You know I'm a pretty good healer without magick, so I thought ... this picture snapped into my mind of Sir George as a good guy when I was yelling about no more evil. And I kind of thought maybe if we did something nice for him, Sir George would stop being evil. Maybe he'll help us now." She stared at the knight.

For a moment, Sir George stopped admiring his new armor. He looked up at Moire Ain, smiled, and saluted. "I heard the old crone say something about becoming the Primacy's Wizard." And with that, Sir George turned and ran, faster than he had before, in his new, unbroken and un-rusted armor. Unfortunately, he ran away from them all.

"Ungrateful." Moire Ain shook her head.

"Nevermore!" Raspberries said, and took off flying. He circled the fleeing knight, dove close, and let loose a signature Raspberries-large raven poop. The little dr'gon, who followed, turned somersaults in the air, almost like he was laughing. Then he zoomed back to Cl'rnce and Moire Ain, with Raspberries right behind. Even with bird dump slipping down his visor, Sir George never slowed. He kept running.

Cl'rnce said, "It's okay. We don't need him. He just told me what's going on. I know why Hedge-Witch wants me dead, and why she kidnapped you and wanted to force you to do magick." He paused as if for dramatic effect.

"Go on," Moire Ain said.

"Hedge-Witch summoned Lasair, the Killer Dr'gon, right? She knows of the old myths about him taking back the Dr'gon Nations, becoming the Primus. She's helping him so he'll make her the second most powerful being and the most powerful wizard ever. Like you said, Great and Mighty, dr'gons have some of their own magick, and combined with a wizard, it becomes unstoppable.

"Lasair needs the powers and blood of a great wizard and two dr'gons to restore his poisonous power. Hedge-Witch intended to provide Lasair with you and me. That just leaves one more dr'gon," Cl'rnce finished.

"So does that mean you and I are powerful enough together to stop them?" Moire Ain asked, feeling the queasy stomach thing that meant she already knew the answer. No matter what Hedge-Witch Themora had said, deep down Moire Ain was only a beginner with bumblespelled magick, no real match for Themora and her dr'gon. Moire Ain was a little shocked that Cl'rnce would even say he had magick when he'd spent so much time denying he had any.

Cl'rnce shook his head. "No. We might not be able to stop them. Well, maybe if we had that other dr'gon. The problem is, I never practiced the lessons on defeating Lasair and, well, employing dr'gon magicks. Instead of preparing for *Dr'gon Magicks* practicum, I had an important practice for the nap-off between the dr'gon students and the first-year knights. I won." Cl'rnce grinned. "I'm pretty famous for thundering snores. I kept all the other contestants awake, which assured me the silken pillow trophy."

"Nevermore!" Raspberries landed on Cl'rnce's shoulder and pecked him on the back of the neck.

Cl'rnce sighed but didn't even swat at Raspberries. "You aren't a fan of sports, bird?"

Moire Ain groaned. "How are we going to find this other dr'gon you don't know about? Do we really need to? I mean, if we just get your Whisper Stone back to the Council, won't that be enough?"

"Maybe," Cl'rnce said, fishing the locket out of his pouch. "But what if the Whisper Stone showed us the dr'gon and where he is? It showed me you, Hedge-Witch, and Lasair, for a short while."

"So we think this whole errand of yours and Hedge-Witch and Lasair's plans are connected?" Moire Ain wondered how long Hedge-Witch had planned this. Moire Ain had always thought it was weird that the witch had allowed Moire Ain to go anywhere on her own, much less not come looking for her when she was so late the day she had found the book.

Cl'rnce pried at the locket, but it wouldn't open. He held it out to Moire Ain. "You try. It's not working for me."

She took the locket. It felt warm, but that was from being stored next to Cl'rnce's skin. Other than temperature, nothing. It wouldn't open like it had before.

She was about to hand it back to Cl'rnce when the little dr'gon sighed, hovered over her hand, and drifted down onto the locket like a hen sitting on an egg.

Moire Ain stood very still, holding her hand out as steady as she could. Purple and gold light leaked from beneath the little dr'gon. He got heavier and heavier and the light beneath him got brighter. She struggled to keep her hand up. Moire Ain wedged the crystal staff under her hand to keep from dropping the little dr'gon and the locket. As the faceted end of the rod bit into her skin, she chewed her lips and concentrated on not complaining or moving.

Cl'rnce edged close to her, sniffing at the little dr'gon. "What's he doing to the Whisper Stone?" he asked, bending down and peering under the little dr'gon. Cl'rnce sounded curious rather than upset that the precious stone was being sat on.

"I don't know, and I can't hold him. He weighs a ton!" Moire Ain finally gasped. "Catch him." Her arm gave out, and her hand fell to her side.

For a second, Cl'rnce didn't move. Then his paw shot out, but there was no need. The locket and dr'gon floated in the air. Still sitting on it, the little dr'gon grinned. Purple and gold light shone out of his mouth.

"What's happening?" Moire Ain whispered.

Before Cl'rnce said a thing, the little dr'gon spit purple and gold beams. Moire Ain turned to watch the arc

236

of light streak through the air and splash against the mountain, turning its face into an amythyst. Then the little dr'gon hiccuped, and the light show was over.

"Hmmm." Cl'rnce held out an arm, and the little dr'gon landed on him the same way Raspberries perched on Moire Ain. Cl'rnce sniffed and kept his nose pressed close to the little guy. "You look like a miniature River D'rgon. I mean, I know you are one, but that wasn't normal." He looked under the little dr'gon's butt. "What was that spitting light all about? Where's the locket?"

The little dr'gon paced up and down Cl'rnce's arm like an oversized pet bird. Moire Ain, Cl'rnce, and Raspberries watched him. Finally, the little guy stopped and stared at each of them like he expected them to know what he wanted them to do next. But all three, even Raspberries, shrugged their shoulders. The little dr'gon snorted, then focused on each, staring into their eyes one by one, but none of them did anything more than stare back.

He snorted a golden flame. The snort-fire was solid and plopped to the ground. Cl'rnce and Moire Ain jumped back from the glob. Moire Ain wasn't sure what this little dr'gon was and what might be in his bodily fluids. The snot simply lay on the ground. Not glowing. Not burning.

Cl'rnce sniffed. "Nothing unusual. This little guy isn't normal, but his boogers are."

Moire Ain groaned. "Boogers. We're standing around looking at tiny dr'gon boogers? Did he destroy the locket and stone? Or swallow it backward? What does that mean to finishing your errand? And ugh, going back in Ghost Mountain to deliver your stone. Hedge-Witch and Lasair are still in there somewhere, looking to kill you, and I don't know what they want to do to me, and we're worried about dr'gon boogers?"

Cl'rnce shrugged. "I think he's somehow hiding the locket. I'll keep an eye on him. My theory is he's a dwarfed River Dr'gon. I've heard of them. Very special. Even have more magick than the ordinary dr'gon. Very shy. Which would account for why he doesn't talk."

"Wait! Magick and dr'gons! You said dr'gons don't have magick! You lied," Moire Ain tried to say it with humor, like a joke, but she felt hurt that Cl'rnce, whom she thought had become a friend, had lied.

Cl'rnce shrugged. "I don't know that much, sort of, so I didn't want to . . . admit I didn't."

Moire Ain decided not to talk about the lie anymore. She went on, "So you said this little guy might be the second dr'gon Hedge-Witch and Lasair need for taking over the Primacy?"

Cl'rnce pursed his muzzle, rubbed behind his left horn, dug something that glowed out of his right ear. Then finally said, "Maybe."

"I'm going with yes," Moire Ain said. "Don't you see?

This is good news. It means we have all we need to defeat Hedge-Witch and Lasair." She took a deep breath. "The only problem is we don't know how."

"We could check your book," Cl'rnce said, swapping stares with the little dr'gon.

Moire Ain pulled her book out of her pouch. "I don't remember any pictures or any other clues in here about special small dr'gons and the Primus." She flipped through the pages, most of which were still too damaged. "No. Hedge-Witch said stuff about worrying I'd never be any better at magick than this book could teach. That was definitely an insult." Moire Ain wrinkled her nose. "You know, there's one thing I know for sure about Hedge-Witch: she's a liar. Since I now suspect she arranged for me to find this book, she had a reason. She must have wanted me to learn from it. So I'd be a powerful wizard she could use." Moire Ain blushed at sounding like she was sort of bragging. "Or something." She turned pages and looked harder, thinking about how to make sure Hedge-Witch did not use her to kill a king, like Cl'rnce.

"Got anything?" Cl'rnce didn't seem to notice her search.

"Well, there's a spell for remembering. That might help you recall what you were supposed to learn in class."

Cl'rnce didn't break his staring contest with the little

dr'gon. "Sure, if I had practiced all the elements."

"Oh, right." Moire Ain flipped a few more pages. "This. I'll try this."

Cl'rnce said, "What?"

But Moire Ain was already humming as she squinted at a mostly readable page. For the first time, the whole spell's words were in Common Language. "Small printing, but I can do this." She put the book down and said very slowly, "Show us the little dr'gon's kind."

She was on her third repeat when the rumble of thunder rolled in from the west. Moire Ain scanned the horizon, thinking they'd need to run and hide from a whopper of a storm. A huge bank of clouds tumbled across the sky, but they weren't rain clouds. Out of the roiling dark emerged a herd of dr'gons, most looking a lot like Cl'rnce, flying straight at them.

"Oh, *NO!*" Cl'rnce yelled. "We're in trouble now!"

CHAPTER 23

The little dr'gon, his scales a shining sable instead of jade, aimed his muzzle at the flying thunder above them.

First looking ahead through the trees, then back toward home, then up at the mountain, Cl'rnce tried to decide which was more appalling. He had to choose from three bad ideas. Was the worst choice facing a herd of dr'gons, possibly killers, or just Lasair in Ghost Mountain, or Hazel when he failed at everything? He decided all of them were the worst.

Before Cl'rnce could shake the little dr'gon off and run for the woods, Hazel soared out of the herd's cloud, zooming so close Cl'rnce choked on her gardenia scent as she exhaled for her landing.

At the same time Hazel hit the ground, she reached out and slapped her brother behind the left horn. "Idjit!" she screamed. "How in the Three Rivers did you mess this up? You called the entire Dr'gon Nations to you for what? You can't possibly claim the succession to the Primacy if you can't do a simple thing like delivering the Whisper Stone to the Council chamber without involving the entire River Dr'gon Nation. And for your information, Mother is in the back with Thomas. You know Thomas, *THE PRIMUS!* You are in so much trouble." She smiled.

Hazel was the only person Cl'rnce knew who could smile and look even angrier. He edged away.

"Primus Thomas isn't dead?" Cl'rnce lifted himself on tiptoes and stared. He turned to Hazel. "You said he was superannuated! You lied!"

Hazel blew hot air out of her cheeks. "I should have known you didn't know. Superannuated means he retired." She snapped her chin over at Great and Mighty. Who is this?" She jerked her head at the little dr'gon. "And tell me you know who *this* is."

"River Rats. I thought you'd know who he is," Cl'rnce mumbled. Often, if he could get Hazel to be the know-it-all and lecture him, she'd forget to be angry, angry, angry. "He just appeared, and . . . ." Cl'rnce shrugged and opened his eyes wide in his most appealing little-brother look.

Hazel held up a paw, her talons sharp and sparking as she flexed them. Gaelyn, Hazel's Wizard Partner, popped into the space beside Hazel. Gaelyn ran her slender brown fingers through her curly hair to plump it up. If there was anyone half as vain as Hazel, it was Gaelyn.

Nudging Gaelyn, Hazel asked, "Gaelyn, is that what

I think it is?" Hazel's tone was somewhere between un-believing and satisfied.

Gaelyn smiled. "I told you he'd do it." Gaelyn had always been much nicer to Cl'rnce than his own sister.

Hazel frowned at Cl'rnce and squinted her eyes as if he had done something so bad she couldn't speak of it. She sighed. "Fine. But that doesn't explain why we've been summoned."

Gaelyn patted Hazel's arm and pointed to Great and Mighty. "I think she explains it. We have before us the Three. You were right. Cl'rnce, with all his flaws, is meant to be the next Primus. His wizard must be very powerful to bring the entirety of the Dr'gon Nations here. And the little dr'gon, well, you know the legends."

"No. Actually we don't," Great and Mighty squeaked out. She looked like she was trying to appear brave, af-ter summoning the dr'gons. Although casting a spell to find out what kind of dr'gon the little guy was and in-stead bringing in a nation of dr'gons. . . well, that felt bumblespelly to Cl'rnce. It didn't feel so much like Great and Mighty had become super powerful.

Hazel rolled her eyes. "He didn't tell you?" She closed her eyes as if she was in pain. "Let me guess. Another of those classes Cl'rnce skipped. Honestly. He doesn't deserve to be the Primus." She opened her eyes and looked Great and Mighty up and down again. "I should have been much more scared at how clueless he was when he agreed to deliver the Whisper Stone with only a little of his usual sniveling. I should have known he didn't understand the ramifications of the Primus superannuating, but there you are."

"Hrumph." Cl'rnce decided against commenting when Hazel bared her fangs in warning. He could accept that he was the next Primus. But if he thought about it, other than getting the Whisper Stone into the mountain, what was the big deal?

Hazel turned to Cl'rnce, saying each word like she was talking to a baby who had only just learned to speak. "The River Dr'gon Primus normally rules forever or as long as he lives, if he chooses against being eternal, but ours has elected the third option, to retire." She lifted her eye ridge and jerked her head to the right.

Cl'rnce followed her motion. At the back of the pack of dr'gons, he saw his mother and the Primus, hand in hand. "Gross!" Cl'rnce said at the sight of his mother staring all lovey-dovey into the eyes of a dr'gon who was older than most mountains.

Hazel slapped Cl'rnce on the back of the head again. "Listen up, slacker. If you'd gone to your classes, you'd know this, but I can tell from your clueless face that you don't. When the Primus retires instead of dying, the traditional heir does not automatically inherit. Anyone can challenge the heir. If there is a challenge, a powerful wizard and another powerful dr'gon fight the heir for the crown."

"Fight?" Cl'rnce gulped. He was opposed to fighting. At least fighting anyone bigger than he was, or stronger, or . . . . If he could sneak up on someone and throw them in a pond, or bind them in slippery bubbles until they were too exhausted to move, or . . . . This was not good news. Was it true Hazel wanted the Primacy? Did he have to fight her?

"By the Three Rivers and all the River Rats, don't you pay attention to anything but yourself?" Hazel stared at Cl'rnce, then snorted. "Someone issued a challenge seven days ago. You two should be handling this alone, but since your wizard brought us here, we will stay and advise," Hazel said, sitting down.

Cl'rnce was relieved that Hazel wasn't who he'd fight, but him fight? Shouldn't a potential Primus delegate that kind of work? "Advice? That's all you're offering? You're just going to hang around and nag? How about gearing up and helping me fight? Do you know who I have to fight?"

Hazel pursed her lips and shrugged. "I do not know precisely. No."

Gaelyn looked at the ground, her lips mashed together.

All of a sudden it fit together: why Nasty Sir George or anyone would want him dead. "Well, I know." Cl'rnce hissed. "It's Lasair!"

"Ah." Hazel's wide eyes flicked to her Wizard Partner, who shrugged. "That's a rough one. What have you done to prepare?"

"Prepare?" Cl'rnce felt himself losing control. "So far I've fought off a knight who was sent to kill me. Rescued Great and Mighty—"

"Hold on! You didn't rescue me," Great and Mighty said. "I got away all on my own."

"Technicalities. I'm trying to get us some help here." Cl'rnce glared at her, willing her to stop talking. Great and Mighty sucked her lips together and nodded.

"Look, Cl'rnce, this is a little complex. Since your wizard has the power to bring the Nations, she is not a usual Wizard Partner. Having a wizard with a dr'gon's power is like having another dr'gon for a Wizard Partner, but one from a different clan." Hazel put a claw to her nose as if she was remembering something. "Long in the past there *was* a wizard Primus, so it's awfully rare but not impossible. And then there is the little one. The Old Language is a little fuzzy sometimes, but I think the legend means any one of you three could defeat Lasair and become Primus. It's that simple. We are not allowed to do more than back you up. If Lasair brings an army at you both, we will fight. But as long as it's you against him, you've got to handle this on your own."

"And his witch," Cl'rnce added. "Her old guardian." He jerked an elbow at Great and Mighty. "That's two against us. So, are you going to help?" The idea that Great and Mighty could end up the one with all the responsibility of being Primus wasn't so bad. He could go back to napping. But no matter what, even he couldn't allow the evil Killer Dr'gon Lasair or Hedge-Witch to become the Primus.

"Interesting but irrelevant. I don't see an army opposing either of you, so we'll settle down here and wait while you handle things. You still have the Whisper Stone, right?" Hazel leaned back and stared upward. "Ghost Mountain. Long time since we've been here, huh, Gaelyn? I'll bet you three spells he lost the Stone."

"I did not lose it. I . . ." He patted his neck and remembered the locket was gone, up the little dr'gon or somewhere. Turning his back on Hazel, he tried to think of a way to come up with a substitute. Desperate, he wished Great and Mighty could hear him and pick up a stone and pass it to him, so he could fool Hazel long enough to find the lost Whisper Stone.

He almost jumped out of his skin when Great and Mighty sidled up close and slipped a pebble into his paw.

Cl'rnce turned back and held it up to show Hazel. He kept his digits covering most of it in hopes she wouldn't notice the difference.

"What has it told you?" Hazel said, studying her claws.

"Nothing. It hasn't said a thing. It showed me Great and Mighty, Lasair, and Sir George. And it spit purple and gold flame out, but it hasn't said word one. Just like him." Cl'rnce jerked his thumb at the little dr'gon. It wasn't a real lie. All those things had happened, if not from this particular rock.

Hazel stopped polishing her claws against her scales. Gaelyn stopped fluffing her hair. Every dr'gon around them became completely quiet and solidly still. "He doesn't talk?" Hazel asked finally, staring at the little dr'gon, whose scales turned back from black to the signature green of a River Dr'gon.

"Not a peep. I don't even know his name. But he is really good at pantomiming. And he sat on the Whisper Stone and gold and purple flame shot out of his rear." Cl'rnce started to laugh at his joke, but he stopped when he realized every eye was no longer on him but fixed on the little dr'gon. And no one was laughing.

Hazel took a deep breath. "River Gods!"

"That's it? River Gods?" Cl'rnce asked.

"Well, things are a little more complicated now. I thought because Thomas instructed me to supervise you and have you fetch the Whisper Stone to the Council Chambers that you were the next Primus, that he had persuaded the rest of the Council that you must be Primus. Not that you deserve it, but when Thomas says to do something from the Primus throne . . . ."

"When you teamed up with a great wizard, I thought perhaps you'd found a more qualified Primus. When you found the little dr'gon, I thought you'd found one of the legendary fae dr'gons who left the River clan millennia ago. I thought you had found the power to be a truly great Primus. But a dwarfed River Dr'gon who does not speak . . . but communicates with the Whisper Stone . . . that's the Phoenix Legend. Your friend—" She nodded at the little dr'gon, who had settled on Cl'rnce's shoulder, his small paws tucked under him like a sleepy cat "—will forge a once in an eon powerful Primus, If you three can defeat Lasair."

Cl'rnce would have laughed that a tiny dr'gon could be powerful, but two things occurred to him. First, the little guy had communicated with the Whisper Stone, and in fact the spot where he'd spit the purple and gold flame still glowed on the mountain side. And second, and even better, if the little guy was the new Primus, then Cl'rnce definitely wasn't. With that burden on the little dr'gon, Cl'rnce would never have to work a day in his life. Once they helped the little guy into the Primacy, Cl'rnce would live life as a retired hero. He and Great and Mighty could go have adventures and lots of naps. *YES!*

"Does he have a name?" Cl'rnce asked.

"Ask him," Hazel snorted.

Cl'rnce would have sassed her back, but it wasn't worth it. "What's your name, little guy?" he asked. Since the little dr'gon hadn't said a word, he didn't expect any kind of response. Which would be good for telling Hazel she'd come to a stupid conclusion, but the little dr'gon began to vibrate on his shoulder. A kind of happy thrumming sent warmth into Cl'rnce.

It was like the little dr'gon had been waiting to be asked. He butted Cl'rnce's chin, and Cl'rnce felt a tingle of happiness, like he'd done something really good. He didn't hear the little dr'gon speak, but a warm purple aura drifted in front of him.

Cl'rnce was about to dismiss the glow as leftover little dr'gon gas from sitting on the Whisper Stone, when he heard Great and Mighty say, "Amythyst. His name is Amythyst."

Cl'rnce stood absolutely still for a moment. It was surely a mistake. There was no way Great and Mighty heard the little guy correctly. Amethyst was a name that would be given only once, and never again. It was the name of the legendary dr'gon who would create the Primus that would rule for a thousand dr'gon lifetimes with complete justice.

The dr'gons sitting in a circle around them bowed their heads for a second, then looked up.

If she'd gotten the name right, why hadn't Cl'rnce heard it? After all, he was a dr'gon, not her. He didn't know if he was happy or sad thinking that he might be excused from being Primus. But he did know this was confusing. "You heard him?" Cl'rnce asked Great and Mighty. She nodded.

"The wizard heard, and you saw," Hazel said in a hushed voice. "You don't deserve it, slacker, but you have your Wizard Partner. And the two of you are thralls to the new Primus."

The awe in his sister's voice made Cl'rnce feel very important. Although he was not sure about the 'thrall' part. It sounded like work. Not what he'd hoped.

"Now get back in that mountain and face Lasair and his witch!" Hazel snapped.

"So much for respect and the good vibes," Cl'rnce muttered.

Amythyst purred and dug his small claws into Cl'rnce's shoulder, as if preparing to leap hard into flight.

Before Cl'rnce could try to tell Great and Mighty what he suspected, she nodded to Cl'rnce. "We'll do this. We have to. We can't let Lasair . . . . I say we head for the glowing hole Amythyst made. Charge!" She slammed her crystal rod into the ground, then stiffened when a flash of light sizzled up her body, leaving her auburn curls standing in fried straw sticks.

"How about let's fly?" Cl'rnce said, snagging the back of Great and Mighty's robe and lifting his partner as he beat his wings. It felt good to let his family and everybody see him fly. There was no getting away from it. He was great. He had a great Wizard Partner and Amythyst. He could feel the buzz of Great through every muscle in his body. He didn't feel a bit afraid. He knew down to his tiniest scale they could win. This was going to be a piece of cake. Chocolate, maybe.

CHAPTER 24

Cl'rnce flew straight at the glowing patch of Amythyst's purple and gold spit on the mountain. He knew they were headed in the right direction, because he felt the excited vibes from the little dr'gon. The little guy definitely knew things, and had some kind of power.

The positive feelings vanished when they were only yards from the mountain. The stench of dead and nasty filled Cl'rnce's nostrils. Among the gagging smells was the stink of Nasty Sir George. The rotten knight was back.

Cl'rnce slowed and hovered, looking around. He waited, expecting to have to dodge, fly sideways, and loop the loop to avoid the knight who must have found his skeleton horse and come back to attack them. It seemed to take forever, but finally Cl'rnce spotted the no-longer-rusty knight on a ledge below.

Nasty Sir George held up his sword and yelled something, but it was gobbledygook from so far away. Cl'rnce dipped to his right to veer away before the knight attacked. But a hard tug pulled him back in line to fly down and close to the knight. Amythyst had a mouthful of Cl'rnce's wing, pulling him to the knight. "That's not a good idea," Cl'rnce said.

"Sir George is shouting something about his sword," Great and Mighty called out. Cl'rnce looked down to see her pointing at the knight, as she swung from Cl'rnce's talons.

"Yeah. He's yelling that he wants to use it to kill me," Cl'rnce grumbled.

"No. He's saying to take it."

"Huh?" When Cl'rnce looked harder, he saw that the knight held the sword out by the tip, as if offering it to them. The sight was too odd not to investigate. Cl'rnce swerved and flapped to the knight, where he teetered on a narrow ledge fifty feet below the still-glowing purple and gold mountain patch.

"My sword," Nasty Sir George called as they neared. "I offer my sword."

"Do you mean you'll fight alongside us?" Great and Mighty asked.

The un-rusty knight shook his head. "I gift you my sword. Take it. The little one will know what to do with it." He nodded his head at Great and Mighty.

Before Cl'rnce could object, Great and Mighty grabbed the sword by its hilt and swung it in the hand that did not hold her rod. A trail of gold light followed the pattern she made as the sword arced through the air.

"It's magick?" she asked. "Why would you give us a magick sword? And why didn't you use the magick to kill us in the first place?" Great and Mighty sounded like she thought it might be a trick. Cl'rnce certainly agreed.

Nasty Sir George looked down the mountain as if he'd just figured out he had a long climb down. "It's not magick in my hands. It's not my sword. When you transformed my armor, you made my sword different. All I ever wanted in life was enough money to buy nice armor. You gave that to me. I'm headed off to earn enough for a horse that likes me."

Great and Mighty laughed. "You want a horse? I'll give you a horse!"

Cl'rnce groaned. "No."

But it was too late; Great and Mighty was already on the third repeat of her spell to make a horse for the knight. "A forever horse for Sir George."

Cl'rnce crossed his digits that the bumblespell in this magick wouldn't backfire. From below them, he heard a whinny. Cl'rnce, Amythyst, Great and Mighty, and Nasty Sir George all looked down. The skeleton horse stood once again at the foot of the mountain.

"Oh, great," Sir George said, sounding more like he was sorry he'd given away his sword than happy he had a horse. "That one doesn't like me at all."

"But I said a forever horse; that has to mean it'll stay with you forever. It has to be your friend," Great and

Mighty tried to explain.

"Nice try, Great and Mighty," Cl'rnce said. "My sister is forever, and she definitely doesn't like me. And she's not a skeleton horse who'll never die." Cl'rnce flapped away from the knight before Nasty Sir George decided he'd been too nice and wanted his sword back.

They circled to Amythyst's purple splot. When they hovered over it, Cl'rnce heard the knight yell. "Use the sword. It's a key. Opens the door."

The side of the mountain glowed, but there was no cave opening, no door. No way in. Cl'rnce felt Amythyst lean against his neck. A picture formed in Cl'rnce's head of the sword flying at the mountain's purple and gold and disappearing inside.

"Throw the sword at the spot," Cl'rnce said to Great and Mighty.

"I heard Amythyst!" Great and Mighty said. "Here goes." She swung back and forth in Cl'rnce's grip, and when she was closest to the mountain, she tossed the sword. Just like the picture Amythyst had shown him, the sword pierced the mountain, passing through like the mountain's rocks and dirt were nothing but soft cheese. Cl'rnce's empty tummy growled at the thought of any kind of food.

From below, a flurry of feathers flashed up and in front of Cl'rnce. Raspberries cawed as the sword disappeared into the mountain. A blast of gold light flared out behind it, seizing Cl'rnce, Amythyst, the raven, and Great and Mighty. They were sucked into the mountain faster than Cl'rnce could finish saying, "River Rats!"

Cl'rnce pulled Great and Mighty closer to his chest as they hurtled down a tunnel that curved this way and that, then turned upward. Faster and faster, they sped along. "I hope we don't end up just passing through the mountain again," Cl'rnce said, shivering at the memory of his failed attempt to rescue Great and Mighty.

"Look!" Great and Mighty yelled.

Ahead of them, the sword's golden glow exploded, lighting a huge cavern. No sooner had they entered the crystal-lined chamber, than Cl'rnce's wings tired out. They felt like lead weights as he dropped like a ton of wet river stones. As he hit, posterior first, Cl'rnce managed to hold Great and Mighty up while Amythyst clung to his shoulder. Other than Cl'rnce's bruised dignity, nothing was hurt. "Everybody off." Cl'rnce let go of Great and Mighty.

Cl'rnce turned his head to Amythyst, but the little dr'gon ignored him. He squinted at the far side of the cavern. Cl'rnce followed the little guy's gaze. Across from them, dark shadows swirled, growing and shrinking, as they moved, first forming a billowy man, then solidifying into the enormous dr'gon.

"Welcome." Lasair's voice dripped with hate. He slid out of the shadows without so much as a slither of noise. "I see we are all gathered." His eyes were slits, out of which red light leaked at the corners. "You who are about to die, I salute you!"

Without another wasted second, the huge dr'gon charged at Cl'rnce, throwing blasts of fire at Cl'rnce's head. Cl'rnce dodged behind a rock, trying to get his flame pit to fire up. He hadn't had enough practice to make fire instantaneously.

Before Cl'rnce had a mouthful of flame, two more jets of fire shot by the sides of his hiding place. When a third blast shot over the top of the rock, Cl'rnce was ready and jumped up to fire back. Lasair was far closer than Cl'rnce thought, but still Cl'rnce missed the other dr'gon when his flame deflected to the left. Something was wrong. Cl'rnce ducked down and tried to think. Lasair had some kind of shield. Cl'rnce needed one, and a way to pierce Lasair's. Cl'rnce looked around for Great and Mighty. She'd made a shield before.

The little wizard squatted behind a rock two paces from Cl'rnce, but her focus was not on Lasair. Instead, she stared as if hypnotized by the boiling shadows to the right of Lasair.

"A little help here," Cl'rnce called. "I need a shield."

"Sure." Without taking her eyes off the shadows, Great and Mighty tapped her crystal rod three times on the rock floor and said, "Shield the dr'gons." She snapped it out all three times before Cl'rnce could stop her.

Cl'rnce watched a golden haze form in front of him. When he stretched to look around his rock, a matching fog hung in front of Lasair. Cl'rnce wanted to whine about the unfairness, but faster than he could waste time sniping, he had an idea. Cl'rnce's years of practical jokes took over. He had a plan.

Cl'rnce popped up and screamed, "You will never be the Primus, you loser. I'll make your skin into a rug for my palace." Then he dropped down, making a loud gulping noise like he was afraid and was shouting to try and fool Lasair. He wanted the dr'gon confused and overreacting.

He had to give the Killer a moment to get riled and dig up a really big flame. After counting to two, Cl'rnce popped up again, this time climbing to the top of his rock like he was going to leap at Lasair. "Coward!"

The red-eyed dr'gon screamed in fury as he let loose a huge burst of fire. When Lasair's first flame bounced off his shield and smacked back into him, the Killer was knocked onto his rear. He screamed in frantic fury. Lasair was one part ambitious killer and nine parts too angry to think. Cl'rnce couldn't hold in his laughter.

Lasair blasted another flame, like he hadn't figured out how he'd knocked himself over. This time his rabid fury had given the fire the black edges of death. When it splashed back over the insanely screaming Lasair, he stopped moving. Shadows wrapped his still body like a funeral cloak.

"*YES!*" Cl'rnce yelled. "I did it all on my own. I saved the day. I'm a hero." An image of Amythyst clutching the Whisper Stone came to him. Cl'rnce said, "Come on, Amythyst, we'll take the Whisper Stone to the Council Chamber and do all the official stuff to make you the next Primus." He looked for the little dr'gon but didn't see him.

What he saw instead was Great and Mighty standing stiff, as if frozen, her face nothing but terror, her skin sliding around like it was trying to leave her skull. Hedge-Witch reached for Great and Mighty's rod.

As Hedge-Witch's fingers neared the crystal staff, Amythyst and Raspberries flew at the crone. She almost had the rod when Amythyst wedged himself between her and the magick staff. With her other hand, the witch reached around him and jerked the rod and dr'gon to her until it dug deeply into Amythyst's back. Raspberries swooped and pecked at Hedge-Witch, but she grabbed the little dr'gon with her free hand and pushed him until her rod sank deeper into him.

He went limp, and she dropped his little body on the cavern floor. "Two before one," she said. She lifted her wand and turned in Cl'rnce's direction.

Before she could do anything more, Cl'rnce was on her. He'd never hated anyone so much as he hated this witch. He knew he couldn't blast her with fire, because the shield would make him fry himself, but he still had his tail. He swung it at her, along with his shield, knocking the witch across the cavern and away from Great and Mighty and Amythyst.

From where she landed on her back, he heard the witch cursing. He might have stopped Lasair, but Hedge-Witch was still a problem. He needed Great and Mighty to wake from whatever trance she was in. She had to save Amythyst, who was leaking royal purple River Dr'gon blood all over the cavern floor. And the little wizard had to save herself.

All his ideas about being a hero, handing over the Primacy to Amythyst, and being able to slack off for the rest of his life were nothing. Cl'rnce didn't care about power or helping power, he just wanted Great and Mighty and Amythyst to live. He wanted Lasair and Hedge-Witch to be permanently imprisoned, stored in a deep river dungeon forever, even if he had to stand guard on them for the rest of his life. But how?

CHAPTER 25

Moire Ain couldn't move. Giant ghost snails sucked at every inch of her body, inside and out. Their gloppy bodies covered her and glued themselves so closely she couldn't even twitch. Their slime sank into her nose and mouth. Her fear was even thicker. She could barely think. Twice, several years ago, Hedge-Witch had bound her with ghost snails. Each time, Moire Ain had been close to suffocation before the old hag relented and freed her.

I can't let her do this to me, Moire Ain thought. *The whole reason for learning magick was to make me so powerful I could stop her. To keep her from hurting me and other people. To keep her from using me to kill the king. I cannot let her do this to me.* The ghost snails sucked the oxygen Moire Ain needed to breathe, and their mucous sealed her arms to her body. They sapped her strength. She felt like a hollow gourd emptying itself of air, crumbling. If she didn't do something fast, she wouldn't have the strength to stand up.

Think, Moire Ain, think, she told herself. *Hedge-Witch can't take your thoughts. Think of a spell. You don't have to talk and move. You can make a spell and make it work, silently. Be Great and be Mighty. Think!* She shut her eyes and pretended the snails were blankets rolling her in warmth. She drank in their almost non-existent heat.

Moire Ain still couldn't move, but her thoughts came clearer when she pictured the ghost snails as comforting warmth rather than steamy slugs creeping through her body and into her brain. *I need a spell to get free. To get rid of the snails. What do you do with snails besides remove them from vegetables?* A vision of Cl'rnce delicately picking snails off squash blossoms popped into her head. He was always hungry, so he'd probably eat the blossoms and the snails. She had it! Moire Ain started to giggle.

Eat the snails! Eat the snails! Eat the snails! She pictured herself swallowing the snails whole. She gagged, and threw up. A stream of gray lumpy ectoplasm spewed across the cavern, slapping into Hedge-Witch where she crouched on hands and knees. The force of the vomit smashed the witch back on her seat.

"I'm free!" Moire Ain yelled. A second later she gagged, and another round of snails hurled up her throat and gushed out. She aimed them at the witch again. This time Moire Ain knocked the crystal stave out of the old crone's grip.

Moire Ain leapt and grabbed for the rod at the same time Hedge-Witch muttered, "To me!" The crystal staff began to slide back to the old witch.

Moire Ain knew that if Hedge-Witch valued a thing, then it had power. It was time to take power away from her. Moire Ain bellowed, "*TO ME!*" She vomited snails again, aiming at the old crone's eyes. At the same time that the staff flew to Moire Ain, her puke took a turn and headed back at her. "Uh-oh. Bumblespelled again!"

The wand was in her hand and the vomit only inches away, when Cl'rnce stepped between Moire Ain and the oncoming snail chunks. "You're going to owe me big," he said.

Moire Ain winced, thinking of his green scales coated in vomit. But the snail chunks never hit him. Instead Cl'rnce did a fast turn and the snails bounced off something invisible around him. The snails splattered back onto the old crone.

"Cool!" Moire Ain said.

"Nevermore," Raspberries cawed from a ledge at the top of the cavern.

Cl'rnce nodded. "That shield you made for me came in handy." But he didn't smile. He walked over to a small pile of purple on the floor. Bending down, he tried to pick it up, but the glowing shield encompassing him made his movements clumsy. He sighed and poked the little thing gently.

Moire Ain followed him over. "Amythyst! What happened?"

For a moment, Cl'rnce just pointed at Hedge-Witch as the old hag slipped on the floor, trying to stand again. "She killed him." His arm trembled, and smoke seeped out of his mouth, filling the space around his head.

Moire Ain was afraid if she didn't dissolve his shield, Cl'rnce would fill it with smoke and suffocate, or worse, he'd get so angry he'd spit flame and burn himself. Without thinking that there was no way she could penetrate the shield, she grabbed his arm. They both stared at how her fingers flowed easily through his shield.

Her heart beating a tattoo of bravery and belief, Moire Ain said, "I can do it. First I'll get rid of your shield, and then we'll make Hedge-Witch bring Amythyst back to life. By the rules of her black magick, I think she can do that. What evil she did she can undo. Right?"

Cl'rnce gave her a doubtful look. He held up a single digit. "Wait." He walked over to the witch, who was almost on her feet. "Stay down!" he yelled. And he smacked her with his tail, sending her skidding across the room.

"We have to work quickly," Moire Ain said, trying to make her brain come up with everything she needed. First, she had to take away Cl'rnce's shield. How? She couldn't make herself concentrate and think of anything but how much she hated Hedge-Witch. For so many years Moire Ain, had tried to undo the cruelty the witch had wrought. Despite Moire Ain's determination to prevent it, the old hag had killed the next Primus, the next Dr'gon King, little Amythyst. Just as the old crone had wanted, she'd used Moire Ain to do it. If Moire Ain and Cl'rnce had not brought the little dr'gon to the cave, Hedge-Witch would never have gotten to him.

Moire Ain examined the crystal rod. The witch wanted it badly, so that meant the magick in it was what Moire Ain needed. "Hold still," she called to Cl'rnce. He turned around. Moire Ain sang, "Break," as she smacked at him with the rod. The stick bounced back, knocking into and cracking a stalactite above Moire Ain. She barely kept her grip on the staff. Trying again, slowly this time, she pushed the rod at Cl'rnce and said, "Break the shield. Break the shield. Break the shield."

There was a cracking noise, and Cl'rnce yelped. Then he sang, "YAY!"

But his voice was drowned out by a roar rolling down the tunnels leading into the cavern. Shadows flew into the chamber, pooling where Lasair twitched as if he had called something evil. The shadows disappeared into the Killer Dr'gon, and he leapt to his feet, snarling.

Before Moire Ain could scream, Cl'rnce charged at Lasair. Cl'rnce jumped into the air to meet the killer, who soared to the chamber ceiling. In midair the two dr'gons attacked each other with flashing teeth and razor claws.

Moire Ain could hardly follow them as they tumbled and slashed in the middle of the huge cavern.

She tried to think of a way to help Cl'rnce. But as she raised the magick rod to cast a heavy-as-stone curse on Lasair, Hedge-Witch tackled her and grabbed at the rod. This was it. Moire Ain had to fight face-to-face the being that she most feared. If she didn't, Hedge-Witch would kill them all. The witch may have seemed to be subservient to Lasair, but she'd pretended the same thing with Sir George the first time Moire Ain saw them together. The witch was a liar. Moire Ain was certain the treacherous crone had all the power she needed with or without Lasair. Hedge-Witch would stop at nothing to accomplish her evil plans—to kill Cl'rnce, to take the Primacy by force.

Moire Ain clung to the stick. The staff thrummed with power. Moire Ain didn't just want to keep that much magick away from Hedge-Witch, she felt a growing need to have it for herself. She'd felt the pure white-magick energy when she'd used the staff before. With this kind of sorcery, she could help Cl'rnce. And maybe, with this surging power, revive Amythyst.

Hedge-Witch began to chant. Moire Ain's heart sped up with the old fear she'd lived with over the years. Hedge-Witch began to smile. For all Moire Ain's life, the old hag had smiled each time Moire Ain showed fear. When the witch was this pleased, next came something truly awful. Moire Ain couldn't think of a spell, so she did the only thing that popped into her mind.

She kicked Hedge-Witch as hard as she could. The old crone folded to the stone floor screaming, "My leg, you little brat. You broke my leg."

Moire Ain was sure this time the witch wasn't lying. Hedge-Witch's leg stuck out at an unnatural angle. For half a second, Moire Ain felt badly, but then Lasair roared. She whipped around to see Cl'rnce on his stomach in a corner, his chin flat on the rocky floor. The Killer leapt at him.

"No!" Moire Ain screamed. Thinking only the word *reduce*, she generated a ball in one hand. With all her strength, Moire Ain threw the silky white orb at Lasair. It splat against the Killer Dr'gon, melting down his scales. Instantly, Lasair shrank to the size of a spider.

Moire Ain wanted to dance her happiness. Her spell had worked. "Was that great or what?" she shouted. "Watch this. Tiny, tiny, bug tiny."

Cl'rnce rose to his knees at the same time Moire Ain tossed another ball. *Splat.* The second sphere missed, flying over Lasair and into Cl'rnce's face.

"Uh-oh," Moire Ain said.

Cl'rnce shrank to the size of the small Killer Dr'gon. Once again, the dr'gons stood face to face. Cl'rnce's tiny voice squeaked.

"What did he say?" Moire Ain leaned down but

jerked back up when Lasair stabbed her nose with a tiny flame.

"Ribbit, ribbit, ribbit, CROAK!" A frog wearing the top half of a suit of armor clunk-hopped into the cavern.

"What?" Moire Ain stared.

"Nevermore! Sir George!" Raspberries cawed.

"It can't be! Can it?" Moire Ain watched the frog's lopsided hop. It leapt up close to her and stared at her. The frog's helmet had the sinking sun crest Moire Ain remembered from Sir George's new armor. "Are you Sir George?"

The frog nodded, turned, and hopped toward the two tiny, battling dr'gons.

"What happened to him?" Moire Ain asked.

"You are a stupid girl," Hedge-Witch snapped. "He's been mermaid-bit. The poison from that pond has finally taken hold. Any fool knows that. First they bite, then you turn into a frog, then they eat you! Usually they hold their food captive, waiting in a circle and humming as the poison takes hold. Somehow he got away from the pond before he turned into a frog and they could eat him."

"Nevermore!" Raspberries cawed and flew over the witch, bombing her with his freshest raven poop. "Spider web," he added and flew to a ledge over the two tiny dr'gons.

"Huh?" Moire Ain watched Lasair and Cl'rnce. She

269

looked up at Raspberries. "You want a spiderweb for what?" The two battling dr'gons were bug-small now. Cl'rnce climbed a stone wall and, flying low, veered into the shadows across the cavern. He dodged and hid. He kept moving, but each time he slowed, the chasing Lasair threw a flame that missed Cl'rnce by fewer and fewer inches.

Moire Ain knew Cl'rnce must be tiring. He wasn't used to life without a nap and lots of good food; Moire Ain was sure of that. On his empty stomach and after days with little sleep, how long could he dodge Lasair? But why didn't Cl'rnce turn and fight? Was this about the old Dr'gon Curse that said if a dr'gon killed, it turned into a killer?

"They're so tiny," Moire Ain said to Sir George. Now the flying dr'gons looked no bigger than a fireflies. "What can I do to stop Lasair?" Sir George sat on the floor watching the pair. His tongue zipped in and out like he was trying to catch a fly. "Oh!" She knew what to do.

She cast the spell. At the same time, Hedge-Witch screamed her own chant. Moire Ain ignored Hedge-Witch. Moire Ain held the crystal staff and focused. She felt like her concentration was a lance, armed and aimed at its target. "Web, web, web," she sang, keeping it simple in hopes that she wouldn't bumblespell it this time. Using the rod to add power and direct the spell, she aimed the web behind Cl'rnce and in front of Lasair.

CHAPTER 26

Cl'rnce scurried behind another stalagmite. Running as fast as he could, he listened to Great and Mighty. After she said, "'Web, web, web,'" her voice seemed to be in his head. He heard her add, "I must be so careful. Use a small motion."

He glanced up at her to watch as she passed her hands in tiny circles, one over the other. When she stopped and cupped her hands together, a white ball formed. He slowed to stare at the orb. But Cl'rnce jumped when Lasair, only an inch away, screamed.

Cl'rnce sped and passed Great and Mighty as she tossed her sphere. Watching it arc, he managed to run fast enough so that it landed behind him and in front of Lasair. Cl'rnce glanced over his shoulder in time to see the ball splat on the floor and unfold into a web. Seeing the web gave Cl'rnce an idea. He turned, leapt into the air, and flew headlong at the web. Lasair kept chasing, his teeth gleaming in a salivating smirk.

Cl'rnce's wings stuttered in the air when he felt

Great and Mighty's panic and confusion. She didn't understand what Cl'rnce had in mind. For a moment, feeling all her emotions rolling off into him confused Cl'rnce. But he heaved his wings harder; there was no time to doubt his plan.

An inch from the web's sticky silk, Cl'rnce swerved sharply to the left. Lasair, flying much faster, slammed into the web. The killer thrashed in the gluey strands, tangling himself from blood-red eyes to tail tip.

"Good one, Cl'rnce," Great and Mighty called. "He'll never get free. Now I'll restore you to your real size."

Cl'rnce was taking a bow when a tiny *ping* rang like a cathedral bell. Lasair broke the first of the web's strands. His neck moved freely. The witch cackled from the floor.

Great and Mighty's voice went terror-high, scraping at Cl'rnce's ears and ringing in his head when her panicked emotions hit him. "I can't remember the spell to restore you, Cl'rnce. How long will the web hold? Will he stay small?" Great and Mighty pressed the palms of her hands hard into the sides of her head. But it did nothing to stop the storm in her head from echoing inside Cl'rnce's.

Using all the focus he'd ever learned in designing and executing exquisite practical jokes, Cl'rnce stared at his enemy. The tiny Lasair snorted flame. With a precision Cl'rnce had never had a chance to practice, the

Killer melted strand after strand with short blasts. His left wing wiggled free. He turned to fire-liberate the other.

"I could send another ball of web. Maybe hold him until we can get out of here. Cl'rnce, move aside," Great and Mighty called.

"RIBBIT! RIBBIT! RIBBIT! RIBBIT!" An armored frog leapt away from Great and Mighty's side.

The web snapped apart as Lasair broke the last string.

In two long hops, the frog was between Cl'rnce and Lasair. The frog leapt again, and in midair, his tongue shot out and slurped back in. Lasair disappeared into the frog.

"Grulp." The frog clattered back to the cavern floor. He swallowed the dr'gon whole and sat very still. "Ribbit. Yack. Ribbit." The armored frog took a small, pathetic hop.

Cl'rnce peered down from the ledge he'd flown to. "He sounds sick."

Great and Mighty ran to the frog. "It's Sir George. He says the dr'gon tasted bad." Great and Mighty bent, peering into the frog's big yellow eyes "You're right. He doesn't feel well."

"Sir George?" Cl'rnce looked harder. Had Great and Mighty bumblespelled the nasty knight into a frog? That was pretty slick.

"Ribbit, rib-bit. Blach."

"Whoa." Great and Mighty jumped back from Sir George. She fanned the air beneath her nose. "Frogs belch? That was so much worse than your burps, Cl'rnce." Great and Mighty scooped up the frog.

Sir George leaned into the little wizard's arm. "Feeling better?" Great and Mighty asked.

"Ribbit. Ribbit. Ribbit. Croakkkk!"

"I see. Sir George says a tummy ache is worth finally getting to slay a dr'gon from this clan," Great and Mighty said.

Cl'rnce squeaked a laugh. "I guess you can't change a nasty knight. He'd rather eat his former employer's boss than miss the chance to slay a dr'gon. Thanks, Sir George. Great and Mighty, thanks for the webs. Can you un-shrink me? I want to go home."

As Cl'rnce spoke, the cave floor rolled like an earthquake was about to tear apart the mountain. Great and Mighty stumbled backward, and Sir George tumbled off her shoulder with a ribbit.

Over the frog's panicked call, the sounds of wind rattling in tree branches, waterfalls pouring into ponds, rocks tumbling down mountain faces, talons scratching on slate, sneezes, and burps filled the cavern. A glistening granite table rose out of the floor. On the tabletop, six stones sparked—red, yellow, purple, green, silver, and orange. The sparks grew to flames. The flames became dr'gons, and then voices. Cl'rnce recognized one at once. "Hazel?" Cl'rnce said.

His sister's voice rang from the transformed jade green stone, "Well done, little brother. You've come a long way from a lazy nap-dr'gon to Stone Deliverer."

"Just Deliverer?" Cl'rnce snorted. "She," he pointed to Hedge-Witch, "killed Amythyst. I have this feeling that makes me the Primus."

"Is that what you want, little brother? To become the Primus at the expense of Amythyst?"

"Hey! I didn't kill him. That witch did. I don't want him dead. I want . . . ." Cl'rnce slowed, not sure what he wanted. For a moment, he'd felt important and like he could do a lot of things that would make him feel good. But the next second, he thought about how much work being Primus would be, being king of the Dr'gon Nations.

"He's not dead, dr'gon," Hedge-Witch said. "But only I can return him to life. Before it is too late."

"She's lying!" Great and Mighty said. She pointed the crystal rod at the witch. The tip of the rod bulged with black.

"But what am I lying about?" Hedge-Witch said. "Is the Primus dead? Can I bring him back? Which is a lie, and which is truth?"

Great and Mighty marched up to the crippled witch. She started to lower the rod at her.

A voice iced into Cl'rnce's head, "Stop her!" It was a voice at once unfamiliar and familiar. It wasn't Great and Mighty's, but there wasn't time to waste wondering where it came from. He knew the voice was right. He couldn't let Great and Mighty kill. He flew to Great and Mighty and leapt at the rod, hoping in his tiny form he had enough force to knock her back.

When he hit the staff, he exploded into normal size. The weight of his usual self against the rod sent it and Cl'rnce crashing toward Hedge-Witch. Cl'rnce snapped at the stick, grabbing it in his teeth, and backpedaled his wings faster and harder than he'd ever even thought to try. The witch reached, her fingers lengthening to grab at Cl'rnce and the wand.

"Use me!" the voice in Cl'rnce's head commanded. He dug into the air harder and moved out of range of the witch. The voice wasn't in his head, but coming from the floor, where Amythyst's body rested. For a second, all he could do was stare. Then the voice roared, "*USE ME!*"

"I know how," Great and Mighty said. She was right beside him. "Give the Stone to me."

"I can't," Cl'rnce said. "I don't have it, remember?"

"Then you have to do as I say," Great and Mighty began.

But Hedge-Witch was chanting. "One then Two, Two then Three. Three then One. End the One."

Before she finished the last, Great and Mighty yelled, "Three again. Three again. Three again. No time." She dropped beside Amythyst's body. As her hand hovered over the little dr'gon, a blast of light hit her and flew on to Cl'rnce.

Everyone in the cave froze. The stone chamber became a hall of statues: dr'gons, wizard, frog, witch. Only one being moved. Raspberries soared to Amythyst's still form, grabbed the Whisper Stone, reformed and glowing in the midst of the blazing light. Raspberries stood with his head cocked to one side as if waiting. "Nevermore?"

Nothing happened.

CHAPTER 27

At the same time that the raven cawed, Cl'rnce felt himself free to move. He trotted over to Amythyst's glowing remains and the raven. Below him, the little dr'gon was no longer a tiny body. In the radiant halo of purple and gold, Cl'rnce thought he saw two glowing figures.

But he didn't have time to examine the lights. Behind him, Cl'rnce heard Great and Mighty. She argued with Hedge-Witch. He turned to watch.

"You!" Great and Mighty said as if she wanted to spit but was trying not to. "You did this. I have lived all my life mending broken bodies you've damaged. This time you went too far. This time you killed the king. You will pay. Whatever the dr'gons' worst punishment is, I will make sure you are given it." Her chest rose up and down in her ragged robe like she was a race horse trying to catch a big breath.

Hedge-Witch laughed. "They will do nothing. It is what makes my plan so perfect. The whole of the Dr'gon

Nations is too fearful of becoming killers themselves. They will never punish me enough to stop me. I murdered their king, and they will do nothing!" She squinted at Great and Mighty. "The dr'gon calls you Great and Mighty? A bit pretentious, Moire Ain, don't you think? Can you do magick enough to defeat me? Are you so very great or mighty? I think not. Your spells are always a little wrong, aren't they?" She scrabbled at the rocky wall behind her, trying and failing to get to her feet. "Give me my rod," she said in the same terrible, threatening tone that Cl'rnce was sure had sent Great and Mighty into hiding in the past.

Great and Mighty stared at Amythyst's glowing remains. She looked around the circle of dr'gons, so still that only the tears in their eyes moved. Cl'rnce could read the defeat in her downturned mouth and begging eyes. Great and Mighty believed the evil Hedge-Witch, that the dr'gons would visit no revenge on the witch that was strong enough.

It was true. His dr'gon race could not. Cl'rnce could think of nothing to help.

But then Great and Mighty straightened her shoulders and turned to Hedge-Witch. "They may not stop you, but *believe me*, I will!" She pointed the crystal staff at the witch and sang out words sharp with a small power that grew in echoing vibrations. He saw Great and Mighty's doubting face tighten with determination and confidence in herself.

He was about to cheer when she sent waves of confidence and power to him. He almost burst with pride to feel that she believed; this time there would be no bumblespelling. "Your life for the Primus," she chanted, her arms steady as a wave of power shot through her fingertips. "His life restored. His goodness unblemished. The Three Again."

Cl'rnce shouted her words along with her, and every dr'gon in the cave joined in. The sound of the words bounced off rock and crystal walls, getting louder and louder. Great and Mighty peered into Cl'rnce's eyes and smiled. She mouthed the words, "I can save the king and punish Hedge-Witch."

Turning to keep her stare on the witch, Great and Mighty backed over to Amythyst. When she smacked into Cl'rnce, she reached a hand back. "Can you give me Amythyst?"

Cl'rnce gently picked up the little dr'gon. He felt the slightest bit of life thump through the fiery purple skin. "You can do it, Great and Mighty. That's one thing Hedge-Witch didn't lie about. He's not dead. Bring him all the way back."

Great and Mighty nodded. But instead of taking the little dr'gon out of Cl'rnce's hands, she whirled around and spoke so fast he almost missed the words. "Live to rule. The king ascends." She tapped the little heart, then threw down the crystal rod and placed both her hands and her forehead against the little dr'gon's chest.

For a moment, Amythyst's eyes fluttered open; warm gold light flashed out. He grinned, his eyes fastened on Great and Mighty, and then turned and looked at Cl'rnce. His wings unfurled, and Cl'rnce got ready to let the new Primus fly. But Amythyst's wings stretched only far enough to touch both Great and Mighty and Cl'rnce at the same time. When he did, a shock ran through Cl'rnce.

Great and Mighty gasped and stood up straight. The next moment, Amythyst burst into pure gold flames. Like a Phoenix, he floated, burning above Cl'rnce's arms and below Great and Mighty's face. With one powerful downbeat, the little dr'gon shot up and exploded into gold-edged amethyst light that swept into the form of a dr'gon as tall as the cavern's high ceiling. He became the biggest dr'gon Cl'rnce had ever seen.

With one more wingbeat, the made-of-light dr'gon split into two. For a moment, the halves hung in the air, all luminescence and warmth, then the parts splintered and showered over Great and Mighty and Cl'rnce.

Cl'rnce was stunned. The Phoenix Dr'gon legend was true. Amythyst had come. The Greatest Primus was about to rule.

Before he could say a word, Great and Mighty whipped around, picking up the crystal rod and screamed, "Stone."

She said it only once, but it was enough to turn Hedge-Witch, who had finally managed to stand on her one good leg, into a rocky column of muddy stone, upright in the cavern shining with crystal walls.

Great and Mighty turned slowly back to Cl'rnce and said, "I messed it up again. I am so sorry. But she will never hurt a dr'gon ever again. I'm sorry you have to be the Primus, Cl'rnce. I really am a bumblespell wizard. I killed Amythyst."

"Well, about time." Hazel stomped over to Cl'rnce, smacking him in back of his horns. "You are the worst, laziest, undeserving candidate for Primus ever, but somehow you bumbled yourself into it, you and the greatest sorcerer of all time." She wrapped her wings around him and whispered in his ear, "I knew you could do it, little brother."

"Huh?" Cl'rnce looked from Hazel to Great and Mighty, to the burnt shadow on the cavern wall that matched the huge dr'gon Amythyst had burst into.

"Now, that's my super intelligent brother. Welcome back." Hazel laughed.

"But what happened? I thought Amythyst was the Primus?" asked Great and Mighty.

Cl'rnce felt like he'd had a bad nightmare and had come awake to a worse reality. If Cl'rnce had this right, nap time was over, forever.

"In a sense, of course Amythyst is Primus. You are

both Primus." Hazel marched over to Great and Mighty and tugged one of the little wizard's sleeves to make it reach to her wrist. "You'll need better robes for your new position. Can you make them?"

Great and Mighty's hand went to her pouch. She pulled out her book. "I don't know. I never tried. What if I make a robe, and it's really a road, or a web, or some kind of . . . poison?"

"Magick exhaustion," Hazel's Wizard Partner, Gaelyn, said. "It'll take a while for it to sink in that she has power and responsibility. Give her time."

Hazel nodded. "In any case, I believe Cl'rnce knows the Old Dr'gon meaning of the Amythyst legend—the Primus within two. Right?"

He nodded.

Hazel smiled at Great and Mighty. "Amythyst is within both of you. You did notice that? Right? Cl'rnce saw the visions, and you, Great and Mighty, heard." Hazel stared hard at Great and Mighty and Cl'rnce.

They nodded.

"You two are really the one Hedge-Witch kept going on about. You two. Cl'rnce is the nominal Primus, but Great and Mighty is his essential sorcerer. You are the ultimate team. Pretty amazing, but according to the Book of Dr'gons, you two will rule over a thousand thousand years of peace. Frankly it's gobsmacking that a practical joker and a bumblespell—"

Gaelyn put a hand on Hazel's wing, and the dr'gon stopped. "You know what Thomas said. Have patience. Your brother had to obtain the Primacy, but he will need you to help rule. It was why Thomas insisted the Council make you the Head and created the provision that the Head could take on Primacy responsibilities."

Cl'rnce liked the helping part. Even if she was his snarky big sister, he knew he'd need Hazel to do the real work. He glanced over at Thomas and their mother, staring into each other's eyes like lovesick dr'gonelles. They wore huge leis around their necks.

Gaelyn laughed and pointed. "Looks like the happy couple are about to leave on a long honeymoon on a distant island with lots of beaches. It's up to you now."

Hazel took a breath, nodded, smiled, and said, "Congratulations. We'll have the dual coronation at home. I've had enough of this place. Let's roll, everybody."

Dr'gon and wizard after dr'gon and wizard disappeared out of the chamber.

"She's pretty bossy seeing as how I'm the Primus," Cl'rnce muttered.

"We're the Primus. And you know you'd rather she helped, a lot!" Great and Mighty said, nodding her head. "Hey, I stopped Hedge-Witch. She didn't kill the king." She smiled as she ran her hand down her arm. A sleeve appeared, long enough to cover her from shoulder to wrist. She kept tapping until she had a new robe, this one a soft green that matched Cl'rnce's scales. "Pretty cool for a bumblespell wizard."

"Pretty good for the wizard half of the Primus." Cl'rnce snagged the back of the new robe's collar, tucked his partner under one arm and said, "Hop on, Sir George, Raspberries. We're going to a party. I love parties."

"Don't forget the crystal staff." Great and Mighty wiggled in his grasp.

"You get it," Cl'rnce said, holding his breath in hopes that the bumblespells were over and Great and Mighty wouldn't turn the staff Hedge-Witch had prized for its power into a frog. Or into raven poop.

Great and Mighty snapped her fingers and said, "To me. To the party!"

They landed in the middle of the chocolate fountain at Cl'rnce's mother's cave.

"Party!" Cl'rnce and Great and Mighty yelled at the same time. Cl'rnce dove deep into the chocolate pond to take a short nap and fill up on the best liquid food in the whole dr'gon, wizard, and knight world.

ACKNOWLEDGMENTS

Once upon a time I drew pictures of my little sister, Patricia Boyd, and wrote a story about a "PB." My grandfather stapled the notebook paper into a book, and I published my first story. (Thank you, Little Sis and Grandpa Jesse.)

Years later as a teaching assistant in Mrs. Whitney's third grade, (yeah, I took the job to stalk my daughter in the fourth grade classroom just down the hall) those sweet and funny third graders awoke a dr'gon and a wizard just as wacky and imaginative.

Forward a few years to me handing openhearted-Joan Broerman my tardy registration fee for my first SCBWI conference. Thanks to Joan I began to learn to put the dr'gon and wizard's story together.

The list of talented writers to thank for selfless support and critique help is long. My second writing group: Joan Broerman, Jo Kittinger, Brenda Moore, Debbie Sessamen, and Han Nolan read it week after week. To this day Joan and Han still give their spot-on critiques and support along with authors Connie Fleming and Aileen Henderson. And thank you, endlessly generous and wise author and friend Ann Dorer.

Since everyone knows the infinite length of a cat's memory and retribution list, even after they are heavenly cats, here is the pantheon of cats who sat on my desk and supervised: Chester, Emy, Pye, Sam, Pete, and Nikki (alive and well, is snoring behind me.) Nikki will eat thank-you treats for all of you.

When my parents, Mary Ann and Clancy Boyd read the very first draft of Bumblespells, they pronounced it a winner. Being the family goof-up, I was stunned. And then they shared it with their friends Rex and Annette Booher, who, after my parents passed away, believed in me and continued their support for the dr'gon and the wizard. Thank you!

I'm so smart! I participated in NaNoWriMo, where I found Jan Buck (aka Ally Shields). We are online critique partners. Jan sets an example of professionalism and talent that keeps me plugging. Thank you, Jan, for never sugar-coating it and setting the ultimate example.

I always wondered why authors thank their editors. And now I know! Madeline Smoot commanded a miracle out of me.

By the fall of 2012, I had failed so often I was discouraged. Deciding I had nothing to lose, I sent entries to each of the CBAY Middle Grade and Young Adult contest categories. Because a month before, a CBAY editor had rejected one of my YA manuscripts, I had no rational reason to believe I had a chance.

I didn't win, but I nabbed the top prize. Madeline started working with me on my Pansy Pants contest manuscript. Some people can teach; some can write; some geniuses can do both. Madeline is one of the geniuses. She helped me put together all those workshops, courses, conferences, and classes and form a book.

In the midst of Pansy Pants revisions, I gathered my courage and risked my precious dr'gon and wizard. I sent her a query and held my breath. She loved Cl'rnce! We began the work that became Bumblespells.

Once upon a time I dreamed of being a published author. Thank you, Mom and Dad, Pat, all my amazing friends. I thank you, Madeline, and so do Cl'rnce and Moire Ain.

ABOUT THE AUTHOR

Kath Boyd Marsh writes about dragons and wizards and the occasional witch. As a teaching assistant, Kath loved the wonderfully funny imagination of her third grade students. She lives in Richmond, Kentucky. *The Lazy Dragon and the Bumblespells Wizard* is her debut novel.

Find Kath online at http://kathboydmarshauthor.com.